W9-AMQ-406

BEFORE THE DAWN

Center Point
Large Print

Also by Cynthia Eden and available from Center Point Large Print:

After the Dark

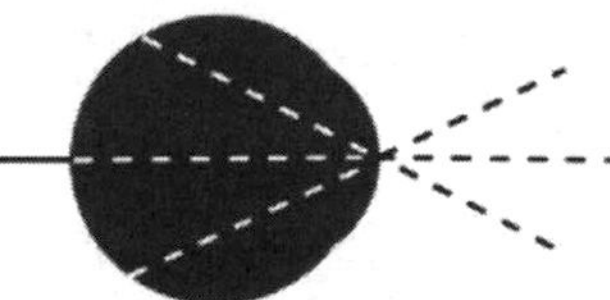

This Large Print Book carries the Seal of Approval of N.A.V.H.

BEFORE THE DAWN

CYNTHIA EDEN

Center Point Large Print
Thorndike, Maine

This Center Point Large Print edition
is published in the year 2017 by arrangement with
Harlequin Books S.A.

This is a work of fiction. Names, characters, places and incidents are either the product of the author's imagination or are used fictitiously, and any resemblance to actual persons, living or dead, business establishments, events or locales is entirely coincidental.

The text of this Large Print edition is unabridged.
In other aspects, this book may vary
from the original edition.
Printed in the United States of America
on permanent paper.
Set in 16-point Times New Roman type.

ISBN: 978-1-68324-601-5

Library of Congress Cataloging-in-Publication Data

Names: Eden, Cynthia, author.
Title: Before the dawn / Cynthia Eden.
Description: Center Point large print edition. | Thorndike, Maine :
Center Point Large Print, 2017.
Identifiers: LCCN 2017040777 | ISBN 9781683246015
(hardcover : alk. paper)
Subjects: LCSH: Large type books. | GSAFD: Romantic suspense fiction.
Classification: LCC PS3605.D4535 B44 2017 | DDC 813/.6—dc23
LC record available at https://lccn.loc.gov/2017040777

I fell in love with romance novels when I was thirteen years old. I've been addicted ever since. So this book—this story is for the other romance addicts out there. For the people who love their happy endings, who love the suspense and the adrenaline . . . for the ones who just love their books.

CHAPTER ONE

"I'm going to teach you to like pain."

Dawn Alexander felt the tears trailing down her cheeks. She could only stare at the man who stood above her, a man with a face that was so heartbreakingly familiar, and shake her head.

Her hands were tied behind her back. The rough hemp rope bit into her wrists. She'd strained to break free for hours, and the rope had sliced into her wrists as she struggled. Each ankle was bound to a chair leg.

And Dawn was in hell.

He smiled at her. A smile that was wide and charming. A smile that flashed the dimple in his left cheek. "Right now, you don't understand how good the pain will be. You still cry out when I hurt you."

He'd hurt her plenty. The nightmare wouldn't stop.

He lifted the bloody knife and pressed the tip to her cheek. "But soon the real fun will begin. By the time I'm done, you'll be begging for the knife to slice you deeper."

He means I'll be begging for death.

"Please," Dawn pleaded then as she had for hours. But he hadn't listened to her. The man she'd *thought* was her friend had turned into a monster before her eyes. "Just let me go."

His bright blue eyes hardened as he stared down at her. “You came into *my* life, Dawn. You came to me. You tried to come between me and the one person who matters most.”

Her breath sawed out of her lungs. They were in a small cabin, far away from the busy streets of Baton Rouge. The man before her—she knew him. She’d known him for years. Jason. Jason Frost. Everyone in the area knew him. Tall, handsome, smart and strong . . . Jason had been the star athlete on the football team. The guy most likely to succeed. Sure, there were plenty of stories that had swirled about his family—or rather, his father—but Jason, with his perfect looks and easy charm, had been the one all the girls loved.

But not me. I didn’t love him.

Because she’d lost her heart to his younger brother. She’d fallen fast and hard for Tucker Frost the first time they’d met.

She’d been thirteen. He’d been sixteen. She’d been so taken by him that no other boy had ever been able to compare. But when he’d turned eighteen, Tucker had left her. He’d joined the Navy, gone far away. She’d heard people say that he’d become a SEAL.

And he’d just . . . vanished.

Until a few weeks ago. Until he’d come back and she’d turned around and found him standing in the library at Louisiana State University. He’d been looking for *her.* And she’d been lost.

"Does Tucker know what you're doing?" The broken whisper came from her. That had been her darkest fear as the hours had slipped by and her pain had continued.

Jason had picked her up from her dorm room. He'd said that Tucker wanted him to give her a lift out to their place. She'd gone so easily, so happily, never hesitating. Only he hadn't driven her to their home. He'd taken her away from the city, to the edge of the Mississippi River. To this little cabin.

The first time he'd hit her, she'd been stunned. Too stunned to move. The second time, he'd hit her so hard she *couldn't* move.

Jason tilted his dark head down, seeming to give her question deep thought.

Her heart pounded frantically in her chest. "Tucker won't like this," she said, desperate. "You'd better let me go. You don't want Tucker angry—"

His head lifted. His eyes—eyes the exact same shade as Tucker's—met hers. And he smiled again. *Tucker's smile.* Oh, God. "Of course he knows. Why do you think he came to see you when he arrived back in town? You've been on our list for quite a while."

Her heart stopped. Dawn shook her head. No. Anger was there, beating just below the terrible fear. Tucker wouldn't do this.

Not Tucker.

He'd . . . he'd seemed to care about her. They'd always been close, secretly so before he left for the Navy. Nothing romantic or sexual, just . . . friends. They'd been friends when they were kids. He'd walk her home. He'd make sure she had all her books.

But when he'd come back recently, when he'd come back as a man and found her at LSU, they'd stopped being just friends. They'd become so much more. He'd become everything to her.

Not Tucker.

The knife lifted and her breath came a little easier.

Then the blade sank into her shoulder, going deep, and he *twisted* the hilt. Dawn choked out a scream.

He laughed at her. "Surely you've read the stories in the paper? I mean, the press seems to be giving our kills a great deal of attention."

Our kills?

"They even gave me a name." He pulled out the blade and gazed at the blood on the weapon. "The Iceman." He nodded once, as if satisfied with that name. "But they are so clueless. They don't know why I freeze the bodies. They don't get it at all."

OhGodOhGodOhGod. Yes, she'd heard the stories about the Iceman in the paper. The guy who'd been abducting women for the last few years. The man who *froze* their bodies and . . . kept them. Kept them so very long before he would call the cops, tipping them off to the locations. And those poor women would be found, so perfectly preserved, in freezers.

She looked up at Jason. His thick, dark hair. His perfect features. His gleaming eyes. That dimple. Dawn could only shake her head.

"The press should have realized it wasn't just one man committing the crimes," he said. "I mean, really, it's more like *Icemen* than Iceman."

"Not Tucker." Her breath heaved out. "You're lying!"

His eyes narrowed. "Why?" That bloody knife came back to her cheek. She knew he was going to cut her face. Dawn tried to brace herself for that pain. "Because you *think* you know him? Because he fucked you?"

She felt her face flame. Yes, he had. And Tucker had been her first. Her only. She *loved* him. She trusted him. She—

Jason laughed. Hard, deep laughter. "You are so clueless. Blood comes before anything else. Tuck has *my* back. He always has. He'll be here soon, and he'll prove the truth to you."

The tip of the knife pressed into her cheek, a shallow cut, taunting her.

"And you'll see the truth for yourself."

He turned away from her.

Dawn twisted her bleeding wrists behind her, struggling as hard as she could against the rope.

Terror clawed at her insides as the stories of the Iceman's kills ran through her mind. All the victims had been young women—pretty, single. When their bodies had finally been recovered, they had been covered in slices. Stabbed again and again. Tortured. Then frozen in time . . . as if . . . as if the killer wanted to savor them.

I won't be another victim.

"They're alive when I put them in the freezer."

For an instant, her struggles ceased. Stunned, she could only stare at his broad back.

"I make sure of it," he added. "The cops haven't released that part to the media, but I always put them in the freezers when they're still breathing. I like for them to feel the cold sliding over them. I know it makes them long for the pain again." He looked back over his shoulder at her, and his profile . . . *It is so like Tucker's.* "I told you, before I'm done, you'll grow to like the pain."

No.

She yanked hard at the ropes and Dawn thought she felt them give . . . just a bit.

She also heard the growl of a car's engine outside the cabin.

His smile stretched. "Right on time. I'll go greet Tuck, then the real fun can get started."

She opened her mouth, ready to scream. She'd done that before, screamed endlessly, but he'd just laughed and said that no one was around to hear her.

This time, though, he leaped forward and slapped his hand over her mouth.

Anger hardened his face. "I'll be the one to talk with Tuck first." Then he slapped a gag on her in mere moments. He shoved it into her mouth, bloodying her lips even more, and then tied it behind her head. He stood in front of her as that growling engine came closer, and he leaned down, until they were eye to eye. "We are going to have so much fun with you."

He kissed her, putting his mouth right over the gag.

"I'll fuck you, too," he promised.

The tears fell again, but he'd already turned away. He rushed toward the cabin's door. Toward Tucker. And she kept yanking on the ropes that bound her wrists. He'd been so busy with the gag that he hadn't even checked to see if she was still securely tied.

The joke is on you, bastard. I'm not. The rope around her left wrist broke free.

Tucker Frost parked his car and jumped out of the vehicle. A thousand stars glittered overhead as he approached the old cabin, a place that he damn well hated.

Jason should hate the place, too. He had no idea why his brother wanted to meet him there. The cabin held only bad memories. Memories Tucker wished that he could forget. He'd gone halfway around the world in an effort to banish that hell from his mind.

Insects chirped all around him. Frogs croaked, and down near the water he could hear the deep growl of a gator. Swamps weren't quiet—most folks had that wrong. Swamps were loud and busy, all the time. *Especially* at night.

And he hated this one swamp in particular. It was too full of dark secrets.

"About time you got here!"

His gaze lifted at his brother's voice, and he saw Jason bound out of the cabin. "I've been waiting over an hour for you to show up."

Tucker rolled back his shoulders. "I stopped by Dawn's dorm. I needed to talk to her." Because he'd gotten orders to ship out. A new mission. He wouldn't be back for a few months and he'd wanted to tell her the news face-to-face. Hell, he hated the idea of leaving her. Little Dawn Alexander. Who would have thought that she'd come to mean so much to him, so fast? He cleared his throat. "But she wasn't there."

Jason glanced back toward the cabin. "You don't say . . ."

Tucker yanked a hand through his hair. He and his brother stood at a similar height, and their bodies were built along the same rough and ready lines. "Why did you want me to come out here?" Before his brother could answer, Tucker gave a bitter laugh. “Unless we’re out here to torch this place, I don’t really want—”

“We’re not torching it.” Anger crackled in Jason’s voice, surprising him. “I don’t like fire.”

Tucker’s brows flew up. “And I don’t like this place.” Too many bad memories. “You shouldn’t, either.” Not after the hell that had happened to them there.

Jason rocked back on his heels. “Family comes first.”

That was a phrase that seemed to echo in Tucker’s mind. It was a phrase his father had used too many times.

Jason cocked his head and studied Tucker. “You believe that, don’t you?”

He didn’t speak. Tension snaked up his spine. This scene was wrong. “Why are we out here?”

Jason glanced back toward the cabin. “I fixed it up while you were out saving the world. Looks good, doesn’t it?”

It would never look good to Tucker. *We should have destroyed it long ago.*

“When you came back, I knew things would be different.” Jason focused on him once again. “I have a surprise for you.” He nodded once. “Inside the cabin.”

The tension Tucker felt grew even worse. “I don’t like surprises.”

But his brother just laughed. “You’ll like this one.” Then he came forward and slung his arm around Tucker's shoulders. Tucker forced himself to relax. This was Jason, the guy who'd always had his back. The guy had been looking out for Tucker his whole life. When he'd been a kid, Jason had made sure no bullies were ever dumb enough to tease Tucker about his worn clothes or the fact that his lunch box was empty most days. Jason had *always* been there to take care of him.

He's my blood. The only blood that matters.

Tucker blew out a long breath. If Jason wanted him to go into the cabin, then he would. Hell, he'd do just about anything for his older brother. With Jason's arm still slung around his shoulders, they headed up the rickety stairs and toward the door. Jason was talking and laughing, and the guy seemed happier than Tucker had seen him in years.

Jason opened the door with a flourish. "After you, bro."

Tucker headed inside. The old floorboards creaked beneath his feet, the way they'd done years ago. But the place didn't reek of the stale scent of old beer. Instead . . .

What is that scent?

"Open the door on the right." Jason's voice had hitched up. "Your surprise is in there."

Okay, he'd play along. For the moment. Then he needed to tell Jason about his new orders. His brother wasn't going to like that he had to leave again. Jason hadn't understood when Tucker had enlisted. But Jason didn't get it. If Tucker didn't let the dark energy swirling inside him have an outlet, then trouble would come.

Tucker grabbed for the doorknob. He pushed it open and—

Terror.

For an instant, Tucker just stood there. He stared into Dawn's beautiful green eyes—eyes that were glassy with terror. Blood and tears trickled down her cheeks and she was yanking at the rope around her left ankle. Her shirt was covered in blood. Her body marked by bruises.

And she looked at him as if he were the devil himself.

Tucker shook his head. No, this was wrong. This was *wrong*. "Dawn?"

Jason slapped his hand down on Tucker's shoulder. "Surprise! Had her waiting for you."

A gag was in Dawn's mouth. A purple bruise along her delicate jaw.

Tucker whirled on his brother, knocking that hand aside. "You did this to her?" A dull ringing was in his ears and rage burned in his veins. "You *hurt* her?"

Jason's eyes widened. "Easy, bro." The words were low and warning. "You know you have to watch that temper of yours. Control, right? It's key?" But his lips were curving. "You lose it and you become just like our old man."

Screw that. Tucker shoved his brother back,

hard, slamming him against the wooden wall then pinning him there. "What the hell did you do?"

Jason's mouth opened to respond, but then Dawn was rushing right past them. She'd leaped out of her chair and run for the door.

"Shit!" Jason bellowed. "Stop her! We have to stop her!"

Was his brother insane? The guy lunged up, but Tucker slammed him back against the wall. *"What did you do?"*

Jason head-butted him. The blow was fast and brutal and Tucker staggered back for a moment, and that moment was all that his brother needed. Jason shot toward the door, chasing after Dawn.

Stunned, Tucker glanced around the cabin. There was blood on the floor. *Dawn's* blood. And she'd stared at him with such absolute terror on her face. No, *no,* it couldn't be happening. Not again.

Not the fuck again.

Locking his teeth, he raced outside. His gaze flew to the left, to the right. He saw Jason, running toward the car that Tucker had just driven up in. Dawn was yanking at the driver's-side door. Frantically, she clawed at the door handle, obviously desperate to get inside.

But I have the keys.

"Dawn!" Tucker yelled her name.

Her head whipped toward him. Then Jason was *on* her. His brother grabbed her head and slammed it against the car. Dawn sagged instantly and a fury unlike anything Tucker had ever known filled his whole body. He heard a roar and didn't even realize that guttural cry had come from him, but in the next instant, he was on his brother. He ripped Jason away from Dawn. *"Not her!"* Carefully, he lowered her to the ground. His hand went to her forehead and he felt the blood on his fingers—

"Hell, yes," Jason snarled. *"Her."* Then he drove both of his fists into Tucker's back. Tucker fell down, nearly landing on top of Dawn, but he managed to turn his body at the last moment. He came up again, swinging this time. A hard cut at his brother because the guy never had been able to take a left hook. Jason stumbled back at the hit, and Tucker went at him again. Punching. Kicking. Using every bit of knowledge he'd learned in the hellholes on earth. SEALs could fight dirty and he sure as hell did. In moments, Jason was beneath him on that ground, his face a bloody mess, barely able to lift up his hands and stop Tucker's blows.

"She's . . . going to die . . ."

Tucker froze with his hands still fisted.

Jason spat blood as he said, "She's . . . running to the . . . river . . ."

He hadn't even heard her flee. Tucker's head whipped around, and sure enough, he saw that Dawn had fled. Only she wasn't rushing down the old dirt road that led away from the property. She was running to the rotted dock that waited yards away. A dock that stretched out over the mighty Mississippi.

"Dawn!" Tucker yelled her name as he leaped to his feet. He left his brother there because Dawn was the priority. She mattered. "Dawn, *wait!*"

She cast a terrified glance over her shoulder and in that moment, with the stars glittering down and showing him her face, he realized . . . *she's afraid of me.*

But . . . he was trying to help her.

"Dawn?" He ran toward her.

She backed to the edge of the dock. She was right over the water, just standing there. Too close because . . .

Dawn didn't know how to swim. She'd told him that less than a week ago. A hushed, embarrassed confession. When she'd been six, she'd fallen into her aunt's pool and nearly drowned. After that, she'd been terrified of the water. At her quiet confession, he'd felt protective. He *always* felt protective where she was concerned. He'd promised to teach her how to swim. Promised to make her whole life safe, always.

And now this is happening.

He'd told his brother that Dawn couldn't swim. He'd told Jason how afraid she'd been and how Tucker had wanted to erase that fear.

"Don't go into the water!" He lifted his hand

toward her and realized that his knuckles were bloody from punching Jason. "Dawn, please . . . stop."

She lifted her hands, as if she'd ward him off. "Don't hurt me." Her voice was a weak rasp and it utterly broke his heart. Until that moment, he hadn't realized just how completely truly she *owned* his heart.

But when he felt it shatter, he knew.

"I wouldn't." He took another step toward her. The dock swayed beneath his feet. "Not ever."

She shook her head.

She doesn't believe me. He could see it. He risked a glance over his shoulder but saw that Jason was still sprawled on the ground. Quickly, he turned his attention back to her. "I don't know what's happening here."

Her laughter was bitter, terrified, and it hurt him. "Your brother . . . is going to kill me."

No. It wouldn't happen.

Tucker took another step toward her. "We're going to get in my car and we're going to get the hell out of here." He kept his palm open to her. He needed her to trust him. To take his hand. "Come on, baby. I swear, I won't let him hurt you." *I won't ever let anyone hurt you again.*

She was shaking, but . . .

"He said you were . . . coming to kill me."

Tucker shook his head. "No."

"Did you . . . kill the others?"

What others? Nausea rose in his stomach. Wasn't this what he'd feared? Oh, shit. *Shit.* He should have stopped this. Should have paid more attention to his brother.

He's too much like our father.

That was the problem. They were both too much like dear old dad.

She put her hand to her shoulder, to the wound that was still bleeding. She was covered in blood, they were near the edge of the water, and he knew there were plenty of gators out there. He could hear their cries. "Let's get out of here." He took another step toward her. He was just going to have to grab her and pull her to his car. He wanted her *away* from that death-soaked place. Right the hell then—

He lunged for her. But Dawn jumped back and fell into the water. She sank like a stone and his heart stopped. In the next second, he was diving off that dock after her. No way was he going to lose Dawn. *Not her. Not her.* The words were a mantra in his head. He swam until he touched her, until his hand wrapped around her body, and then he kicked them up to the surface. He felt something brush against his body but he didn't stop. The gators were there, he knew the blood and thrashing would just be drawing them in closer, and Tucker knew that he *was* getting Dawn out of that water.

He pushed her toward the dock and helped

to heave her body up onto the old wood. Water streamed down her body as she crawled across the rotting dock, and Tucker hauled himself right up after her. He reached for Dawn.

Jason's laughter froze him.

"That was impressive," his brother said. "Very hero-like, the way you dived in after her."

Tucker was on his knees. Dawn was about two feet away from him, and Jason . . . he had a gun pressed to her head.

"This isn't how I planned things." Jason's left hand swiped at the blood that fell from his busted lip while his right held that gun against her temple. "But it can still work."

Tucker didn't look at Dawn's face right then. He couldn't.

"You knew it would happen," Jason said. "Only a matter of time, for us both. The urge was always there. The violence—it's a rush, isn't it?"

His hands fisted at his sides. "Let her go."

"You won't believe what I've learned. I want to show it to you. Share it with you. But this one . . ." He jabbed the gun into Dawn's temple. Dawn didn't make a sound. "She's messing things up. You think I didn't see it? Even years ago, you watched her too much. But you didn't touch her. *Hands off, right, bro?* You broke that rule this time, and everything changed." His shoulders slumped. "So maybe it's your fault this is happening to her."

"Jason . . ."

"It's your fault she's dying."

Tucker reached his right hand beneath the leg of his wet jeans. He grabbed for the knife he kept there, but he made sure not to let his brother see the weapon.

"She *has* to die. I mean, if I let her go . . . she'll run to the cops. She'll tell them what happened. They'll lock me up. You don't want that to happen, do you?" Jason demanded, a desperate edge creeping into the words. "You don't want me in a cell? A cage?" His voice roughened even more. "We've both been in a cage before. We swore neither of us would go back."

Yes, they had sworn that.

"Choose." Jason stared straight at him, his eyes glittering. "Choose right now and let her know it. Tell her the truth that we've always both known. Blood is thicker than anything else. Blood binds."

Tucker rose to his feet, making sure to keep the knife behind him and out of his brother's sight. "Blood comes first." Those were the words their father had battered into their minds.

Jason nodded and he lifted the gun away from Dawn's head.

"Tucker?" she rasped his name. "Please, don't . . ."

"You do the honors," Jason said. He offered the gun to Tucker. The guy was smiling at him, as if this was some kind of game.

It wasn't a game.

Dawn tried to crawl away.

Jason yanked her back. He locked one hand around her throat. The other still held the gun, but now the barrel was pointed down at the dock.

"She's more of a fighter than I thought," Jason murmured. "Sometimes, they don't fight at all. They just beg."

My brother is a monster. And Tucker had let this happen.

Dawn was clawing at Jason's hand, but his brother didn't even seem to feel the pain. He just stared straight at Tucker, that stupid smile on his face as he *choked* Dawn.

With his right hand, Tucker reached for the gun. But at the same time, his left hand came up in a rush—and he drove that knife straight at his brother's chest.

Jason let out a bellow as he staggered back. He freed Dawn and she scrambled away.

Tucker snatched the gun from Jason. Then Tucker twisted that weapon around in a fast, practiced movement, aiming it at Jason even as his brother yanked the knife out of his chest.

"Don't!" Tucker snarled when Jason took a lunging step toward him. Dawn had run down the dock, heading back toward the old cabin. "This is ending, right here. You aren't hurting anyone else." *Dear God, Jason . . . how many people have you already hurt?* He was afraid to find out that truth.

"You stabbed me." His blood was dripping on

the dock. "To save her, you stabbed *me.*" Fury burned in this words. Disbelief.

"I will kill you in order to save her." Just so there was no confusion. *But it doesn't have to be this way.* He moved his body, making sure to block the exit off that old dock, stopping any attempt Jason could make to charge after Dawn. "Jason, drop the knife." Jason still gripped it tightly. "Drop the knife and put your hands up."

Jason didn't drop the knife. "What are you going to do? Call the cops? Play the hero?"

His phone was in the car. "Yeah, I'll be calling the cops."

"I said *no cage!*" That rage was getting hotter. "You know that! You know I can't handle that!" And Jason laughed. A wild sound. "Just as I know you won't kill me. You can't. That knife barely even went into me. You weren't trying. Just for show . . ."

He was coming forward.

Tucker couldn't hear the thud of Dawn's footsteps any longer. Where was she? "Don't take another step."

But Jason did. "I'm going to slice her all over. I'm going to make her beg."

Tucker's rage burned, too. "You aren't touching her."

"You're going to help me. You're going to be at my side, the way you always are. You understand me. You want the same things I want."

Jason was a foot away from him.

Tucker shook his head. "I want Dawn." He eased out a low breath. "Drop that knife, now." But he knew Jason wasn't going to do it. "Don't—" he began, but it was too late. Jason had surged forward. He didn't swing at Tucker with his knife. Tucker wasn't his goal. He slammed his body into Tucker's, shoving him out of the way.

Because Jason wants Dawn.

But Tucker wasn't letting that happen. He caught his brother, held tight when Jason fought and then . . .

He fired.

The blast of that gun seemed deafening. For a moment after that terrible thunder, there was no sound at all. Even the insects had stopped chirping, as if they were afraid. Jason was staring at him, his face easy to see under the bright, full moon.

Shock.

Betrayal.

Then Jason was plunging that knife at Tucker, slicing down his arm, slicing his hand and trying to make Tucker drop the gun.

He didn't drop it. Tucker fired again.

Jason staggered back.

"You won't touch her again."

Tucker fired once more. His brother was on the edge of the dock, he staggered back—

And fell into the water, sinking deep with a splash.

CHAPTER TWO

Seven years later . . .

Second chances didn't come around often. If a man was lucky enough to have one, then he should grab on to that opportunity and hold tight to it with every bit of strength that he had.

It was a good thing Tucker Frost was strong.

He hurried into the conference room at the FBI's Washington, DC, office. It was early June and the sun glinted through the window, shining right through the blinds. The other agents were already inside, seated at the round table. Their laptops were out. Their manila files were open. Their phones were on the tabletop, probably already turned to mute.

He took the last seat, had his laptop out and open in seconds and was adjusting the volume on his phone when Samantha Dark delicately cleared her throat.

"I want to thank all of you for joining me on such short notice."

The meeting had been called ten minutes ago. He'd been outside the building, already anticipating just how he'd be spending the weekend.

"I know that our unit is still in the development

phase, but you were all handpicked to join this team because I know that you bring a unique set of skills and a perspective for targeting killers that others just can't imitate."

Her voice was low, calm, and she turned her golden stare on all of the agents at the table.

Samantha Dark.

He was damn glad she'd come back to the FBI. He'd always respected Agent Dark. From the very first moment that they'd met at Quantico, he'd known just how sharp she was. Samantha had been the profiler to watch, but when her ex-lover had turned out to be a vicious serial killer, she'd retreated, pulling away from everyone close to her. He'd hated that.

But Samantha was back now. She'd stopped not just *one* serial killer on her last case, but two, and since she'd also managed to save the life of the FBI's executive assistant director, Justin Bass, she'd been given carte blanche to try her experimental unit.

"Some folks would say," Samantha began as her stare turned pensive, "that we aren't the best ones to profile killers. They'd say our personal connections to murderers are weaknesses."

His jaw locked.

"But those people would be dead wrong." She gave a grim nod. "The fact that we've had serial killers intimately involved in our lives means that we understand them like no other person can." She paused. "They were friends. They were lovers."

She'd taken down the lover who'd tried to hurt her and who *had* hurt so many others.

"They were family." Now her golden stare came back to him.

Beneath the table, his hands fisted. *Blood always comes first.*

Then her stare tracked to the red-haired agent on his left, Macey Night. "They have been our tormenters."

From the corner of his eye, he saw Macey stiffen.

But then Samantha's focus was on the last agent at that little table as she stared at Bowen Murphy and said, "And they have been our prey."

Bowen inclined his head toward her.

"We have all been in life-and-death situations with serials. We know how dangerous they are. We don't underestimate them. We see them from a unique perspective that no one else can fully appreciate." She exhaled as she moved around the table. "And that perspective is going to help us. It will allow us to think outside of the box. It will allow us to notice things that others cannot. It will allow us to stop the perpetrators before they take more innocent victims."

Hell, yes. That was what he wanted. Why he'd agreed to join this group when Samantha had approached him. He'd been working in Violent

Crimes for years now, but going back to profiling, it was exactly what he needed.

Maybe the guilt will finally stop. If he could stop enough serials. If he could make a difference, if, if, *if.*

"You all know that there are currently 25 to 50 active serial killers hunting in the United States." Her lips thinned. "Or at least, that's the number we're supposed to be working with." The number that the FBI bandied about to the media.

"I think there are more," Bowen said, his voice rumbling. "I think there are hunters who are so good at killing, the authorities have no idea they're out there. They're flying right beneath the radar, picking victims that no one will miss, and they're getting away with murder."

"That's where we come in," Samantha said with a nod. "Part of our job will be to try to find those *unknown* killers. We will unmask the ones who are hiding in shadows. We'll find the victims that they don't want anyone to know about."

"That's easier said than done," Macey murmured.

Samantha smiled. "Yes, it is." Her shoulders rolled in a shrug. "But I think we're up to the challenge."

Tucker didn't speak.

"That's part of our job," Samantha continued in that mild, calm voice of hers. An oddly soothing voice. "But another part . . . another part is immediate mobilization when we think local authorities have uncovered an active serial. At the first hint of serial involvement, a team will immediately deploy to the local area and begin cooperative action with the authorities there."

He liked that. Damn straight they needed immediate action. When it came to serials, the locals were often in way over their heads, and time lost meant lives lost.

"That brings me to the reason I called this meeting . . ." She glanced at the watch on her slender wrist. "At seven p.m. on a Friday night." She headed toward her laptop and pressed a few buttons. She had a projector hooked up and a screen had already lowered from the ceiling. "Agents, we have our first target."

And an image appeared on that white screen. Even though he'd prepared for it, Tuck's whole body tensed. *No, hell, no.* Not happening. It *shouldn't* be happening—

"Is she . . . frozen?" Macey asked.

"Yes," Tucker gritted before Samantha could speak.

Because the crime scene photo they were staring at . . . it showed a woman with skin that appeared almost blue. Her lashes were covered with small ice particles. Her lashes, her lips, the tip of her nose. He could see the slices on her body, slices that were wide and deep, obviously from a big knife. And her body—

Samantha hit a button on her laptop. Another picture appeared. This one wasn't as close up. Instead, it was a distance shot of the crime scene, and it showed the victim's body perfectly.

She was inside an open freezer.

Tucker wanted to jump to his feet. He wanted to snarl . . . *No fucking way. This can't be happening. Not again.* But he knew Samantha was watching him. He knew Samantha needed him.

And he knew he was going to give her exactly what she wanted.

"The Iceman."

He could feel the other agents staring at him.

He rose to his feet and headed toward the screen. He stared at the victim's arms, her bare torso. Her neck. "The angle of the cuts . . . it appears to be the same." Because the Iceman had enjoyed inflicting maximum pain on his victims. "He'd start easily, just little flicks of the blade. Then he'd go deeper. Starting with the arms. The stomach. Then driving the blade into the shoulders. The right first, then the left." And the guy had only been getting started at that point. His torture would last much, much longer.

Tucker stared at the victim's face. "She's in her early twenties. A young, pretty female. Just his type."

Only it wasn't possible.

"Uh, yeah . . ." Bowen cleared his throat. "I

was under the impression that the Iceman died seven years ago."

Tucker forced himself to turn away from the victim. "You're not the only one who thought that." He'd been under that same impression, until Samantha Dark had given him a heads-up when she first told him about the meeting. She hadn't wanted him walking into that room blind. And, in fact, she'd given him the option not to come in at all.

He'd been late to that meeting for one reason . . . because he'd gotten lost thinking about the ghost of his bastard brother.

There were some things a man couldn't forget, and there were some things that he couldn't, *wouldn't,* hide from.

"The original Iceman was Jason Frost, and, yes, I'm the man who shot him one long-ago Louisiana night." He kept his voice flat with an effort. Tucker valued his control above all else. "It's safe to assume that we're looking at the work of a copycat. It could be as simple as some jerk who wanted to get rid of his girlfriend, so he thought he'd imitate the work of an infamous killer, or—" he rolled back his shoulders "—it could be one of those guys who gets obsessed with a serial killer's work. Who tries to imitate and duplicate the kills." Of the two options, that was the one that worried him more. If someone was duplicating Jason's work, that meant there would be more death coming.

They couldn't have that.

Macey's fingers tapped lightly on the table. "If I remember correctly, Jason Frost's body was never recovered."

"No, it wasn't." Though dive teams had searched for days. "But his body isn't the first to disappear into the Mississippi, and it won't be the last." By the time the cops had arrived, his brother's body had been long gone. It had taken two hours for the cops to get there . . . mostly because it had taken a very long time for Tucker to call them in. If he'd called sooner . . .

Then maybe we would have pulled him from the water. But my priority was elsewhere then.

"If they didn't get a body—" Bowen's head tilted as he studied Tucker "—then how can you be certain he's dead?"

He didn't let his expression alter. "I'm a former SEAL. When I shoot at something, I hit it. Before he went into the water, I shot Jason Frost three times." The breath he inhaled felt cold. "With my last shot, I was aiming for his heart."

Bowen's eyes narrowed. "But he was your brother. Your blood."

Blood is all that matters.

"In that last second," Bowen continued, his brown eyes narrowed, "are you sure you didn't hesitate?"

"Yes." He stared straight at Bowen. "I'm sure."

"Fair enough." Bowen's gaze slid from his and

focused once more on the woman's image. "Do we know who the victim is?"

"Right now, she's listed as a Jane Doe," Samantha replied. "She doesn't match with any missing person's report, and her fingerprints haven't turned up any hits in our system. But this is still early in the investigation, so I'm expecting to hear more news soon."

Macey swiveled her chair toward Samantha. "Just how early are we talking?"

"The victim was discovered less than twelve hours ago."

Bowen gave a low whistle. "That is early."

Samantha nodded. "And that means we have an advantage. Luckily for us, one of the detectives who is working on this case in New Orleans was familiar with the Iceman's work. He knew instantly what he was seeing, and he put in a call to my office."

When the Iceman's crimes had first been uncovered, his kills had been flashed on every news channel in the United States. But then time had passed and other killers had taken his place. More tales of gore and death had pushed the Iceman out of the spotlight. That was the nature of the beast. In a 24/7 online world, there was always another sensational story waiting.

Always another killer hunting. Always someone out there to satisfy the public's need for bloody details.

"We can hit the ground running on this one. We can get down there and we can hunt. We can stop him." Samantha's gaze lifted to meet Tucker's. "We can prove that this unit is exactly what the FBI needs. We know killers and now it's our turn to show everyone just what we can do."

Tucker eased out a slow breath. "You know I want to be on the plane." The one that would be leaving to fly down to New Orleans that very night. She'd told him about that flight during their brief premeeting chat, too.

"And you're going." She nodded. "You and Macey are heading out tonight. Evaluate the scene, see exactly what we're dealing with and then make contact with me again. If you need additional backup, Bowen and I will be ready to go."

Back to Louisiana. "The location is different." That was something that was already nagging at him. "Jason Frost killed in Baton Rouge, not New Orleans." And he had to ask. "Was the victim alive when she went into the freezer?"

He saw Macey flinch.

"The coroner doesn't know yet. When you get down to New Orleans, visit the coroner's office and see what she's learned." She pointed toward Macey. "The fact that you're a medical doctor is going to come in handy for us—I want your eyes on the victim. Make sure nothing gets missed with her."

"Absolutely."

"Okay, then." Samantha straightened her

shoulders. "You all have files that I passed out earlier—take a look at them. They contain information on Jason Frost and his victims, including the one woman who managed to escape."

Slowly, Tucker returned to his seat. He opened the folder that had been set out for him, and he found a picture of Dawn Alexander staring back at him. It was a picture that had been taken of her when she'd been at the hospital. Her big green eyes were blank, glassy. Bruises and cuts covered her body.

Sonofabitch. Pain knifed right through his heart. Time should have lessened the pain. It hadn't. He didn't think it ever would.

"One of the things that concerns me most about this case is Dawn Alexander," Samantha murmured. "Because the only surviving victim of the Iceman? She's living in New Orleans . . . The exact place our new perp is using for his hunting grounds."

"Dawn!" He turned, frantic to find her. He'd been screaming her name, but she hadn't called back to him. She wasn't at his car. She wasn't in that shit-forsaken cabin. She wasn't on the old dirt road that led out of that place.

She'd vanished. She'd run from him. Because she was afraid.

"Dawn, I swear, I am not going to hurt you!" He'd taken a flashlight from his car and he'd shone it onto the ground. That was when he saw the blood drops, leading into the thick, twisting woods behind the cabin. One drop, another, another . . . Tucker started following them. "Jason isn't here any longer!" He hadn't seen his brother's body come back up because he'd been so frantic to find Dawn and make sure she was all right. She'd been covered in so much blood. He needed to check her out. He needed to make absolutely certain she wasn't going to die out at that cabin.

Another soul taken.

He pushed through the woods. The branches tore at him, but he didn't care. There was more blood there. Some high up on a tree, forming a bloody hand print as if she'd stopped to brace herself. Other drops were low, on leaves, as if they'd dripped from her body as she fled.

He kept walking ahead, calling for her, following that blood trail, but she never spoke back to him. Never called out for him to help her.

He knew why. Because she was afraid. Because Dawn thought that he was just as much of a monster as his brother.

And the problem was . . . she was right.

"We're about to land."

He jerked at the soft voice, his gaze shooting to

the right. Macey Night gave him a worried frown. “Sorry. Did I wake you up?” Her unusual eyes—one blue and one brown—showed her concern as she stared at him. “I was talking to the captain. He said we’d be touching down soon.” She slid into the seat across from him and hooked the seat belt over her lap. “I thought you’d want to know.”

He hadn’t meant to fall asleep. He’d been staring out of the window, trying to get into the head of the killer they were facing, but memories of Dawn had come back to haunt him.

“You said her name.”

His hand tightened around the armrest. “Didn’t realize I talked in my sleep.”

Macey stared straight at him. “May I ask . . . what was it like?”

“To kill my own brother?” His voice was cold. He was cold. He had to have that ice to block off his emotions. Otherwise . . .

Iceman.

“I had a choice to make. I could let a killer destroy an innocent woman or I could stop him. Since I’m not a sadistic bastard, I stopped him.”

“You were involved with Dawn Alexander before her attack.” She pulled at the sleeve of her top. Long sleeves. Macey always wore long sleeves. “What happened between the two of you?”

“You’ve seen the photos of Jason Frost.” *Jason*

Frost. He always tried to refer to him formally. He couldn't say *my brother.* Because he had to keep it separate. His brother had been the guy who kicked the ass of any bully who'd tried to mess with Tucker. His brother had been the one to teach him how to ride a bike. His brother had been the one to hold his hand when their mom was buried.

Jason Frost had been a depraved killer. His brother had been his best friend.

Tucker cleared his throat. "You've seen photos," he said again. "You know we look . . . similar." Even more so now. Time had sharpened his features so that he resembled Jason even more.

"You guys could be twins."

Right. Because fate was cruel and twisted. "Would you want a lover who had the same face as the man who tortured you for hours?"

Her face went white. She pulled on her sleeve again. "No."

He swallowed. "Right. So . . . that's what happened with me and Dawn. I wanted to stop causing her pain, and the best way to do that was to stay far away from her."

"When we get to New Orleans, do you want me to be the one to make contact with her?"

Because one of them would have to meet with her. Once they'd talked to the local cops and learned the latest details of the case, it would be necessary to have a sit-down with Dawn. Her being in New Orleans while a crime like this occurred? He wanted it to be just a coincidence, but he couldn't take any chances.

"Tucker?" Macey prompted. "You want me to handle the interview with Dawn?"

He looked out the window. He could see the lights from the Big Easy. "I think that would be best." Because he'd never responded just right when he was around Dawn. She stirred his emotions too much. She made him want . . . too much.

No, that was seven years ago. He hadn't touched her in seven years. "You don't have a personal involvement with her," he continued, clearing his throat because his voice was too rough, "so you should handle the interview."

"You don't have to lie to me." Her voice was a gentle rebuke. "It's not about personal involvement. It's because you don't want her to hurt," Macey added softly. "When she sees your face."

He glanced back at her. There was no need to reply.

"You might look like him, but that's just skin deep."

Easy enough to say. But having a lover who was blood kin to the man who'd spent hours making you scream? That wasn't exactly something a woman could get past.

The captain's voice floated over the speakers and the plane began its descent.

"Before we're done, I'll teach you to like the pain." He smiled as he trailed the knife over her face. "You'll hurt at first. When the blade cuts you. You'll cry."

A tear trickled down her cheek. "Please . . . let me go . . ." Her voice was a desperate rasp. "I . . . I won't tell anyone . . . about you . . ."

She was a liar. Straight to her core. He let the tip of the blade slice into her cheek. She screamed, a high-pitched, desperate sound. No one was around to hear that cry.

"You'll beg," he continued. He moved the knife down her neck, making small cuts, enjoying the desperate sobs that broke from her. "You'll promise anything if I stop the pain . . ."

He let the bloody blade slide down her arm. Her hands were tied behind her back. Her feet were tied to the chair legs. He'd stripped her so that she wore only her bra and panties.

"But then . . ." He backed away and smiled down at her. "When the pain does stop, you'll wish for it to come back. You'll be so desperate for it."

She shook her head. "L-let me go . . ."

Never.

"I'll teach you to like the pain." He rolled back his shoulders. "And your lesson will start right now."

CHAPTER THREE

Dawn Alexander sat at the table in the little interrogation room at the New Orleans Police Department. It wasn't her first trip to the station on Royal Street, and it wouldn't be her last, either. She'd been working in the city as a PI for the past three years. She often butted heads with the local cops, and she often worked with them as a team. Depending on the case, they could be best friends or worst enemies.

"Okay, Anthony . . . Why did you drag me in here first thing this morning?" Mornings weren't her thing. She worked at night, and, in fact, she'd just crawled into bed at 3:00 a.m., only to be woken right back up by the detective knocking on her door four hours later.

Anthony Deveraux stood near the back wall—only it wasn't really a wall. A large pane of glass stretched for five feet near him. That glass threw Dawn's reflection back at her. Or, it would have, if she'd been staring at herself. Dawn made a point of never looking into a mirror too long.

She didn't always like what she saw staring back at her.

It was one-way glass, of course. Cops or the DA would usually be on the other side of the glass as they watched suspects get grilled.

Her green eyes narrowed. "Just what am I suspected of doing?"

"Nothing," Anthony said quickly, his handsome face tensing. Anthony was a good detective. She'd met him shortly after her move to the Big Easy. One of her first contacts. He was tough and fair, and he seemed to like going after the especially dark cases. His black hair was close-cropped and his golden eyes were shadowed as he glanced at her, then away.

Away? Alarm bells had been going off in her head ever since she opened the door to see him nervously standing there.

"Were you sent to collect me this morning because you're my friend?" She was feeling her way as she tried to figure out exactly what was going on. So she'd done a bit of spying on her last PI case. She hadn't *technically* broken any laws.

Anthony gave a slight jerk of his head. Not really a nod. Not really a denial, either. "You . . . You're related to a case that I'm working on."

A case. She waved to him. "Okay. Tell me more." Why was the guy just leaving her in suspense? It wasn't like him to leave her hanging.

But Anthony licked his lips and his stare darted toward the interrogation room door. "We have to wait. The FBI is joining us."

What? She wanted to bolt out of her chair. She didn't. The FBI . . . Dawn gave a low whistle. "This must be some case."

He looked at her, and she saw the quick flash of sympathy on his face. "It is."

She blinked and that sympathy was gone, but Dawn knew she'd seen it. She rose to her feet and the chair legs squeaked as they slid across the floor. "Anthony . . ."

He tensed.

She stalked toward him. "What's happening here?" Because her heart was racing too fast. Her stomach was tying into knots.

He rolled back his shoulders. "Told you . . . it's a case I'm working on. The FBI came in to consult, and they asked to see you first thing this morning. Just be patient a little longer, okay?"

"I'm not real good with patience." Not any longer she wasn't. Like she wasn't good with many things. *Being alone at night. I suck when it comes to being alone when it gets dark. That's why I hunt then. Better to be on the streets than locked in my home.*

He glanced back at the door, looking over her shoulder. Since she stood at just five foot four and he was easily over six feet, it was simple enough for the guy to glance right over her.

She didn't like being glanced over.

She also didn't like finding out that the FBI was about to burst into the room. *Easy, Dawn. There are hundreds, thousands of FBI agents. What are the odds that he will be the one to walk inside right now?*

He . . . Tucker Frost. The man who haunted her, waking and sleeping.

She shook her head. No, there was *no way* fate would be that cruel to her. Besides, she kept tabs on Tucker. He was working in DC now. He wasn't part of the local FBI branch. He wouldn't be coming in that door.

The door began to squeak open. She whirled around.

Fear.

God, he'd forgotten how much he hated to see fear on Dawn's face.

Tucker stood just behind the one-way glass, watching her as she whirled to confront the agent who'd just walked through the door. For an instant, there had been no missing the fact that Dawn was afraid.

But . . .

When she saw Macey, Dawn's shoulders relaxed.

And he knew why she'd been afraid. *She's still afraid of me.*

Some things didn't change, no matter how much time passed.

His arms were crossed over his chest as he watched the little group. Anthony Deveraux. He'd been the cop who contacted the Bureau, the guy who'd instantly feared that they had another Iceman on their hands. A guy who didn't want a serial, not in his city.

Like anyone wanted one. It wasn't as if folks went out hoping for death and despair to hit close to home.

"I'm FBI Special Agent Macey Night," Tucker's partner said as she closed the door behind her. She was wearing her neatly pressed suit, with the sleeves that fell just past her wrists. Her red hair was tucked behind her ears. Her gaze swept over Dawn. "And I really appreciate you coming in this morning, Ms. Alexander—"

"Just Dawn," she said, shaking her head. "Just call me Dawn." She paced around the room, moving quickly, energy seeming to bubble off her. For a moment, he just stared at her. She'd changed in the last seven years. Her blond hair was shorter, barely skimming her pale jaw now. Her green eyes were still bright, gleaming, but now her stare seemed to carry suspicion. Her cheekbones were high, her chin was slightly pointed and her lips were full and red. Sexy. She'd always been sexy to him. But now . . .

She carried herself differently. She moved with fast energy and, except for that flash of fear . . . confidence.

A scar sliced around her neck, faint now, white and faded, but he'd always remember that mark. Just as he remembered the others.

So many others.

Jason, you bastard. I hope you're burning in hell right now.

"Dawn." Macey inclined her head. "I just want to begin by saying that I know your life hasn't been easy. And I know you probably don't want to talk about your past."

Dawn shot a disbelieving glance at Anthony. "Tell me you did not bring me down here for this." Her hands fisted at her sides. "My past? Seriously? My past is dead and buried." Her chin notched up as she focused on Macey once more. "And you're right. I *don't* want to talk about it. I'm not going to talk about it." She moved toward the door.

Macey stepped into her path. "I should tell you more about my work with the FBI. I studied with the Behavioral Analysis Unit." She gave a weak smile. "Though it's not the technical term we use, you could say I'm a profiler—"

Dawn flinched. "And you want to understand killers better, right? You want to talk to a living, breathing serial killer survivor so you can figure out how those psychos tick?" She shook her head. "Sorry, lady. I don't want to be your science project. I'm not going to let you poke and prod me so you can see all of my pain and learn more about those sick freaks. I'm leaving, so do me a favor and *move.*"

Macey did move. She pushed up her right sleeve, then her left, and she raised her arms in front of Dawn.

From the angle he had, Tucker couldn't see

Macey's arms clearly, but he did see Dawn's expression. Surprise. Pain.

"I have plenty of experience with a 'living, breathing serial killer survivor,' as you put it," Macey said softly. "So believe me when I say . . . I understand. I understand that you're scared. You're angry. I understand that some days you hate the very world around you. You see people living their simple lives and they just don't get how dark and twisted the world around them truly is." She exhaled as she pushed her sleeves back down. "Believe me, I understand."

Dawn was no longer staring angrily at the other woman. Now curiosity was on her face. "What is it that I can do for you, Agent Night?"

"Detective Deveraux and I wanted you to be aware of a crime that was recently committed in the New Orleans area." Macey motioned toward the table. "Why don't you and I sit down so we can talk?"

He saw Dawn lift one delicate brow, but she turned and made her way back to the table. She took one of the seats and then Macey sat across from her.

Anthony wasn't speaking. He was just watching. Waiting.

So was Tucker. He'd held his breath when he'd first seen her. That initial view of Dawn had been like a punch straight to his gut. As he watched her now, his hand rose and pressed to the glass.

This was the closest he'd been to Dawn in years.

There was another knock on the interrogation room door.

Dawn's shoulders stiffened, but a young cop came running inside, and he handed Macey a manila file. She thanked him and—

Dawn is looking at me.

Her head had turned and she was staring at the one-way mirror. It actually seemed as if she were gazing at him. For a second, he almost fucking forgot to breathe.

But then she looked away.

"These are crime scene photos," Macey began as her fingers slid into the folder. "I asked Officer Higgins to bring them into us but before you see them, I wanted to warn you that they are very graphic."

"I'm used to graphic," Dawn replied. Her voice was husky. Soft. It rolled over him as he stood there.

He wanted to be in that room. Wanted to be with her. But . . .

Fear.

It held them both back.

Anthony cleared his throat. "I found a body recently, Dawn. One that set off every alarm bell in my head." His lips thinned. "Because of you, I was . . . familiar with this kind of work."

Her head tilted as if she were considering his words. "I'm not sure I understand."

Macey opened the file and she pushed a picture toward Dawn.

Dawn immediately jumped to her feet and the chair shot back behind her, its wheels screeching. Fear didn't just flash on her face. Horror came, turning her skin stark white, and Tucker found himself lunging for the door.

She needs me.

"No." Dawn's voice was surprisingly strong. *"No."*

He froze.

She couldn't take her eyes off the first picture.

She'd seen pictures just like that one before. She'd *made* herself see them. Dawn had wanted to learn everything she could about the Iceman's other victims. And they'd all looked just like this . . . when he was done with them.

Ice covered the woman's thick lashes. Her skin was blue. Her lips—they were so dark. There were cuts on the woman, cuts that had long since stopped bleeding.

The pain had stopped.

I'm going to teach you to like the pain.

The woman appeared young, perhaps barely twenty-one. She was dead. Frozen.

"I found her in a warehouse downtown. An anonymous tip came into the station and I followed up on it," Anthony said. "At first, I thought it was a hoax, then I saw the freezer.

There was power in the building, but it looked as if the place hadn't been used in months. Cobwebs were everywhere. The air tasted stale but the freezer was . . . humming."

Look away from the picture.

She jerked her gaze up to him.

"I had to look inside." His eyes squeezed shut for a moment. "And I found her."

"Who owns the building?" The words came from her, flat, calm. Surprising when she didn't feel calm at all. "Get the person who owns the building. I mean, if the freezer was running . . ." *How long? How long were you in there?* She cleared her throat and made herself keep talking. "If the freezer was running, if the power was on in that building, then the owner has to know *something*."

"The owner was questioned first thing. He'd moved his operation out of the warehouse seven months ago. He'd kept the power on because of a clerical error in his office. He didn't even realize he was still getting billed for it. The freezer . . ." Anthony shook his head. "He swore he knew nothing about it."

"And you believe him?" She didn't, but then she didn't usually trust anyone. People hid too many secrets. They told too many lies.

"At this point, he appears to be telling the truth."

Bull. She'd like to talk to the guy herself. She'd like—

“We may be looking at a copycat here,” Macey announced.

Dawn backed up a step. *“May?”* She gave a rough laugh. “Considering that Jason Frost is dead, I think there is a bit more than *may* involved right here.” Her temples were throbbing. Her heart racing. *Jason has to be dead. He has to be.*

But in the last few months, hadn’t she started to wonder . . . hadn’t she started to fear . . . ?

“It could be a onetime situation,” Macey continued briskly. Her head inclined and her red hair gleamed under the overhead light. “It could be a person who was trying to take advantage of a serial killer’s fame. Perhaps this individual had someone he wanted to eliminate from his life, so he used the Iceman’s MO to do it.”

Anthony had edged closer to them.

“That’s actually what I hope it is,” Macey continued, her head cocked a bit to the right. “And not a true copycat. Because in that instance . . . there will be more deaths.”

No, no, she did *not* want to hear this. Dawn’s gaze cut to Anthony. “Way to warn a woman what she’s walking into.”

He winced. “I was under orders not to talk about it. Not to—”

“Our department wanted to speak to you first.” Macey’s interjection was smooth.

And . . . interesting. “Why?” Dawn demanded. “Because you wanted to watch my reaction?”

That just didn't make sense to her, not unless . . . Her spine straightened. "Surely you don't think I'm involved in this?"

There was the faintest of hesitations before Macey said, "You were the Iceman's only surviving victim. You knew Jason Frost well before your attack."

Not as well as I knew Tucker.

"Sometimes, victims can . . . associate with their attackers. They can believe that a connection exists between them."

The lady needed to be bullshitting.

"The Stockholm syndrome is the greatest example. Victims sympathize with their attackers, they've even been known to assist—"

Dawn held up her hand. "Just stop right there, okay? I know about Stockholm and I know plenty of psychological BS that folks like to throw around about displacement and emotional attachment and blah-the-fuck blah."

Macey's eyes widened.

"Let's cut to the chase. I didn't kill that poor woman." Her gaze darted to the chilling photo. "I'm not some copycat. I'm not some insane killer who's trying to emulate the man who attacked her." The very idea made her stomach twist. "And if that's the profile you're going with, then maybe you need to head back to Quantico for some refresher courses on behavioral analysis because you are seriously off the mark."

Macey eased out a slow breath. "You being in

this town while this murder has occurred isn't a coincidence."

No, Dawn didn't think so, either.

"The coroner is working on the time of death now, and once we have that, we will be asking you for an alibi."

This was bullshit. "He froze her. We both know that you'll be lucky if you can pinpoint her death down to a period of a few weeks. No way you're going to get it down to an exact day. I know the Orleans Parish coroner, and Julia Bradford is a great doctor, but she's not some kind of wizard. She can't do the impossible." She'd just called the FBI's bluff there.

Macey and Anthony shared a long stare.

"I know a bit about forensic science," Dawn murmured. "Call it a hobby." And that wonderful Orleans Parish coroner? Well, Julia happened to be one of the few people Dawn could call a friend in that town.

"We're hopeful," Macey said slowly, "that a general time of death can be identified."

Don't hold your breath on that one.

"But . . ." Macey's stare had sharpened on her. "If you're not involved—"

"I'm not." They could be clear on that. She didn't get her jollies by murdering people.

"Then that could mean something very dangerous for you. It could mean that the killer is here because you are."

Enough. She'd heard more than enough from the woman with the scars that snaked down her arms and the hint of pain that shadowed her unusual eyes. "I'm done here now." Because she couldn't breathe in this little room. The dead woman's image was in her head, her heart was about to burst out of her chest and the tiny walls of the interrogation room seemed to be closing in on her.

"I understand." Macey inclined her head. "But if you decide you do want to talk more, I hope you'll contact me." Macey pulled a small white business card from her pocket and offered it to Dawn.

Dawn took the card without glancing at it. She headed for the door, but something was nagging at her. Her fingers curled around the doorknob. *Walk out. Walk away.* But . . .

The victim was still in her head.

And the *tick, tick, tick* of the clock on the wall seemed far too loud.

"Not as easy to walk away as one would think, is it?" Macey murmured.

No, it wasn't. "Do you know who she was?"

"Not yet." It was Anthony who replied. "She's listed as a Jane Doe, but we hope to learn more soon."

Dawn licked dry lips. "What a terrible death. Tortured and frozen away, then when you're found, no one even knows who you are." She looked back at Macey. "That could have been my death."

And now someone is here, using the Iceman's MO. Dawn had to ask, "Was she dead when he put her in the freezer?" *Or did she die in that cold hell?*

Macey was watching her so carefully. "We don't know yet. That's one of the things we hope to learn soon."

Sounded to Dawn as if they didn't know one whole hell of a lot. "One more question . . ." She glanced over her shoulder, looking first at Anthony then at Macey. "Who's been watching me?"

Macey's eyes widened the smallest bit. "Excuse me?"

"Who's behind the glass, watching me?" Because she knew someone was there. "Your partner?" In her experience, no FBI agent ever went into the field alone.

Macey shared a quick look with Anthony.

Her partner. Hit that one dead on.

"We thought you might be more comfortable speaking with a female agent," Macey said, her voice smooth and her expression giving nothing away.

Sure, sometimes agents used that ploy, but . . .

They're dealing with a killer who is acting like the Iceman. And one of the FBI's own agents has personal experience with that SOB. Would the powers-that-be at the FBI have sent him in? Would they have thought he was an asset on this case?

Or would they have wanted to keep Tucker Frost far away from this scene?

"Tucker." His name slipped from her, helplessly.

And there it was . . . Macey's gaze jerked toward the glass. A fast glance, one that, if Dawn hadn't been monitoring the other woman so closely, she would have missed. But in the last few years, Dawn had worked hard to stop missing things. To study her environment. To watch others. To learn their secrets.

Macey Night had just revealed one secret to Dawn.

Tucker Frost was in New Orleans. He was in the police station. He was behind that glass.

Her hand fell away from the doorknob. Slowly, she turned to face the one-way mirror, but she didn't focus on her own reflection. Instead, she imagined she could see right through the glass. To him.

"Hello, Tucker. It's been a long time."

Oh, hell. She was talking to him. And he was just standing behind the glass in the observation room like a fool. He took a step back, then another. But . . .

On the other side of that glass, Dawn turned on

her heel and grabbed for the door. She yanked it open and vanished from the interrogation room in mere moments. Macey spun toward the glass and mouthed, *I'm sorry,* because she knew that she'd given him away.

It didn't matter. Dawn had always been smart. Once she'd realized what was happening, it hadn't taken her long to realize that he'd been pulled down to the city.

And it had taken no time at all for her to run from him, just as he'd feared. He squared his shoulders and headed for the door, more than ready to get out of that damn observation room. He'd get Macey and they'd head over to see what the coroner had discovered. Then—

Before he could reach it, the door flew open.

"You can't go in there!" A man's desperate voice cracked.

But she was already there. Dawn stood just inside the doorway, breathing hard, her eyes locked on his face. "Found you."

The uniformed officer tried to grab her arm. "I told you, Dawn, that room is off-limits. You know better—"

"Let her go," Tucker said flatly. "We need to talk." He leveled his gaze at the officer. For the life of him, he couldn't remember the guy's name. "Alone."

"You heard him, Higgins," Dawn muttered. "He wants to be alone with me."

The officer immediately backed away.

Dawn took a step forward and she shut the door behind her.

Tucker kept his hands at his sides. He tried to figure out just what in the hell he was supposed to say to her. The silence stretched a little too long—uncomfortably long. Her gaze was on his face, sweeping over his features one at a time, and he knew what she was thinking.

I look even more like him now. Time had thinned his face more, hardened him, and when he looked in the mirror, most days Tucker swore he saw his brother staring back at him.

He cleared his throat. "You . . . you look good, Dawn."

She blinked.

Shit. That had been the wrong thing to say. He wanted to yank his hand over his face or pace or do *something* to get rid of the fierce energy pulsing through him.

"That's what you have to say to me? After all this time?" Her voice was still husky, but he could have sworn he heard an echo of pain in it.

He'd always hated her pain.

"Why didn't you come in there to tell me about this case?" She put her hands on her hips as she stared up at him. "Why send in your partner?"

He wouldn't lie to her. "Because I knew you didn't want to see me." That was the same reason he'd left her so long ago. Why he hadn't talked to her in the last seven years.

"You know bullshit." She shook her head. Her blond hair hit her sharp cheeks. "No, you just know your own fear. You don't know anything about me or what I *want.*"

Her words surprised him and he took a quick step toward her. But . . .

She tensed. He saw it and the telling movement knifed right through him.

No, Dawn. I do know you. Better than you know yourself. I always knew you.

The problem was that she hadn't truly known him. He'd been afraid for her to know the truth. He was still afraid. *You won't like who I really am.*

"What's happening in this city? Who killed that poor woman?"

"I don't know." He'd be finding out soon. "We thought you had a right to hear about the crime first, before any news leaked to the media." He hadn't wanted her learning about this killer when she turned on the five o'clock news.

"Maybe that's true, but I also think you wanted to see my reaction. You know, just in case I'd gone psycho and started killing like Jason." She pursed her lips, as if thinking about that situation. "What would that be? Some serious PTSD shit, right? Your buddy Macey sure acted as if it were a possibility."

"Dawn . . ."

"He *didn't* break me." Her eyes glittered at him. "I get that you think he did. I get that you think I was so shattered by what happened that you left—"

"That wasn't what—"

"But I'm stronger than he was. I'm stronger than you gave me credit for being."

He'd always thought she was the strongest woman he'd ever met.

"I'm strong," she said again, "and I want in on this investigation."

It took a moment for her words to register. Then he could only blink and shake his head. "What?"

She pulled her ID out of the small bag that was slung over her shoulder. She advanced toward him and her scent—soft, vanilla—wrapped around Tucker, reminding him of things he should forget. Of things he had *no* business remembering right then. "I'm a PI now. A damn good one. I know this city, I know the people here and I want in on the investigation."

He glanced at her ID, but he'd already known she was a PI. He'd researched her . . . He'd peeked into her life many times over the years. He'd always thought that, one day, he'd check up on her and discover that she was married. That she had a family. That she was happy.

He'd both longed for her happiness and feared it. *Because I couldn't imagine her with anyone else.*

"I want in," Dawn said again, her expression determined.

Tucker shook his head. "It's a preliminary investigation. And right now, the local authorities are handling things. We're here in a backup capacity, just in town long enough to prove that the killer *isn't* Jason Frost . . . and to assist the NOPD in finding the man who murdered that victim."

Her delicate jaw hardened. "What makes you so sure?"

He didn't understand her question.

She took another step toward him even as she shoved her ID back into her bag. "They didn't find his body. His body was *never* found."

He could hear the drumming of his heartbeat. That dull thud seemed to shake his eardrums.

"What makes you so sure this isn't Jason? Your partner was talking about a copycat, talking about some guy who might just be taking advantage of Jason's MO . . ." Another step toward him.

Tucker locked down his muscles, refusing to move so much as an inch.

"Tell me, Tucker. The truth. Why don't you think it could be Jason?"

He couldn't believe she was saying this to him. "Because he's *dead,* Dawn. Jason Frost is dead." The idea that she still thought his brother might be hunting—

Oh, Dawn. I am so sorry. So sorry for the pain he is still bringing you.

"No body, no proof." Her stare was unflinching. She was absolutely serious. "You think my brother is still alive?" He reached out and his hands curled around her shoulders. She stiffened and immediately pulled away.

He let go. Just like he always did.

"No, Dawn." He made his voice flat with an effort. "I shot him that day. I killed him. He is gone."

"I thought so, too, but . . ." Her lips parted, as if she'd say more.

A knock sounded on the door. "Tucker . . ." Macey's voice drifted through the closed door. "The coroner just called. She wants to see us."

"Let me work this case with you," Dawn said. Her voice was almost pleading. He hated for her to plead. Dawn should never have to beg anyone for anything.

But Tucker shook his head. "This case could be about to end with the coroner's report."

Her eyes turned to angry slits. "I don't like being shut out."

There was no choice that he could see right then. He couldn't pull her in, not with the local cops running the show.

She spun on her heel and yanked open the door. Macey hurriedly stepped aside.

"Dawn!" He couldn't let her go like this. *God, I missed her. So fucking much.*

She paused.

"After I meet with the coroner, I want us to talk again." *I'll share what I learn.* He could give her that much. He hoped that she could see the message in his eyes.

Her head moved in a grim nod, and then she was gone, cutting through the station and leaving him behind.

Macey didn't speak until Dawn was long gone, and then she let out a soft sigh. "That did not go well."

Fucking understatement.

"Could have gone worse," Anthony noted as he joined their little group. "Dawn has one hell of a temper when you get her going."

Dawn? She'd never had a temper before. Seven years ago, she'd been the most easygoing woman he'd ever met. Always sweet to everyone. Always kind.

And why the hell was the detective speaking as if he knew her so well? *Intimately?*

"Ah, right, we haven't been officially introduced yet." Anthony offered his hand at Tucker's questioning glance. "Detective Anthony Deveraux."

Tucker shook his hand. The guy had a solid grip.

Anthony smiled at him. "You're his brother, huh?"

"Yes," he gritted, "I'm his brother."

Anthony's smile dimmed. "When I first met

Dawn, I made a point of . . . learning everything about her." His stare was assessing as it slid over Tucker. "I don't think she was happy to see you."

He knows Dawn and I were involved. Once upon a time, everyone had known. Their story had been too sensational for the reporters to pass up. *Her lover's brother tortured her. He tried to kill her.*

"No," Tucker murmured, "I don't think she was." And her words kept ringing in his head, playing over and over again.

No body, no proof.

He hadn't realized until that very moment just how much his brother still haunted her.

CHAPTER FOUR

"The killer took his time with our victim." Dr. Julia Bradford, the Orleans Parish coroner, moved briskly around the lab. She spoke with sympathy flowing in her voice. "There were over a dozen knife wounds to her body."

"A dozen?" Macey repeated. He saw her eyes briefly close. "That poor woman."

Macey always responded to the victims because she knew them so well.

She knew what it was like to feel their pain.

"Many of those wounds were shallow." The coroner's hand moved toward the victim's face. "Like these here on the cheek . . ."

"As if the killer was just getting started," Tucker muttered, disgust rising in him. It wasn't a disgust he'd allow to show. All of his emotions were locked down right then, and he'd keep them locked tight.

The way he always did. Seeing Dawn had rattled him, and he was having to fight harder to keep his control in place.

"But here . . ." Dr. Bradford's glove-covered hand moved to the victim's neck and the mark there. "As you can see, the wounds became deeper."

"Dawn has a scar like that one," Anthony said, leaning closer to the body.

Tucker's gaze swept over him.

"The wound is deeper here, too." Dr. Bradford's hand went to the woman's right shoulder.

"Dawn has—" Anthony began.

"I know where her scars are," Tucker growled. But Dawn didn't have over a dozen scars, thank Christ. Tucker had stopped Jason before the bastard could finish his ritual on her.

Anthony's brows rose. "Sorry." He cleared his throat even as a light flush stained his cheeks. "I was just pointing out that the wounds seem to be following the Iceman's pattern."

Because the Iceman had used a particular pattern with his victims. A very thorough pattern designed for maximum pain and disfigurement. But not for death.

"I compared the wounds on our Jane Doe with the wound patterns from the Iceman's attacks," Julia said. "They're the same."

Tucker and Macey shared a long glance. *Not good.* But they'd already suspected this. When they'd first gotten the crime scene photos, the similarity had been obvious. However, a similarity was one thing . . . an exact copy was another entirely.

"The wounds didn't kill her . . ." She took a deep breath. "They weren't severe enough for that. Just like with the Iceman, no major arteries were damaged. The wounds were given to inflict pain, to maim, but not to kill." Dr. Bradford swallowed as jazz music played lightly in the background. "Our victim died in the freezer."

"Shit," Anthony muttered. He backed away from the exam table. "Talk about torture. She was in there, knowing she was dying, knowing there was no way out. Freezing to freaking death."

The Iceman's MO.

"I'm running her DNA, hoping for a hit on her identity." Julia's lips turned down. "Her fingerprints weren't in the system, though."

"We should release her photo to the media," Anthony said, nodding. "She could have family out there, people who can identify her. People who are looking for her."

"Those same people haven't filed a missing person's report for her," Macey stated quietly. "Don't you think that is odd?"

Anthony didn't speak.

So Tucker did. "Maybe she didn't have family," he said. "Or maybe they just weren't close any longer. Families grow apart. Everyone knows that."

Julia covered the victim. She took off her gloves and tossed them into the trash. She turned to face them, her dark cream skin smooth and unlined. She was a young doctor, he knew that, but he'd done some checking on her. Julia Bradford had graduated at the top of her class at Tulane. She was smart, thorough and well respected by the prosecutors in the area. She might be new on the scene, but she knew how to do her job. They weren't going to have to face amateur hour on this one.

"How long was she in there?" Tucker asked her.

Julia hesitated.

"If we know how long she was frozen," he said, "we can figure out more information about the man who took her."

"Freezing the victim helped to obscure her time of death." She shook her head. "I'm working on that, but . . . I don't have a definitive time for you. Considering the way she was stored, I doubt I'll ever have that for you."

Exactly what Dawn had said . . . and, unfortunately, what he'd suspected given his own knowledge of forensics. "Did you find any evidence on her?" Tucker asked. "Skin cells beneath her fingernails? Fibers or—"

"Her wrists were tied together when we pulled her out of the freezer. From what I can tell, she never had the opportunity to fight back." Sorrow flashed on Julia's face. "The killer was very organized, I can tell you that. No trace evidence was left behind."

So basically, they had jackshit. "I want to see the crime scene."

Anthony nodded. "Sure thing, but . . . the freezer was transferred to Evidence. We ran a check on the serial number and got a hit because, years ago, the freezer was registered under warranty. We found that owner, but it turned out that she'd put the freezer out as garbage two years ago. She thought it was hauled to the dump. Hell, maybe it was . . . or maybe someone just took it when they saw it outside. Either way . . . we turned up empty when it came to tracking it."

Son of a bitch. "I'll be wanting to talk to that woman."

Anthony shrugged. "Yeah, okay, but I already interviewed her. She didn't know anything about the case and when I told her about just what had been found inside of the freezer . . . I thought she was going to have a heart attack."

His attention shifted back to the woman in that freezer. "She has a name. She has a family."

"She had a life," Macey murmured.

Had. Until some sick bastard stole that life.

"Someone is looking for her," Tucker said. Somewhere out there, someone was looking.

But Anthony shook his head. "Maybe they're not." He paced near the exam table as the coroner watched him. "Jules, you know as well as I do that the lost flock to our city. The Big Easy is a great place if you're looking to escape a troubled past. If you just walk down Canal, you'll see our homeless. Those are people that slip under the radar every day. People who could vanish and . . ." His lips tightened. "And no one would be looking for them."

Tucker cocked his head as he studied the victim's covered body once more. "She didn't look malnourished. Her hair was cut neatly and . . ." Now his stare darted to Julia. "Any sign of needle marks or drug use?"

"No. Other than the knife wounds, there were no marks on her at all. No distinguishing birthmarks. No tattoos. Nothing that stood out."

He nodded. "I don't think she lived on the streets."

"That doesn't mean she wasn't running from someone," Anthony continued doggedly. "Hell, just ask Dawn. People come here for a fresh start. 'Cause they are trying to escape someone or something."

Tucker's shoulders stiffened. "I know plenty about Dawn."

"No," Anthony denied, "I'm not so sure you do."

The guy was pissing him off. He took a breath, focused. *Keep your control always.* And a dick detective wasn't going to get beneath his skin. Tucker motioned toward Macey. "Dr. Bradford, my partner, Macey Night, has her medical degree."

Julia's brows rose. "So you want to review my findings?" She jumped right to the point, but didn't seem upset or territorial, responses that Tucker had certainly seen in the past.

"I'd like to assist you," Macey clarified.

"Because when it comes to serials, I have experience."

That was an understatement.

"Sometimes I can see things—particularly relating to a killer's signature—that might be missed during the course of a normal exam."

Julia nodded her head toward a box of white exam gloves. "Help yourself. I'm not into any pissing match, so you want to help me find justice for this woman?" She nodded grimly. "Then I appreciate the help."

And while Macey was working with the coroner, Tucker had plans of his own. "Thanks for your time, Doctor," he said to Julia. Then he made his way outside. Anthony was right behind him. He waited until they'd left the coroner's building, when they were outside—and then he turned on the guy. "Just what is the nature of your relationship with Dawn Alexander?" The words came out quiet, flat, as he stared at the other man.

Anthony blinked. His expression was bemused. "Excuse me?"

"Do you have a personal relationship with her? Because that's something I need to know about." Right the hell then.

Anthony's face tightened. "Look—"

"No, *you* look. We have a killer imitating the Iceman in New Orleans, the same city that the Iceman's only surviving victim just *happens* to live in. And then we have you . . . the detective who found the body based on a tip. Then I learn that you and Dawn . . . You two seem close. I'm thinking the killer knew that, too, and that's why he chose you to receive the tip." His breath felt cold in his lungs. "So I'm going to ask again, just what is the nature of your relationship with Dawn Alexander?"

A muscle flexed in Anthony's jaw. "We're friends. I help her on cases and she helps me."

Friends. "Nothing more?"

Anthony's mouth opened.

"No, nothing more."

That had *not* been Anthony responding. Tucker glanced to the right and saw Dawn step from the side of the building. She came toward him with slow, determined steps.

"Eavesdropping?" Tucker demanded.

She tucked a strand of hair behind her left ear. "I've found that cops don't always want to share directly with me. But you'd be surprised what you can pick up from folks if you just stop . . . and listen."

And hide out of sight.

"I need to get back to the station," Anthony mumbled. "Captain Hatch is going to be wanting a report from me. Agent Frost, we'll finish this conversation later."

"Nothing left to finish," Dawn said. "I think I gave him a solid answer for us both."

"Dawn . . ." Anthony's voice had a warning

edge. “Watch your step with him. The FBI might not play as nicely with you as the NOPD does.”

She didn’t speak until Anthony was gone. Then she swept her gaze over Tucker. “I asked you to play nicely before, but you shut me out of the investigation.” She shook her head. “That’s okay. I don’t give up easily.”

Obviously not.

“You followed me here?” Tucker asked.

She smiled. For an instant, he could have sworn that his heart stopped.

“Don’t be silly. I know where the coroner’s office is. Julia and I go out for beignets every Thursday.” She paused. “And po’boys on Tuesdays.”

So she had an in with the coroner. “You’re planning to get her to tell you what she’s learned on the case?”

Her smile dimmed. “I was actually hoping *you* would tell me what you learned.” She paused a beat. “Is it him?”

Him? And he found himself reaching for her. This time, he was prepared when she flinched away from his touch, but he still kept his hands wrapped around her shoulders. “Jason Frost is dead.”

“Was the MO the same? Was the pattern of slices the same?”

“Yes,” he ground out, “but . . .”

“Was she alive when he put her into the freezer?”

He didn't speak but he could tell by the way her face paled that his silence was answer enough.

"So . . ." Dawn licked her lips. "If this is a copycat, we're dealing with someone who has closely studied Jason's work. To get all of the wounds just right, to attack with a knife *that* many times . . ."

"I'm going to find the guy," Tucker swore. "I will stop him."

Her thick lashes swept down, concealing her gaze. "Right. That's what you do now, hmm? No more out saving the world by fighting the secret missions you couldn't talk about with me. These days, you go after monsters much closer to home."

Because I had monsters in my home.

"I want in on this investigation." She was still not looking at him. "I *need* in on it."

"I get that you want closure." Oh, hell, yes, he got that. "But the FBI doesn't pull in civilians when—"

Her gaze flew up and he saw the anger burning in her eyes. "I'm not a civilian. I'm a PI. My specialty is missing person cases, and I am very good at my job."

And I don't want you in danger. Not on my watch.

"You're going to say no again." She backed away—no, pulled away.

His hands fell to his sides.

"Why can't you see that I'm not the same broken woman you knew before?"

Her words pierced right through him. "I *never* thought you were broken."

"Then why did you leave? Why did you leave me?"

He took a step toward her. "Dawn—"

"Someone has been watching me."

For a moment, all he heard was the thunder of his heartbeat. Again, too loud. Drumming in his ears. Nearly bursting. Rage heated his blood. *"What?"*

"It started a few months ago. I *felt* someone watching me."

He grabbed her arm and pulled her with him, moving too fast, knowing that his touch was too rough, but not able to help himself. He steered her to the side of the building. The same spot she'd been hiding in before because that spot gave them perfect privacy. "Why the hell are you telling me this *now?* It should have been the first damn thing you revealed—"

"I have no proof. If I'd had proof, I would have brought the evidence to the police long ago. If I go to them with nothing, I'd look like the woman crying wolf. With my past, folks would jump to the conclusion that I'm suffering from PTSD. I have built a solid reputation with my clients. They know me. They trust me. If I start throwing claims of some shadow stalker without any evidence . . .” She shook her head. “I’d lose everything I’ve worked to build.”

His hands pressed into the rough stone on either side of her head. He wasn’t touching her then, he didn’t trust himself to touch her, but he caged her with his body because she wasn’t getting away, not until she’d answered all of his questions. “At the police station, you should have told me—”

“You keep looking at me as if you think I’m going to shatter. I didn’t want you to think I was crying wolf, either.”

Fuck. “There’s something you need to understand. Right the hell now.” He stared into her eyes. Got lost in her gaze, like he used to do. “I will always believe you. I have *never* doubted you.”

She sucked in a sharp breath. “But I doubted you.”

Oh, shit. “That wasn’t what I—”

Her hand came up between them and her palm slid over the stubble that covered his jaw. He hadn’t shaved that morning. Deliberately.

Because if I have stubble or a beard . . . maybe I don’t look quite as much like him. Jason had always been freshly shaven. He’d always been so fastidious about his appearance. *An organized, obsessive killer—*

“It’s his face.”

Every muscle in his body locked down at her soft words. “His face. *But I am not him.*” He wouldn't be, fucking ever. But had Dawn sensed the darkness in him? All that seething energy that he kept bottled up every moment? He wouldn't let it out. He'd never let it touch her.

"It hurt me, at first, to see you."

He knew that. When he'd tried to make love to her after the attack . . .

Her screams haunted him.

"But then you were gone—" her hand was still against his cheek "—and that hurt worse."

What?

She swallowed. Her hand fell back to her side. "But that's in the past. We both moved on."

"Someone didn't move on. Someone is out there, starting his crimes again." And that had him breaking out into a cold sweat. "Why do you think someone has been watching you? Tell me everything, right now."

Because he truly did believe her. He would always believe her.

Only you're wrong, Dawn. We both haven't moved on.

If only that part was true.

The players were together. He'd waited. He'd been so patient. So careful. But now they were all there.

He watched as Dawn led FBI Special Agent Tucker Frost away from the coroner's building. They'd been having quite the conversation moments before, but now they were hurrying from the scene. Did Tucker realize he had a tendency to stand too close to Dawn? That was a dead giveaway.

He knew plenty about body language. About the unspoken cues that could give away a person's real emotions. People lied with words, but their bodies always told the truth.

Tucker still cared about Dawn. That was his weakness. But just how *much* of a weakness, well, that remained to be seen.

Tucker had left the scene. He and Dawn had vanished. He'd find them later. He kept his gaze on the coroner's building. His victim was still in there.

Eventually, they'd find out who the woman was.

But he'd planned for that. Just as he'd planned for everything.

How much will you be able to take, Tucker, before you break? Because he knew there was a darkness inside of Tucker. And it was time to let that darkness come out and play.

I've been waiting for this moment. For a very, very long time.

Seven years, to be exact.

CHAPTER FIVE

Dawn's home was on the second floor of a historic building in the French Quarter. Years ago, the house had been converted into two condo units. Dawn had jumped at the chance to get the upper condo. She loved the view of the city that she had from her balcony. Loved watching the tourists on her street. Loved listening to jazz music drift on the breeze.

And the second floor should have been safer. I picked it because it was harder to access. And this updated building had top-notch security.

She should have been safe.

Only she didn't feel that way.

"As you can see," Dawn murmured as she gestured to the security control panel near her door, "I always set my alarm. It's never gone off, never warned me that any intruder was inside . . ."

Tucker had paced toward her den. He stood there, glancing around the space curiously.

Tucker is here. She swallowed and would *not* let her emotions push her to say something she wouldn't be able to take back. He was there to help her. Nothing more, nothing less.

"The alarm didn't go off, but you think someone has been here."

She nodded. "I do." She walked toward the

window. "It's small things that I notice. Things that other people might brush away." She pointed toward her bedroom. The door was open, and from her vantage point she could see the pictures that hung on her wall—a dark blue wall. She'd painted it blue because the color was supposed to soothe, to help her relax.

Only I haven't been relaxing at all lately.

"My pictures . . . One day, I noticed that two of them were moved. Just . . . switched in position." A mocking laugh came from her. "Try telling the cops that someone came in and moved your pictures for you. This is New Orleans. We had the biggest homicide rate in the US just a few years ago . . . The cops are too busy to worry about swapped pictures."

He stalked into her bedroom and studied the photos hanging on the wall. Dawn followed him, her steps slower. She'd taken both photos. Photography was her hobby. Another thing that was supposed to *soothe* her. When she'd been in therapy, her psychiatrist had been big on *soothing*.

He'd actually been right about the photography, though. She liked taking her pictures. When she looked through the lens of her camera, she got lost in the moment. She forgot her past and only focused on the image she was trying to capture. She focused only on the moment. The present.

The present mattered. The past didn't. And the

future? Why plan for something that could go so terribly dark?

Her breath eased out as she looked at the framed images. In one of the photos, she'd captured the sunset over the Mississippi. In another, she showed the imposing figure of the St. Louis Cathedral at nighttime.

"You and Detective Deveraux are friends. Surely he would have listened to you if you'd taken your fears to him."

It was because they were friends that she hadn't gone to him. He looked at her with respect, treated her as a colleague. She hadn't wanted him to start doubting her. *And did I doubt myself? Maybe, at first, when I glanced at the photos, for a moment, even I wasn't sure* . . . "I need more proof." She still needed it. She'd worked as a PI long enough to know that she didn't have enough evidence for the cops. So she'd tried to get evidence. Only it hadn't worked.

"Anything else happen?"

"I woke up one morning, and I could . . . smell him." Yes, even as she said it, Dawn knew her words sounded crazy. *This is why I didn't go to Anthony.* "That aftershave that Jason used to soak himself with . . . I smelled it. I woke up and it was all over the place." She pointed to her bed. "It was strongest right there, right next to me."

Her bed, a brass four-poster that she'd bought from an antiques store just down the street, sat in the middle of the room. A lounging chair that she used for reading was to the right of it, and a heavy cherry dresser leaned against the far wall. "Sometimes, you can think your mind is playing tricks on you. A familiar scent . . . Maybe you're just imagining it." Her fingers skimmed over the pillow on her bed. "But the scent was so strong. It was like he'd been standing right next to my bed, watching me. Like he was here with me." *While I slept.* She breathed out, nice and slowly, then turned back to face Tucker. "After that, I upgraded my security system again and . . . I don't think anyone has been back inside."

He was watching her with that too-bright blue stare. Goose bumps rose on her skin.

Why does he have to look so much like Jason? Her breath came faster, nearly shaking her chest. *Before I'm done, you'll grow to like the pain.* Jason's voice. Always in her head. Always, damn it.

Tucker moved toward her. "Dawn?"

She shook her head. She needed to get the rest of the story out, fast. "There have been a few other times, when I was out in the city that I *thought* someone was following me." She bit her lower lip. "I'm pretty good at spotting a tail." Mostly because she tailed others and she'd learned all the tricks of the trade. "But I could never spot him."

"Yet you're sure someone was following you?"

She faced him fully. "You know when you're being hunted."

His gaze drifted to her bed. If anything, his expression hardened more. "You should have contacted me."

She blinked.

"I get that you thought you didn't have enough to show the local cops. You didn't want them thinking you were imagining things, didn't want to put your business at risk, but . . ." He took a step toward her.

The back of her legs bumped into her bed. *He's the only one I back away from.*

When he should have been the man she always ran to.

"But you should have contacted *me.* Some creep is in your *home, in your bedroom.*" His hands were fisted. "I would have been on the first fucking plane down here. Jason is *dead*. But there are people out there—people who get obsessed with serials. Women who fall in love with them. Men who want to *be* them. As the only surviving victim, shit, that makes you a target for people like that. It makes you—"

"Why do you think I moved to New Orleans?" She gave a sad shake of her head. "I needed to get away from all that. From the letters that came from strangers who told me what they'd like to do to me." She'd given all of those twisted letters to the authorities in Baton Rouge. They'd assured her they would investigate, but no one had ever been arrested.

That was years ago.

"I had a normal life here," she continued determinedly. "People had forgotten. I had a business. I had clients who trusted me." A job that made her feel as if she were making a difference. *And not just being a victim.* "But someone started trying to unravel that life."

He watched her with a hard gaze. "You think it's the same man who killed our Jane Doe."

"I think . . ." She stopped, then tried again. "I think I want to be a part of your investigation because *someone* has been screwing around with me." She wanted to believe that Jason Frost was dead. Oh, God, she wanted that to be true. But his body had never been found and fear had haunted her. The fear was a companion that had dodged her steps for years.

And . . .

She was lying to Tucker. Well, a little. Only a little lie. In those first few months after her attack, she *had* imagined that Jason was after her. Everywhere she'd turned, she'd seen him. She'd thought for sure he was tailing her. She'd been so certain that she'd hired a PI.

Timothy Roth had been in his late fifties, a tough, grizzled, no-nonsense PI. He'd taken her money, he'd tailed her and he'd looked for someone who might be stalking her . . .

Jason.

And after six weeks, he'd given her the money back. No one had been following her back then. He'd found zero evidence.

The PTSD had gotten to her.

She'd seen a shrink.

She'd gotten better.

But I can't have that dark time brought up again. I can't have people saying that I was just imagining everything again. And *that* was the real reason she'd held off on contacting the police until she had solid proof. Not just scents in her home. Not just two photos that had been switched. Not just goose bumps on her arms when she was out late at night—the primitive, instinctive response to being hunted.

More evidence. Real evidence that couldn't be denied.

Timothy had been the one to teach her that she needed more. Timothy had been the one to teach her how to be a PI. Only she wouldn't tell Tucker any of that because she wanted him to keep believing her. There couldn't be any room for doubt in his mind.

But Tucker had just turned and headed away from the bed. She hurried after him. "Tucker?" Her fingers itched to reach out and touch him again.

He opened the French doors that led to her balcony and stepped outside. She hurriedly followed him, and the heat of a June New Orleans day sank on her like a hot, heavy blanket.

Since she'd grown up in Baton Rouge, Dawn was used to the South and the heat it brought. But tourists . . . they usually melted down on the street below. They'd strip off their extra garments and sag as they walked down the worn sidewalks . . . just as they were doing right then.

"The only way to your condo is by taking the stairs that were inside the building, right?"

"Right." The door to her building opened to a landing—her downstairs neighbor's place branched to the left, and the stairs that led up to Dawn's place were nestled to the right. But just to get into the building, you had to have the security code. It was supposed to be a *safe* place.

"Who lives below you?" His hands had curled around the wrought iron railing.

"A tattoo artist. Jinx Donahue is the best in New Orleans." Dawn had even gotten inked by her. "I asked Jinx if she saw anyone, but she said she didn't."

"You and Jinx both know the security code to access the building."

The security system was in place to keep the vagrants out of the building. Vagrants, curious tourists, ghost hunters—they'd all tried to get in at some point. She nodded.

"You've both probably given that code to friends . . . to lovers."

"I don't give the code to anyone."

His blue stare slid to her face. "But Jinx does."

"Yes." She eased closer to him. *He won't bite. Why am I afraid?* She'd been strong, she'd *felt* strong, for so long . . . until the watcher began to mess with her mind again. At first, he'd made her doubt herself. *Is this happening? Am I just imagining things again? Seeing a ghost when the real killer is long gone?* "But those people can only access the bottom floor. You saw that I had my own separate security system up here—"

"Getting into the building would be step one. Breaking into your place would be step two." He rubbed his chin. "I want to talk with Jinx."

Dawn checked her watch. "Her shift at the shop doesn't usually start until noon. We can probably catch her downstairs." She turned to go—

His hand curled around her wrist. "I hate that you're still afraid of me."

"I'm not afraid of you." Her immediate denial.

But he smiled. His dimple flashed. And her heart rate sped up.

"I would never hurt you. I want you to know that." He turned his body and . . . with his grip on her wrist, he pulled her closer. She could have broken away. She didn't. "I killed to keep you safe before. Doesn't that tell you anything?"

It told her they were very dangerous when the two of them were together.

He was staring down at her. He was as tall and

strong as she remembered. Actually, he seemed a little bigger. She'd had dozens of self-defense classes over the years. She'd gotten her black belt in Tae Kwon Do. She'd trained to fight with knives and guns. She'd worked damn hard to make herself strong. *I won't be helpless. Not ever again.*

But when she looked into Tucker's face . . .

Fear still snaked through her.

It's not him that I fear. She wanted to banish that terror. To sever the tie to Jason Frost once and for all.

"If this killer is after you, there is no way I'd let him get close to you."

It wasn't as if he could protect her 24/7.

"We should go downstairs and talk to Jinx." She was making an excuse to slip away from him. Being so close to Tucker made her feel nervous, anxious.

It was absolutely terrifying to want a man who looked so much like the twisted bastard who'd tortured her for hours. Her shrink had said that she should try working through her tangle of emotions. That she had to see the two men as separate and distinct.

Easy for you to say, buddy. You've never seen them side by side.

But it wasn't that simple. It wasn't just about the physical similarity.

Because of me, Tucker killed his own brother.

Their relationship had been doomed, no question. "A pity," she whispered.

His brow furrowed.

"I still want you, after all this time."

His lips parted. *"What?"*

Her eyes stung. She hadn't cried in years—literally hadn't let herself—but he was back and the bittersweet memories were filling her and she had to blink the moisture away. "I remember what it was like the last time we were together." She'd *lost* it. "I'm sorry."

"No." The word was an angry growl. "*Fucking*, no. You *never* have to apologize to me for anything, do you understand?"

He didn't understand. When you wanted and you feared the same man, you were screwed up.

His hand lifted and curled around her chin. "You have *nothing* to be sorry for." And a long shudder worked the length of his frame. "I missed you, Dawn."

She sucked in a sharp breath.

I should back away. I should put space between us. I should—

She rose onto her toes and—

She kissed him.

It wasn't the kiss of friends. It was a kiss of desperation. A kiss because she was suddenly frantic to prove something to herself. To him. *That I've changed.* That she could still want. That she could let the fear go. That the past wasn't going to control her life—or destroy her again.

He stiffened against her. She actually thought he was going to push her away and pain pierced through her. Her lips were against his. Her hands had fisted in his shirt when she'd pulled him toward her.

Please kiss me back. She needed this moment. She needed him.

And after a tense moment, he kissed her back. Not carefully. Not softly. But with a wild, ferocious hunger that she hadn't expected. He took over the kiss. His desire was consuming. He thrust his tongue into her mouth and pulled her even closer.

For just a moment, all of the years between them vanished. It was like it had been so long ago. They'd meet at her dorm or at his house, they'd kiss and they would ignite. The rest of the world wouldn't matter. It would just be the two of them and the wild pleasure they gave each other. Pleasure that was addictive. Pleasure that ripped her world apart. Pleasure that told her he *had* to be the one for her because surely she would never be that happy with anyone else . . .

His head lifted. His eyes were sharp with desire, his face tight with need. "What—" his voice was that rough, ragged growl she remembered so well, the growl that used to turn her on so easily "—are you trying to prove?"

She could taste him. Her nipples were tight.

Her breath came in quick pants and she wanted his mouth on hers again.

"Dawn?" He stepped back, taking the heat of his body with him.

But then . . . it was New Orleans. There was plenty of heat to go around.

Her hand flew out and clamped around the balcony.

"What were you trying to prove? That I still want you?" He gave a ragged laugh. "Baby, I *never* stopped."

She'd never stopped wanting him, either. Even when she'd been afraid.

"Be careful what you start," Tucker warned her. "Be sure you can finish it." Their gazes held. His desire was plain to see, and she wondered . . . what did he see when he looked at her?

He took a few nice, long breaths.

So did she.

She'd had lovers in the years since she and Tucker had parted. There had been one guy that she'd even been engaged to—for a very short period of time. All of two weeks. Then she'd realized she didn't love him, that she was just going through the motions. Trying to be normal when normal was the last thing she'd felt.

She hadn't loved Martin, but she'd wanted him. She'd wanted her other lovers, too. She knew what it was to desire someone.

But it still seemed as if she wanted Tucker

more than she'd ever wanted any of the others. The desire she felt for him . . . it was so much stronger. Stronger. Hotter.

Darker.

He rolled back his shoulders. "Let's talk to the downstairs neighbor."

Right. That had been their plan before she'd decided to start testing herself. And before she made any other moves that she might regret, she needed to get her thoughts together. *Because I'm not sure I can finish what I'm starting.* That had been the problem years before. She'd begin with desire when she touched Tucker, but then the dark, twisting fear had consumed her.

"I'm sorry," she whispered as she turned away from him.

But he caught her wrist in a lightning-fast move. "I told you already . . ." Again, his voice was that rough growl that sent a shiver over her. *Not a shiver of fear.* "You *never* have to apologize to me."

She looked back, staring into his eyes. At that moment, she just couldn't speak. Seven years. God, that was such a long time. She hadn't expected her emotions to ignite this way. That fierce tangle she felt inside when she was near him . . . it should have been gone.

But . . .

It wasn't. When it came to Tucker, her feelings were as strong and twisted as ever.

Without another word, Dawn led the way out of her condo, making sure to lock the door and reset her security system. If anyone came through that door, the alarm would sound instantly. That door, her balcony doors and even her windows, just to be safe. The den area was also outfitted with a motion sensor.

She believed in being safe.

They went silently downstairs and she paused in front of Jinx's place. It was edging close to twelve already, but . . .

Dawn knocked. And she knocked again. She listened intently, but there were no sounds from inside Jinx's place.

"Tell me the name of her tattoo shop," Tucker said as he stood to her right. "I have several stops to make today, and I'll add that to my list."

"It's Voodoo Tats, just off Bourbon Street." She knew his "stops" had to do with the case and she sure wished she could go with him on the investigation. "Will you keep me informed, when you find out something new about Jane Doe?"

He nodded. "I will." He turned to leave the building, but stopped.

She tilted her head as she studied him. "Tucker?"

"You tasted as good as I remembered."

So had he. Dawn swallowed.

"But keep in mind what I said. Don't start what you can't finish." He glanced back at her.

"You've changed over the years, and so have I."

Once more, his words sounded like a warning. Probably because that was exactly what they were.

"If something happens again, if anything goes down at your place that scares you, call me."

Easy to say, but . . . "I don't have your number."

His gaze sharpened. Then he pulled out his phone.

She blurted her number quickly, and when he tensed, she wondered if he'd already known it. Tricky FBI guy, he probably did.

A moment later, her phone vibrated.

He stared at Dawn as her phone rang. "Now you've got my number. If you need me, you call me."

Right. She'd be doing that.

He walked away, heading out into the busy street. She stood there a moment and just watched him. He had changed. He'd spent the last seven years hunting killers with the FBI. Had he been forced to take another life? What would it have been like to always be targeting monsters? To make hunting them your life? What would that do to a person?

She heard a soft creak from inside Jinx's apartment. Frowning, she stepped closer to her friend's door. "Jinx?" She knocked on the door again. "You in there?"

Silence.

The place had been updated, but it was still a building that had been erected in the 1800s. Dawn heard creaks and bumps all the time as the place continued to settle. At first, those little noises had unsettled her, and then she'd slowly gotten used to them.

But . . .

She still had her phone in her hand. She swiped her finger across the screen and dialed Jinx. Even as she dialed, she put her head closer to the door. Dawn thought she might hear the phone ringing from inside her friend's apartment . . .

But she didn't.

Her call went to Jinx's voice mail. *"This is Jinx. You know the drill."*

"Uh, yeah, hi, Jinx," she said quickly as she straightened away from the door. *What am I doing?* Her friend wasn't in there, in some kind of desperate peril. She needed to stop letting the case wreck her mind. "Call me when you get this, okay? I need to ask you some questions. And . . . a friend of mine, Tucker, will probably be coming to your shop today. He looks like a Fed." She turned away from Jinx's place and made her way up the stairs. "Mostly because he *is* a Fed, but he's trying to help me out, so be nice to him, okay? I know you and cops don't exactly get along well . . ." *Understatement.* "But he's not a cop." The FBI was different. "And . . . like I said . . . he's my friend."

Or he had been. Once, he'd been nearly the only friend she had.

It was a shame their lives had changed so much.

Don't start something you don't intend to finish. She hurried up the stairs. Tucker might not be allowing her to participate in the FBI's investigation, but that didn't mean she couldn't do some digging on her own. The days of her just sitting on the sidelines of life, too afraid to make a move, were long gone.

He waited until Tucker left and . . . like clockwork, Dawn hurried out of her building just minutes after him. She jumped in her car and rushed off down the street.

When he saw her vehicle turn the corner, he headed toward her building. He had flowers in his hand. Fresh flowers that he'd made special arrangements to get. He hoped Dawn enjoyed them.

He keyed in the code that would allow him access to the ground floor. He'd learned that code long ago.

Jinx was helpful that way.

He stepped inside, immediately enjoying the cooler air. Then he turned to the left. He pulled the key out of his pocket and he let himself inside Jinx's place.

"Oh, honey," he called out, smiling, "I'm home."

There was no response. But then, he hadn't expected one. He put the flowers down on the kitchen table and then he pulled a pair of gloves from his pocket. After all, he didn't want to leave any prints behind. That would just be sloppy.

He walked toward the pantry. He could hear the low hum as soon as he opened the door.

Jinx had been such a helpful woman. She had a refrigerator in her kitchen, but . . . she did enjoy her frozen meats and ice creams. So she'd sprung for a big, 10.6 cubic foot freezer that she'd had delivered a few months back.

His hand slid over the surface of that freezer and he just had to lift the lid up for a moment.

He smiled at what he saw inside. *"Perfect."*

He shut the freezer and eased out of the pantry. After retrieving the bouquet from the table, he headed toward Jinx's bedroom. There was a naughty secret in there. One she'd made the mistake of telling him about. It had always been so easy to get Jinx to talk. The more alcohol she had, the chattier she became. And the harder it was for her to remember just *what* she'd said the next day. What she'd said and what she'd done. Because of her family trouble, Jinx had been drinking a lot more lately. He'd helped with that.

He went into her closet, and there he found the little passageway that waited. Once upon a time, it had been a dumbwaiter that connected to the upper floor. Dawn didn't realize the passage was there. Jinx had only found it by accident. A handy thing . . .

He slid inside, making sure to bring his flowers with him. The actual elevator part of the dumbwaiter had been removed long ago. All that remained now was an empty tunnel that connected the first and second floors. He'd left a rope in there before, so it was an easy enough matter to climb up. Hell, even without the rope, it was a pretty easy climb. But he'd wanted to be fast, and that rope made maneuvering so much easier.

And soon he was just where he wanted to be. In Dawn's home.

All that security, love. You think you're so safe with all the alarms, but that system never lets you know when I'm inside. Because he didn't have to break in through the front door or sneak in from the balcony. He just walked right out of her closet and into her bedroom. He never made the mistake of going into her den. After all, tricky Dawn had a motion sensor in there.

He took the flowers toward her bed. He put them on her pillow.

She'd find them when she came back that night. The flowers that he'd selected especially for her. They'd be in her safest place.

They'd terrify her.

Her terror was exactly what he wanted.

CHAPTER SIX

"No, Jinx isn't here." The guy behind the counter—a tall, thin man with sleeve tats and a dragon that circled his neck—frowned as he stared at Tucker. "We got plenty of other artists in the back, though, if you're looking to get inked."

He wasn't looking, not at the moment. Tucker pulled out his ID. "I need to ask Jinx some questions and I was told her shift started at noon."

The guy's expression immediately became shuttered when he saw the badge. "Look, I get that Jinx had trouble with the law a long time ago. She told me all about that, and I hired her because I believe in her. This is the first time in a year that she hasn't shown up like she was scheduled. Jinx is a good—"

"She didn't show up for work today?"

The man glowered. "Didn't I say she wasn't here already?"

"Did she call to say where she was?" *The first time in a year.* That wasn't a good sign.

"She didn't call." The man crossed his arms over his chest. "But she's probably just sick. Like I was saying, she's a good tattoo artist. The best I've seen in this town. I don't want the law hassling her."

He needed to play this better. So he switched gears. “I know a friend of hers, okay?”

“What’s that friend’s name?” Suspicion was heavy on the man’s face.

“Dawn Alexander.” The name would probably mean nothing—

A wide smile broke across the guy’s face. “Should have started with that.” He shoved aside Tucker’s ID and offered his hand for a shake. “I’m Malone Blade. I own this shop.” He pumped Tucker’s hand. “Dawn . . . How’s she doing?” He cocked a brow. “Still loving those tats?”

Dawn has tats? He kept his face expressionless. “Absolutely.”

Malone nodded. “Jinx did a great job on them. When you’re dealing with scars, you always have to be extra careful. Covering them can be a tricky business.”

A lump rose in Tucker’s throat, but he swallowed it back.

“Covering scars, though, that’s a specialty with Jinx. She can turn something that was an ugly reminder into something beautiful.” Malone gave a low whistle. “I swear, those roses look *real* on Dawn. The detail that Jinx did with the petals is truly amazing. Got to give my girl props. She is one talented woman.”

And she was also a woman who wasn’t there. “Any idea where I can find her?”

Malone sighed. “Honestly, I’m not sure. Like I

told you already, she's not usually late like this."

"You tried calling her?"

His eyes narrowed. "Yeah. But I just got her voice mail." He shrugged his shoulders. "I'm not the kind of boss who keeps twenty-four-seven tabs on his employees, you know?" But there was still an edge of worry in his eyes. "Why did you need to ask her those questions?" He put his hands on the counter once more. "Did something happen to Dawn?"

"Dawn is fine."

A relieved sigh slid from Malone. "Good. Because I owe that woman and getting Jinx to tat her . . . hell, that isn't payback. Not even close to payback."

He owed Dawn?

Malone reached behind him and pulled a framed photo off the wall. In the photo, he had his arm around the shoulders of a young, redheaded girl. "My baby, Melanie." He swallowed. "She got involved with drugs. I *told* her to stay away from that lifestyle, but she got hooked and then she ran away. The cops couldn't find her. Hell, I don't think they even tried. Another junkie on the street. Not exactly high priority for them."

Tucker tilted his head as he listened.

"Dawn took my case. She found my girl within the week. And twenty-four hours after that, Dawn and I had Melanie in rehab." He smiled as he stared down at the photo. "She's at Tulane now—

going to be a lawyer. Turned her whole damn life around." Carefully, he put the framed photo back up on the wall. "The tats were supposed to be part of my thank-you to Dawn, but she and Jinx, they got to talking . . . and the next thing I know, Dawn found a place for Jinx to live."

She moved Jinx into her building.

"She's a fixer," Malone murmured. "You tell Dawn your problems, and she makes them go away."

But no one makes her problems vanish.

"I owe her," Malone said again. "So if there is troublc, I want to know about it."

Tucker slid his card to the other man. "Like I said, Dawn is okay right now." *And I'm not going to let that change.* "When Jinx comes in, get her to call me."

Malone nodded.

Tucker left the shop, but unease nagged at him. They had a copycat working in the city. And at the exact same time the bastard started hunting, Jinx Donahue had her first ever unexplained absence from work in a year?

Maybe she'd pulled an all-nighter. It was the weekend, after all. Maybe she'd stayed up late partying, but . . .

She didn't answer her door.

And Tucker didn't like coincidences.

If someone had been sneaking into Dawn's place, if the guy had come into her building and

Jinx saw him . . . then the tattoo artist could be a person their perp wanted to eliminate.

She could be a target.

As he walked out on the street, his phone rang, vibrating in his pocket. He pulled it out and saw Macey's name on the screen. He swiped his finger across the screen and put the phone to his ear. "What have you got?"

"We know who our victim is."

Hell, yes.

"Her name is Heather Hartley, she's a twenty-one-year-old former student at Louisiana State University."

His heart rate sped up.

"We used her dental records to track her." Macey was speaking quickly. He could hear the murmur of voices in the background. "The woman had no police record. From what I can tell, she never had any trouble with the law. Not so much as a speeding ticket."

"Why wasn't she reported missing?" He walked quickly down the street.

"Her parents are both dead. She was failing her classes at LSU, so she dropped out last fall. Her friends thought she just went somewhere to start new. They had no idea . . ."

That she'd become a victim.

"She grew up in Baton Rouge," she continued, and now her speech sounded more . . . measured. "Even went to Rondale High School."

He stopped walking. “I went to that school.” He’d gone there. Jason had gone there. Dawn had gone there. “Shit. She’s not some random victim.” No, she was a deliberate message. “We need to see if she has any links to Jason Frost. Because maybe she—”

“She is linked to him.”

The heat was blistering.

“Her cousin was the first victim of the Iceman.”

They had a big fucking problem on their hands. “Call Samantha and let her know what you’ve found. I need to get to Dawn. She thinks someone has been stalking her, and I damn well believe she’s right.” A killer was playing a very deadly game with her.

He heard Macey’s quick inhale.

“If this guy is targeting victims related to the Iceman, then Dawn is going to be his big prize. He’ll go after her.” No doubt in Tucker’s mind.

“There’s something else . . .”

He crossed the street and jumped into his rented SUV.

“Heather’s wounds were all made with a knife that matched up *exactly* to the weapon that Jason Frost used. The cuts were all exact duplicates of the ones he inflicted on his victims.”

Duplicates. Because that was what a copycat did. He duplicated.

“This guy knows the Iceman, inside and out.” He cranked the SUV and transferred the call over to the Bluetooth system. "He's going to want to finish what Jason Frost started."

He'll want to kill Dawn.

Not happening. "Dawn needs to be under protective custody." She needed to be a million miles away from the city. "I'm getting her now."

Dawn stared at the line of yellow police tape. That small, plastic line was supposed to keep the perimeter safe from intrusion.

There wasn't even a cop stationed there to keep prying eyes away. And that little bit of tape? It certainly wasn't going to keep Dawn out. She headed toward the warehouse, her gaze scanning the perimeter. There were no other cars there, no sign that anyone else was nearby. She could smell the river and the sun beamed down from overhead. Dawn slipped on gloves—she always did that when she went to investigate a scene.

Don't ever leave a trace behind. Especially if you're doing something not exactly legal. Advice she'd learned from Roth. *Roth's Rules to Spy By.* That was what he'd called them. *Never leave a trace because you don't want to give the cops any reason to come down on you.*

She didn't go to the front entrance. She slipped around the building and, yes, not surprisingly, she found a broken window. Dawn slipped inside.

The building smelled musty. Light shone in

through all of the windows, so she could see easily as she searched the area. The police had certainly left signs that they'd been there. Evidence tags. More tape and—

She heard a rustle behind her. Dawn didn't hesitate. She yanked her weapon from her bag and spun around, her grip dead steady. "Freeze!" Dawn yelled.

And the rustle stopped. She saw a man standing in the shadows, his shoulders hunched, his chin pressing to his chest. "I . . . I don't want no trouble . . ."

"Then you shouldn't sneak up on a woman." Her heart drummed frantically in her chest but her grip never wavered. Getting a concealed carry permit had been one of the first things she'd done when she got her PI license. No way was she going to walk around without a weapon.

He shuffled back. "Y-you're in my h-home."

Goose bumps rose on her arms as she studied him. Older, maybe nearing seventy, with a long, grizzled beard. There were dirt smudges on his cheeks and his clothes were mismatched. He wore one flip-flop and one sneaker. His jeans were held up thanks to a heavy rope around his waist and his dress shirt had been tucked in to try to keep the jeans in place.

"Sorry," she murmured but didn't lower her gun. "I'm a PI. I was investigating the crime that took place here." *My home.*

He took another shuffling step back. If possible, his shoulders hunched even more.

"How long has this been your home?"

He licked his lips. "Don't . . . don't really know." He lifted up his thin wrist. "Don't have a . . . a watch, you know?"

She considered him a moment. "You knew the building had electricity, didn't you?"

His gaze cut away from her. "Maybe . . . I saw a light one night."

And he'd come in from the dark.

"What else did you see?"

His lips had clamped together. "Didn't do nothin' wrong. Empty building . . . No one was usin' it."

"Someone was. Someone killed a woman here. And they kept her body in a freezer." When he didn't speak, she added, "If it were my home, I'd be aware of what was happening inside. If I saw a freezer, I'd look in it, thinking maybe there was some food in there."

She could hear the rasp of his breath.

Her phone began to ring, vibrating in her pocket. She ignored it. She wasn't about to take her attention off the man in front of her. "What's your name?"

"Red."

She could see that part of his gray beard contained the faintest streaks of red. Maybe once upon a time, he'd gotten that nickname. Or maybe it was his given name. She wasn't going to push on that just yet. "Red, did you see a freezer here?"

He gave a quick, nervous nod.

Her phone stopped vibrating.

"And did you look inside it?"

His hands came up from behind his back.

"Stop!" she yelled, thinking he was pulling a weapon, but . . . he was just showing her the gloves he had cradled in his hands. Expensive gloves from the look of them. Leather?

"Left these . . ." he murmured. "Saw him put them behind the wall. I . . . I never touched them before t-today . . . was scarcd . . ."

The *killer* had left those gloves?

"Didn't want police to take 'em . . ." His jaw jutted out. "I can use them m-more . . ."

So he'd taken the hidden gloves. Dawn licked her lips. "Did you see anything else?"

His shoulders dropped. "I was . . . hungry."

He was skeletally thin, so she was sure that he had many hungry nights. Pity twisted through her. "When you looked in the freezer, you saw her, didn't you?"

"Frozen lady. Blue, icy." He lifted his gloved hands and pressed them to his eyes.

She stepped toward him. "Why didn't you call the cops?"

"My home!" Now he sounded angry. "They would have t-taken me from my home! I didn't hurt her! Never hurt *anyone*."

So he'd stayed there, with the dead woman . . . for how long? "Did you see the man who hurt her? The man who left those gloves?"

Red licked his lips. "He . . . visited."

Her goose bumps got worse. She needed to get Tucker down there. Needed Anthony to hear this guy's story.

Her phone vibrated again.

"Did you see him when he visited?"

"H-hid." His head lowered. "Didn't want to get . . . f-frozen."

Those words made her heart hurt. "Red, may I buy those gloves from you?" Because there might be evidence on them. Especially if Red was telling her the truth and this was the first time he'd gotten them from their hiding space. "It's warm outside. You don't really need them now, anyway."

He frowned at her.

"I'll give you a hundred bucks for them."

He dropped the gloves on the floor.

"Great." Wonderful. She pulled the money out of her bag and offered it to him. He inched forward, his gaze darting to the weapon she hadn't put up, not yet. "I'm not going to hurt you," she promised. She lowered the gun.

He reached out his hand. She put the money on his palm and then—

He snatched the bills and ran.

"Red!" She chased after him, but that guy

was *fast.* He shot through the building, zigging and zagging. He knew the building, she didn't, and she was getting lost in the tangle of rooms. *Like being in a maze.* She stumbled after him, doing her best to follow his pounding footsteps, but then he was bursting out the front door. She yelled after him, but Red wasn't stopping. He tore through the yellow tape and kept going.

And her phone was still ringing. She yanked the phone from her pocket, not even stopping to see who was calling. *"What?"* She scampered down the steps, her gaze jerking to the left and to the right.

There was a pause and then . . . "Dawn?"

Tucker. She swallowed and edged toward the little gap between two buildings. Too small to be called a real alley. "I could use some backup," she told him. "It would really be appreciated right now." Because there was too much ground to cover. Red had her at a disadvantage. He would know all the hiding spaces around that area. All the quick exits. And she was just following blindly.

"What? Where are you?"

"I'm at the warehouse. The scene of our Jane Doe's imprisonment. And a witness just gave me the slip."

"How did your team miss the witness?"

Tucker was pissed. Dawn thought that was pretty evident to everyone gathered at the warehouse. When she'd said she wanted backup, Dawn hadn't quite realized just how big her cavalry would be.

Tucker had arrived. Macey had arrived. Anthony had come running, along with his partner, Detective Ronald Torez. The group was assembled in front of the now-ripped line of police tape, and Tucker's low, cutting voice contained more than enough fury to torch New Orleans.

"I don't know," Anthony growled back. His eyes were covered by a pair of mirrored sunglasses. "But you can bet I'll be finding out. Uniforms cased the scene. They should have found our guy."

"Not if Red didn't want to be found," Dawn said. Maybe he'd felt intimidated by all of the uniforms and he'd hidden from them. But when it had just been her there . . . *he came out to play.*

Anthony's lips thinned. "The guy was really living here the whole damn time that woman was in the freezer?"

"She has a name," Macey spoke up. "Heather Hartley." Her gaze cut to Dawn. "We ID'd her. Heather was only twenty-one. Former LSU student. A girl who went to the same high school you did."

And I was twenty-one when Jason took me. Even though she was sweating under the hot heat of the sun, the breath that Dawn took seemed to chill her lungs. “Red gave me the guy’s gloves.”

Gloves that had already been bagged and tagged by Macey.

“Maybe there is some DNA evidence on them. Something we can use. Red said they’d been hidden the whole time.”

“I’ll get the FBI’s team to check them,” Macey said.

“But—” Anthony began, his cheeks red.

“Our team is faster.” Macey wasn’t mincing words. “We can let the NOPD handle it and get caught in your backlog or I can contact my boss, Samantha Dark, and she will give this evidence priority. We’ll have results faster than you can blink.”

He blinked.

“The FBI is taking point on this now.” Tucker’s voice was still that lethal rasp. “Every bit of evidence we are collecting is pointing to the fact that we could be looking at a serial. This isn’t a one-and-done deal, not if our guy went to the trouble of finding a victim from the Iceman’s home turf. He’s emulating the Iceman too perfectly. There *will* be another victim. We have to act, right now, and by getting these gloves to our team, we will save valuable time.”

A muscle jerked in Anthony’s jaw, but he nodded grimly.

Torez rubbed the back of his neck as he studied Dawn. Everyone called the guy Torez, never

Ronald. He *hated* being called Ronald, she knew that from past experience. In his midthirties, Torez had transferred from Biloxi just last year. He was a quiet guy, intense, but he always seemed to have Anthony's back—a good trait in a partner. "You gonna be able to give us a good description of Red?"

"Five foot nine, maybe one hundred and thirty-five pounds." He'd been so terribly thin. "He was bald, but he had a long, grizzled beard, one with red streaks. Dark eyes, thin cheeks." She quickly described the clothing he'd worn. "I think this guy is a loner, so I doubt he'll show up at any shelters. You can still check them but—" her gaze swept back to the building "—my money says he'll come back here." *Home.* "So you should put a patrol on the warehouse."

"A patrol might stop folks from just busting inside a crime scene," Anthony murmured.

Her cheeks reddened at that *not* subtle hit. "I found a witness *and* evidence that we can use on this case. Evidence your guys missed. Do we really want to play the blame game now?"

He shook his head. "Just tell me you were carrying." And worry was there, creeping into his voice. "You go alone into a place like this, with no backup in sight . . . What in the hell were you thinking?"

"I was thinking that I didn't want anyone else dying by this man's hand." Her chin notched up.

"I was thinking that I'm a licensed PI who, yes, does carry a weapon. I've been to scenes a whole lot worse than this before and I will be at them again." She wasn't going to back down and play the helpless victim.

That won't be me again. She'd sworn that to herself. Her gaze darted around the group and she caught the dark look exchanged between Tucker and Macey.

Alarm bells went off in her head.

I am not going to like what's coming.

The detectives headed back to their vehicle. She knew they were calling this in to headquarters and, hopefully, getting an all-points bulletin out for Red. Macey inclined her head toward Dawn. "There anything else about the scene you think we should know?"

"Red is our key." *And I wish I'd caught him.* But Red knew this area too well. He'd been able to disappear between the maze of buildings, snaking away and vanishing like a ghost. "He said the killer came to see Jane—Heather," she quickly corrected. "The guy left his gloves and Red took them."

"Why didn't he report what he'd found?" Macey shook her head.

"He was afraid." Once more, her gaze swept the building. "This was his home. If he called the cops, they'd force him out." And that was the same reason she was worried about the APB.

"He's going to stay far away from cops. I should hunt for him. I have some contacts in the homeless community. I can put out the word about Red and see what turns up." She was betting she'd get a hit faster than the NOPD.

"Do it," Tucker said. "But do it on your way home." His hand curled around her elbow. "I want to talk to you and your friend Jinx."

He . . . he hadn't talked to Jinx yet?

He led her to her vehicle as the detectives called out for Macey once again. She knew he was angry, but his touch was incredibly gentle on her. "You didn't flinch this time," he murmured.

They were beside her car. She looked up at him, frowning.

"When I touch you, you usually flinch away." His fingers slid carefully down her arm. She could feel the calluses on his fingertips. "You didn't this time."

"Tucker . . ."

"I'm worried you're a target."

She'd been worried about the same thing ever since someone had slipped into her home.

"I need you safe, Dawn. I will do whatever is necessary to ensure that safety."

Her gaze searched his. "Why do those words give me such a bad feeling?"

He looked away. "I'll follow you home. We'll talk there."

She didn't want to go home. She wanted to

pound the pavement and find Red. She wanted to find the jerk out there who'd killed Heather Hartley. She—

"I can pull rank and put you under protective custody right now. I can have you in a safe house within the hour."

Her jaw dropped. "No. Absolutely not." She wasn't going to be shut away. Now she was the one to grab on to him and hold tight. "You're not serious."

He looked down at her hands, then back up at her face. "When it comes to you staying alive, I absolutely am." He inched closer to her and his body brushed against hers. "Haven't I proven that already? That I will do *anything* to keep you alive?"

Even shoot his own brother.

She looked away, her emotions too tangled for her to understand, and she saw Anthony, frowning at her. He took a step toward her but she shook her head. She was okay. She didn't need him riding to her rescue. She didn't want anyone doing that. *I can save myself.*

"Dawn?"

Her gaze was pulled back to Tucker's. She gathered her emotions and when she was sure she could speak calmly, she said, "You aren't pulling rank. We're working this case together."

His eyes glittered at her. "Your friend Jinx didn't show up for work."

He'd said he hadn't talked with her yet, but she'd just thought maybe he'd gotten sidetracked. "Jinx always goes to work. That job means everything to her."

"Her boss tried calling her, but Malone said he only got her voice mail."

And Dawn had gotten her voice mail, too.

"I'm not liking this shit, okay? You think someone's been in your home, another girl from our hometown is already a victim and now your downstairs neighbor is suddenly off-grid."

"I have a key to her place." A key that she used to water Jinx's plants when the other woman went out of town. But Dawn shook her head. "What am I saying? We aren't going into Jinx's place. I'll try calling her again. I'm sure she's fine." *She has to be fine.*

She dialed her friend as Tucker watched. One ring, two, then—

"This is Jinx. You know the drill."

She didn't leave a message this time.

CHAPTER SEVEN

"Jinx?" Dawn pounded on her friend's door. "Jinx, please open up if you're in there, okay?"

There was no sound from inside the condo.

Dawn turned toward Tucker. "I don't like this."

Neither did he. Not for one damn moment. Dawn didn't think he'd been serious about the protective custody bit. She was dead wrong. The way this game was playing out—hell, no, it wasn't going to end well. He could see the danger and the death coming. Since he'd been working in Violent Crimes, he'd learned too much about killers.

And the bastard who'd killed Heather? He wasn't going to be the one-and-done type. If he truly wanted to be like the Iceman, then more bodies would be piling up.

Hell, there *could* already be more victims out there. Victims that just hadn't been found yet. Victims who were already in their frozen graves.

"I think I should get my key." Dawn bit her lower lip. "Just to make sure everything is okay in there."

Sounded like one hell of an idea to him.

"It's upstairs. Come on."

He was right behind her. She'd scared the hell out of him when he couldn't get her to answer the phone earlier, and then when she'd said that she needed backup, he hadn't been able to get to her side fast enough. When he'd gotten to the scene, he'd wanted to race up to Dawn and pull her into his arms.

Instead, he'd locked down his emotions and gotten the fucking job done.

But . . .

She breaks my control. She always has. That was one of the most dangerous things about Dawn.

He watched as she unlocked her door and tapped in her alarm code. "The key is in my bedroom," she threw over her shoulder as she headed toward the room. "Just give me a second to get it—"

She'd vanished inside the bedroom. And her voice had abruptly cut away.

"Dawn?" He took a step toward her room, expecting her to reappear. In just a second. Exactly as she'd promised.

But she didn't appear. And it had gone dead silent in that condo.

"Dawn!" He shouted her name even as he yanked his gun out of his holster and ran after her. He rushed into her bedroom, searching for a threat, but Dawn was alone in there. She'd frozen just steps inside of her doorway.

He kept his gun in one hand even as he reached for her shoulder with the other. "Baby, you just—"

He saw the roses. Blood red. A bouquet of them, placed right on her pillow.

"They weren't here when I left," Dawn whispered.

Rage boiled inside of him. He'd seen her turn off the alarm himself, and there had been no sign of forced entry at her front door. He hurried around her bedroom, checking under the bed, going into her closet, searching the bathroom . . . then searching every room in her condo to make sure the SOB wasn't still inside the place.

But no one else was there. Nothing else was disturbed. *Exactly the way Dawn described the other break-ins.*

He went back to her side. She was still standing just inside her bedroom, her eyes on the bed.

"He knows about my tattoos." Her voice was quiet, whispery, as if she were afraid someone would overhear her. Her head turned and she stared at him with eyes gone dark. Her pupils were too big. Her expression too stark. "I put roses over the worst of my scars. Jinx did that for me. She . . . she tried to make my past less ugly."

And some bastard had just delivered roses to her bed.

His gaze flew around the room. "You have a motion detector attached to your security system?" She'd told him that before, but he needed to be sure.

"In the den, yes, there's one in there. I made

sure one was in there because any intruder would have to come in through the front door in order to get to my bedroom."

Not necessarily.

"Not like he could scale the side of the building and come in through the balcony," she murmured.

Maybe. Maybe not.

His gaze swept the floor. He didn't see any dirt there. No tracks left behind. Slowly now, he backed away from her. He went back to her closet. A big, walk-in closet. He opened the door there.

"Tucker?" She followed behind him.

He surveyed the clothes that were neatly hung, and the shoes that were arranged so carefully. "Everything look the same to you in here?"

"Yes."

The bastard was in her bedroom. He'd believed her story before and now his rage was even greater. It was—

"Everything but that rose petal." She brushed past him and knelt on the floor. "That wasn't here before."

And sure enough, there was a small rose petal—actually, more like half of a petal—that had been dropped and forgotten on the floor of the closet.

Dawn stared up at him, not touching the petal.

Think, fucking think. "You said this building was historic."

She nodded as she rose once more.

He glanced at the wall behind her. And then he went to it. He started rapping his knuckles against the wood.

"What are you doing?"

"Checking to see if anything is—" He rapped again. Only this time, the resulting sound was different. *Pay dirt.* "Hollow."

His hands slid around the wood. It *looked* like a wall, but at the very bottom of that frame, he found a ridge of wood that stuck out. He pulled on that wood . . .

The wall popped open.

"You are freaking kidding me," Dawn said, voice stunned.

No, he wasn't.

He pulled out his phone and used the flashlight app to shine light down into what looked like an old laundry shoot. "It goes down to the bottom floor." And there was a damn *rope* there. Tied off right near the small door he'd just managed to open. The bastard had been using that rope and climbing up to her room.

The perp had been letting himself inside her home, slipping right past her security when she was gone.

Only . . . Hell. He might not have gotten inside just when Dawn was away. The bastard could have been sneaking into her room when she was asleep. She wouldn't have even realized it. She'd said that when she woke up, she smelled him.

Because he was with her when she slept.

His head turned toward her.

"Tucker . . ." Horror was on her face.

"He came up from downstairs. Get that damn key to Jinx's place, right now." His temples were throbbing, his blood heating. This guy had been *stalking* Dawn. Coming into her home. And she'd been all alone.

Again, I wasn't there for her. A second time I've let her down.

She grabbed the key from her nightstand drawer. She hadn't touched the flowers on her bed. Neither had he. Tucker planned to get a crime scene analysis team in there right away.

As they rushed back down the stairs, he put in a fast and urgent call to his team. And when they got to Jinx's door, this time, Dawn didn't bother knocking on the door to her friend's home. She shoved the key in the lock and they ran inside.

No alarm beeped. No lights were on. The place was as dark and quiet as a tomb.

"Jinx?" He could hear the worry in Dawn's voice as they searched the rooms. There was no sign of Jinx, though. No sign of her, no sign of any struggle, either, but . . .

He looked up at the ceiling, then gauged where he thought Dawn's closet would be.

"Our condos are almost exact duplicates of each other," Dawn said, as if reading his mind.

He went into Jinx's closet. Sure enough, he

found the entrance to that shoot. Easy to spot, since the SOB who'd used it had left it partially open.

"I need her to be okay." Dawn's voice was quiet. He looked back at her and saw that her skin had turned ashen. "I need it." Then she turned and began to walk very slowly and very determinedly out of the closet.

Out of the closet.

Out of the bedroom.

Down the hallway.

Into the kitchen . . .

Then she paused. "I saw her get a delivery a few months back." She was staring at a white door to the right. And her hand rose and she pointed. "That's her pantry. It must be in there."

It?

Eyes narrowed, he opened the door. And he saw the freezer.

"I need her to be okay," Dawn said again.

He needed to get a team out to that building.

"Open it." Dawn was close beside him in that narrow space. "I have to know." She grabbed his arm and when he looked at her, there were tears gleaming in Dawn's beautiful eyes. "I have to be wrong. She has to be out on a date. Or . . . or she has to be at the tattoo shop now. She has to be *anywhere* but here."

She was breaking his heart. "Dawn . . ."

Her lips trembled and she suddenly jerked

away from him. She yanked open the top on that freezer—

And when he heard the sob that broke from her, he realized that her friend was far, far from okay.

Her skin was ice. Her breath was cold. She couldn't stop shaking.

Dawn watched as Jinx's body was removed from their building. *Not just the body. They're taking everything. The freezer, too.* Because they hadn't wanted to lose evidence. Julia had wanted to move the entire machine so that when Jinx thawed out, all of the potential evidence would still be present.

When she thaws out. My God.

A crowd had gathered on the street. Everyone was watching and whispering. News crews were filming.

She heard a reporter saying the coroner had to be careful with the body transfer. The man stared earnestly into a video camera and explained to the viewers at home that there could be evidence in the freezer. Evidence that they didn't want washed away as the body melted.

I'm so sorry, Jinx.

"She wasn't in there long." Macey came to Dawn's side. Her voice was low, probably because she didn't want her words carrying to any of the reporters who watched the scene with eager gazes. "I could tell that much. She wasn't—"

"I saw her two days ago." Just two days. So she'd already known that her friend hadn't been in the freezer for an extended time. *Is that supposed to make it better? Because it doesn't. Knowing that she was alive forty-eight hours ago means that she died while I was close by.* She could have been dying when Dawn was pounding on her door that morning. She could have still been alive then—

Macey caught her hand. Squeezed tight. "This isn't on you."

"No, it's on the sick bastard who tortured my friend and then shoved her into her own freezer to die."

An image flashed in her mind. Jinx, tied, bound, slices all over her body. She squeezed her eyes shut, but when the vision was forever branded in your head, there was nothing you could do to block it out. "She died when I was one floor above her." And Dawn had never heard a thing.

"We are going to find him."

Her eyes opened. She stared into Macey's gaze. Dawn saw the other woman for exactly what she was. A kindred spirit. A survivor. She'd known that, though, long before she'd seen the scars that Macey carried.

It's in our eyes. The truth is there. She'd gone to a few support groups over the years, and the survivors always looked the same.

"Two more of our team members are flying

in from DC," Macey told her. "With the second victim—"

"It confirms he's a serial." She already knew this.

But Macey nodded. "And the fact that he killed your friend, that he left roses on your bed . . . that means he's put a big, shining target on you."

Tucker was just steps away. He'd looked different ever since they'd found Jinx. His features were sharper, his gaze harder. She could practically feel the tension rolling off him. He hadn't wanted her opening that freezer, probably because he didn't want her to have that last image of Jinx branded in her mind.

"She was my friend," Dawn murmured. "I had to lift up the freezer and look inside. I had to find her." Her gaze was on Tucker as she said those words. Was he close enough to hear her?

Macey looked over her shoulder. "There are things we all have to do." She squeezed Dawn's hand and then let her go. "I hope you remember that. I hope you understand just what he has to do now."

Dawn opened her mouth to reply, but Tucker was already there. He lifted his hand, offering his palm to Dawn. "We need to go now."

"But . . . that's my home." She'd left a light on in the bedroom. She could see it glowing as the sun started to dip beneath the sky. Just how long had she been out there, watching the authorities work? Watching as Jinx was slowly removed and taken away by Julia? “I have to stay here.”

“Both floors are crime scenes. You’re not getting back in there tonight.” He still had his hand out, waiting for her. Her hand lifted and pressed to his. Seemed to *fit* his. “I’m going to take you someplace safe.”

Safe. She stiffened.

“I’ll follow Julia and assist with the exam,” Macey murmured. “I’ll see you both later.” Then she slipped away.

Dawn didn’t move. “You’re talking about a safe housc.” Hc was talking protective custody again. Basically, locking her up.

“I’m talking about a secure environment for the night. A place I know that bastard can’t get to.” He stepped even closer to her. “He was in your bedroom. He killed your friend. He *is* coming for you. The son of a bitch wants to finish what the Iceman started.”

What if the Iceman didn’t die? What if it’s Jason, finally coming back to kill me? But she didn’t say those words. She’d already told Tucker what she feared once. He’d been so adamant that Jason was long dead.

What if you’re wrong, Tucker?

“So I’m just supposed to run and hide?” Before he could speak, she shook her head. “That’s not really my style.” She didn’t hide from life. “Not anymore. But then, I guess you wouldn’t know that, since you don't know me any longer." He only knew the girl she'd been. The broken girl who hadn't even been able to let her lover touch her without seeing a monster coming at her.

"What you're supposed to do is stay alive." Flat. Hard. His fingers closed around hers. "And I know you. I know you soul-fucking-deep. You're torn up right now because your friend is dead and you're putting the blame on yourself." He gave a grim shake of his head. "Not happening. He did this—some sick bastard who wants to be like the Iceman. And he did it deliberately." With his left hand, he gestured toward the reporters. "So they'd swarm in. So he'd get his fifteen minutes of fame at the cost of an innocent woman's life."

"You're profiling him." Because that was what he did now. He profiled killers.

Has he ever tried to profile me? If he really knew her "soul-fucking-deep" then he must have wondered about the dark spaces inside of her. Those yawning places that had grown over the years, after they'd been created by Jason.

And by Tucker.

Do you see what I've become?

"We're taking this one step at a time. Step one . . . let the crime scene guys do their job. We brought in backup from the local FBI *and* Detective Deveraux is on hand, too. They're securing the scene. And my job right now—my priority—is to protect you."

Not because of any personal reason, she got that. "You're supposed to protect the only surviving victim of the Iceman."

"And the next potential victim of this bastard."

She didn't flinch, but her heartbeat stuttered.

"Step two is getting you away from this scene. I know who you are . . . and any moment, one of those reporters will be figuring it out, too. They'll figure out your past."

Her anonymity would be blown to hell.

"They'll pull records on this building. They'll get your name. They'll make the connection. They wouldn't be worth their salt as reporters if they didn't." He looked toward his waiting SUV. "So come away with me now. Let's get away clean for the night. I'll take you away from the crowd, to a place where we can regroup for the night. By morning we'll have more evidence to follow. The rest of my team will be here. We can hit the ground running."

He kept using that tempting word, *we.* "You're going to let me help? No more trying to shut me out?"

"I'm going to make sure you're at my side. He's coming for you. I'm not going to bullshit and tell you that you're safe. We both know that's not true. So I figure the best place for you is with me. With my team. You proved today at the warehouse that you've got good instincts. I'm not going to shove you on the sidelines. I want you with me."

That was where she wanted to be. It took two tries but Dawn swallowed the lump in her throat. "Jinx is—was—my friend." She didn't let too many people get close. Occupational hazard. "This shouldn't have happened." A tear leaked down her cheek. Her hand rose to brush it away, but Tucker beat her. His fingertips slid over her cheek.

"No," he said quietly. "It shouldn't have. But we're going to find the son of a bitch. We will stop him."

She nodded and peered up at him a moment longer. Dawn could feel stares on her. They'd already attracted attention from reporters. She knew he was right. Her identity would come out. With this case, with this situation, it would have to come out.

Without another word, she turned and headed for his SUV. Her clothes were upstairs. Her bag—upstairs. But all of that was part of a crime scene now.

How many times did he come in my home and I didn't know it?

Tucker opened the passenger door for her. She slid inside and when the door shut, she glanced back at the scene.

Was he there when I slept? Was that bastard right beside me and I didn't know it? He must have been. That was why she'd woken to his scent all around her.

Tucker slid into the driver's seat and slammed the door.

"This is different," she murmured. "Jason never broke into my room. He never came inside. I don't . . . I don't think he did that with any of his victims."

"This *isn't* Jason. It's some bastard who's obsessed with his crimes and living out a fantasy where he becomes the Iceman." He cranked the vehicle. "That fantasy is about to fucking end."

His darkest dream was finally a reality.

Dawn's home was lit up with the swirl of police lights. Uniforms made sure the crowd didn't get too close. Local FBI agents were all over the scene. And Jinx . . .

They found you. He'd hoped they'd make that discovery soon. He'd waited patiently for so long, but now everything was falling into place.

The Iceman lived again. The press would be spreading his story to the world. All eyes would be on him. They'd see just what he could do.

Justice was coming. Payback.

And it would be an ice-cold son of a bitch.

CHAPTER EIGHT

She'd come with him. Holy hell, but that had been a gamble. He'd been pretty sure Dawn would tell him to screw off with his offer of a safe house. And if she'd said that . . .

Then there would have been no choice. He would have been forced to take her into protective custody because there was *no way* Tucker could leave her on her own.

"There were only nine roses in the bouquet." The words slipped from him as he drove through the city. He risked a quick glance at Dawn and saw that she was staring out of the window, as if searching the crowd.

"I have nine rose tattoos on my body, just nine." Her voice was soft. "He knew."

Yes, because . . . "I think he knew Jinx." He stopped at a red light. She had turned her head to look at him, but it wasn't bright enough in the SUV's interior for him to see her eyes. He wished that he could see them. "If this guy has been coming into your home like you said—and I fully believe that—then he had to be using the passage from her place for a while." It had looked like some kind of old-school dumbwaiter. "So this was a man that she let into her home."

"Jinx didn't let some jerk break into my home! She didn't let some guy terrorize me!"

The light changed. He accelerated even as he shook his head. "That's not what I meant. I don't think she was involved in anything he did. I think the guy was using her . . ."

Silence. "In order to get to me?"

"Yes." He had been building a profile on this perp, one step at a time. "I think we're looking at a meticulous killer." He had to be, in order to duplicate the Iceman's work so completely. "And he wanted to be sure he was capable of committing the perfect crime, so he needed a trial victim."

"Heather."

A victim from Jason's old stomping grounds. *Homage to the master?* "And then he had to get rid of Jinx because she knew who he was." That was part of the reason. He didn't tell Dawn the other part—that Tucker believed the bastard had killed Jinx . . . *in order to hurt you, Dawn. He knew she was your friend and he wanted that pain to rip straight through you.*

And it had. He'd seen Dawn nearly collapse when she'd opened that freezer.

There were many forms of torture. The worst kinds didn't always involve the slice of knife.

"We have to find Red." Her voice had sharpened. "He saw the killer, too. We can get him to the police station, have him work with a sketch artist . . ."

Tucker wasn't sure how reliable Red's memory would prove to be, but he was willing to give the guy a shot.

"There's a restaurant on the next street. The owner, Jones, usually gives the day's leftovers to the homeless. Let's stop and talk to him."

After everything that had just happened, she wanted to keep hunting? He wanted her off the streets, he wanted—

Her hand curled around his wrist. "Please, Tucker. *Please.* I need to do this. Jones is a friend of mine. He can help us to find Red. I meant to call him earlier, but then . . ."

Then she'd found Jinx dead.

"I have to do something to help her. It won't take long, I promise. Just a quick stop. And you're with me. I'm safe when you're with me, right?"

Always. Without another word, he turned at the next street. Dawn knew the city and the people there. If she had a contact that would help them find Red, he would use it.

"It's that one." She pointed. "Dressed."

The small restaurant seemed packed. Lights glowed from inside and he saw a line of customers spilling out from the entrance.

"Jones has the best po'boys in town."

Dressed. Right. The name made more sense now. Dressed—with lettuce, tomatoes, pickles and mayonnaise—well, that was the only way to eat a good po'boy. He parked at the curb. There were plenty of people strolling on the streets. Tourists always seemed to be out in this city.

Dawn jumped from the vehicle, but she didn't head toward the front of Dressed. Instead, she went to the back, snaking through a small alleyway, and Tucker followed right behind her. She rapped on the door back there, and it opened a moment later. A man stood there, towering over Dawn. He had bright white hair and dark skin—and forearms that looked decidedly like tree trunks. The man wore a faded white apron and he held a white paper bag in his hand. But he blinked when he saw Tucker and Dawn.

"Hi, Jones." She gave him a weak smile. "Do you have a moment?"

Jones put the bag down on the counter. Then he grabbed Dawn, pulling her close in a crushing hug. "Been too long."

Tucker saw Dawn squeeze the man back. "I know. Julia's been sneaking me your po'boys because she understands I need my fix."

He grunted and released her, and a wide smile spread over his face. "I thought she was taking a bit extra when she came to the restaurant." His gaze slid to Tucker. "And just who is this?" His stare turned assessing as it slid over Tucker. Jones studied Tucker a moment, then accurately called him out as, "FBI."

Tucker inclined his head. "Guilty." He offered

his hand to the man. "My name's Tucker Frost."

"Jones." He gave a brief, strong shake. "It's the suit that gives you away." The kitchen workers were hustling behind him and a dozen tantalizing scents drifted in the air. "I can always spot you guys from fifty paces." His smile was gone as he focused on Dawn once more. "Why are you bringing a Fed to my back door?"

"Because we need your help." Her hands were at her sides. "There's a man doing some very bad things in this city, and so far, there's only one person who has actually seen him."

One person who was still alive. There had been a hitch in Dawn's voice when she spoke and he could tell by the sudden stiffness in Jones's shoulders that the other man had noticed. *She's in pain.*

Tucker hated Dawn's pain.

Jones narrowed his eyes. "Tell me more."

"He's killing, Jones. Julia is working on . . . on another of his victims tonight." Her breath whispered out. "This victim was my friend."

The man's face hardened. "What can I do?" His hand squeezed her shoulder.

For a moment, Tucker thought Dawn would cry, but instead she pulled in a long, hard breath. "We're looking for a homeless man named Red." She gave a quick description of him. "If he comes knocking on your back door, will you keep him here? Keep him here, call me . . . and Tucker and I will be at Dressed as fast as we can."

Jones nodded. "I can do that."

"Thank you." She gave a brisk nod. "I know you need to get back to work, but we had to stop by. Word about your place has spread. I know if Red needs a meal, he'll show up here. And maybe you can put the word out to the others . . . when they come for food . . . let them know we're looking for Red, and that I can pay them for information."

"I'll put out that word."

"I need him to stay safe." She rubbed her face. "I gave him a hundred dollars. That could last him a while or . . . or he could drink it away in a night. Just . . . if he comes here, you call."

One of the cooks yelled out to Jones.

"We'll let you get back to work," Dawn murmured.

Jones dropped his hand from her shoulder. But there was still worry in his eyes as he stared down at Dawn.

"Thanks for your time, sir," Tucker said. They slipped away. As they were leaving, a woman with long blond hair and hunched shoulders hurried toward the back door. She knocked, and Jones opened the door to hand her that white bag. The woman whispered her thanks and hurried off.

Tucker paused in the alleyway, watching the scene. "How long has he been doing that?"

"Ever since he opened the business five years

ago. Jones has the biggest heart of anyone I've ever met."

"And let me guess—" he thought of Malone "—you met him while working a PI case? Who did you find for him?"

She frowned at him. "I met Jones when his daughter, Julia, brought me here for the best po'boy of my life."

Julia. The coroner. No wonder they'd been talking so casually about her.

"He's helped *me* on a few of my cases. No one knows the city better than Jones. If Red comes calling, we'll know." She turned and stalked down the alley. He followed behind, and then found himself reaching out to touch her shoulder.

She stilled.

"Why did you come to New Orleans?"

"I couldn't stay in Baton Rouge any longer. It hurt too much." She turned toward him. Their bodies brushed. "But Louisiana is in my blood. New Orleans just seemed to . . . call to me at the time. Plenty of people escape here. Plenty of people start over here. And that's what I needed. A place to start over."

Only that fresh start was being destroyed. "I'm sorry."

Her head tilted back. "For what?"

"My family wrecked your life." His family. His fucking twisted family. And most folks thought Jason was the only problem in their family tree.

Those folks were wrong. Jason hadn't been the first monster in the family. *What if he's not the last?*

"You never hurt me, Tucker." She stared up at him. "But I hurt you."

"Dawn . . ."

"I couldn't see past him, when I looked at you." Her voice had become a whisper. "And I'm sorry for that. You were the person I needed most back then, and you were the one I pushed away the hardest."

He wanted to pull her into his arms. Hold her tight and never let go.

"I won't do it again." If possible, her words were even softer. He had to lean in close to hear her. "I swear, I won't."

"So how did an MD wind up working for the FBI?" Julia Bradford asked as Macey followed her into the morgue.

The victim hadn't arrived yet. A special crew would be bringing her inside any moment. Macey shivered a bit as she stood in the lab. She didn't have a whole lot of experience when it came to working with the dead. "A necessary career change."

Julia quirked one brow at her. "That sounds mysterious."

Macey had been a senior resident when the stalking had begun. Small things, at first. Simple things. She'd been so busy that she hadn't paid them much attention. She glanced down at her sleeve. "I wanted to be a doctor so that I could help people. My mother . . . she died of cancer when I was a kid. I thought being a doctor would let me make a difference. That I could change lives."

Julia stared back at her.

"Then I learned there were other ways to help people." Ways that called to her.

And she also hadn't been able to step back inside an operating room. *Not after what he did.*

"Your hands shake when you get close to the exam table." Julia's voice was quiet.

Surprise rushed through her. *I know. I can't help it.* "You're very observant."

Julia smiled. "My dad taught me that. Said you have to watch the world around you. See the things that others miss. That way, you have an advantage."

"Sounds like some dad you've got there."

"He's incredible." She turned away.

Macey bit her lip, then asked, "Why do you work with the dead?" Because it was her turn to watch closely, Macey saw the slight stiffening of Julia's shoulders. "You're an MD," Macey pushed. "Why not work with the living?"

"I was going to focus on pediatrics . . ." Julia's voice had turned musing. "Make sure kids grew up strong and healthy. I even had plans to start up a clinic back in the parish where I grew up."

"And your plans changed."

Julia turned to face her. "My brother was shot and killed one night on Bourbon Street. In the middle of that crowded street, with a hundred people staring at the shooter. Those hundred people? They should have been able to identify his killer . . . but I swear every single damn one of them gave a different description of the perp."

Macey waited. Her heart ached for the pain she heard in Julia's voice.

"Some of those people were too drunk to remember shit. Some didn't look at the killer, they just looked at the vic—at my brother. But others . . . they stared straight at him, and they couldn't pick him out of a lineup."

"I'm sorry." She'd heard of it happening before. Eyewitness testimony was actually one of the weakest forms of evidence. Two people could describe the exact same attacker in wildly different ways.

Or a hundred people could fail to see the killer right in front of them.

"I was afraid my brother wasn't going to get justice. I went to the police. My dad stood in front of the station for *days.* And then you know what happened?"

She shook her head.

"My brother spoke."

Macey blinked.

"The coroner—Dr. Burns—he never gave up.

He examined my brother again and again. He found trace evidence from where my brother had grabbed the bastard who came at him. Evidence that tied the piece of trash directly to the crime. He's locked away now and will be rotting for the next twenty years. All because the coroner did his job. He was thorough. He *didn't give up.*" She sucked in a quick breath. "Sorry, I just . . . I get emotional about that."

"You don't have to apologize to me."

Julia's smile came again. "When my brother's killer was convicted, I realized I didn't have to be in my own clinic to make a difference. I realized the world needed more people like Dr. Burns."

"I'm glad you're on this case." She took a step closer to the exam table. Her hands started to shake and she balled them into fists. "And I'm sorry about your brother."

"And I'm sorry about the pain you carry." Julia's head cocked to the side. "Did they catch the man who hurt you so badly?"

Macey sucked in a sharp breath. There hadn't been a need to catch him. "I killed him."

"Good."

The door swung open behind them before Macey could say anything else. She looked back and saw Detective Deveraux standing there. "They're about to bring in the victim." His face was grim. His gaze darted to Julia, then back to her. "Where's your partner?" he asked Macey.

"He's taking Dawn to a secure location for the night."

If possible, his face hardened even more. "The PD has plenty of safe houses that she can use. I can guarantee her around-the-clock protection."

Julia laughed. "You know Dawn isn't going to be locked away. That isn't her style."

"For her safety—"

"Tucker is taking care of her tonight." Macey kept her voice firm. "The rest of our team will be here before daylight and we can reevaluate then." She didn't want a pissing match between their departments. To catch the perp, they needed cooperation, not competition.

Anthony gave a quick nod and backed away. He exited the doors, his steps fast. Angry.

Julia pulled on a pair of gloves. "He needs to let that go."

Curious, Macey lifted her brows.

"He and Dawn are not happening. He might want that to be the case, he may want to play her knight in shining armor, but . . ." Julia sighed. "Dawn doesn't want someone to save her. That is the *last* thing she wants. She shuts down guys like him faster than you can blink."

"You know her well."

"As well as anyone can know her. Dawn doesn't exactly let a lot of people come in close. I just found her weakness, so I was able to worm my way closer."

"What's her weakness?"

"Po'boys." She pulled on her exam coat. "And, if I had to guess . . . I'd say your partner."

Macey didn't let her expression change.

Julia checked her instruments. The scalpel gleamed on the nearby tray. "If you think she hasn't told me about *him,* you'd be wrong. He's the man who's haunted her for seven years. He's the guy she's never been able to let go."

"There are two rooms in the suite." Tucker pointed to the room on the right. "You can take that one, and I'll be in here." He moved his hand to indicate the door on the left. They were on the top floor of the hotel, the club level. The only way to access that level was via a special key card. Added security that he'd wanted for the night.

"Where will Macey be staying?"

"She has a room across the hall." And two more rooms were reserved for the other team members who'd be coming into town. His gaze swept over Dawn. She was too pale. Her eyes were too dark. And her body looked far too fragile. "You should get some sleep."

"I'd rather get a drink."

He blinked, surprised by her response, but . . . hell, yeah, they could both use a drink. He made his way over to the bar and checked the selection. "Looks like we've got wine, beer and some

Jack." He didn't remember her liking whiskey, but . . .

"Wine." She'd come toward him, moving silently on the lush carpet.

He poured her a glass of the deep red liquid. Wine for her, Jack for him. He gave her the glass and watched as she drank it. God, but he'd missed her. Sometimes he'd find himself reaching out for her at night.

Sometimes . . . he'd found himself searching for her.

Sometimes I just had to see you. How fucked up is that?

He downed the Jack in moments and set the glass back down with a bit too much force.

She watched him, her gaze shadowed. He needed to step away. She was hurting, her friend was dead, and the woman was being *hunted.* She didn't want him—

"I missed you, Tucker."

Fuck.

Every muscle in his body tensed. "Be careful." The warning slipped out of him.

Be careful, baby. Don't push me too far. My control only works with other people. Not with you. I've wanted you too long. I might not be able to hold back, not now that we're finally alone.

I can't walk away from you again.

"I have been careful. I've always been the careful one. I was the good girl in college, and that got me a swift trip to hell. I've been *careful* in New Orleans, and now my friend is dead. I've come to the conclusion that careful sucks."

He hated her pain. "Dawn—"

But she shook her head. She put her glass down next to his. "Good night." Then she turned on her heel, starting to walk away—

Can't let her go.

He snagged her wrist, curling his fingers around her delicate bones. "Do you still see him?"

She looked up at him. Her eyes were even bigger. So big he could get lost staring in them.

"When you look at me . . ." His voice was gravel-rough. "Will you always see him?"

Her lips trembled and he knew the answer. How could he *not* know? He let her go. "You'll be safe here tonight. Just . . . if you need anything, I'm here."

Like she needed him.

We look too much alike. Every time she sees my face, she will always see him.

He paced toward his room.

"Tucker . . ."

His shoulders stiffened.

"I *want* you."

He kept walking. The last time they'd tried to be together, the night had ended with her screams. He couldn't, *wouldn't*, do that again.

Because she'd looked at him as if he were the monster.

And she'd been right.

He shut the door and knew he needed one hell of a cold shower to get through the night.

Dawn lay in the bed, the covers soft against her skin. She stared at the ceiling but she saw the past.

Tucker.

Her.

In bed.

"Baby, I want you so fucking much." His touch had been so light. His fingers had slid down her neck. *"I need you."*

Her heart had thundered in her chest. She needed him, too, but she hadn't spoken. His lips feathered over her throat and she couldn't help but stiffen. The wound had faded. Weeks had passed since the attack. She had a scar on her neck now, but . . .

As Tucker touched her so carefully, she couldn't help but think . . .

Jason put his hands on me there.

Tucker's fingers trailed after his lips and she had to squeeze her eyes closed.

Jason choked me there, just for fun. Just to show me that he could. He choked me, then he sliced me. Not deep enough to kill me. Just enough to forever mark me.

"Dawn? Dawn, look at me."

Her eyes had opened. All of the lights had been

on in that room. A hotel room because they'd fled to escape the reporters. The crowd. Everyone else. People who just wouldn't let their story go.

At Tucker's command, Dawn looked just over his shoulder.

"At me."

Her gaze came to his. Jason stared back at her. Jason had Tucker's eyes. Jason had Tucker's face. She shivered.

"I would never hurt you."

No, Tucker wouldn't. Jason had lied. *He'd lied.*

Hadn't he?

Tucker had kissed her and tears slid from her eyes.

"Baby?" He had tried to pull back because this had happened before. He'd tried to touch her before and she'd lost herself to terror. *Jason took this from me. He took us away.*

He'd broken the bond she had with Tucker, just as he'd promised to do.

No, she couldn't let that happen. Her nails had bit into Tucker's skin as she'd held him tighter. *"Stay."* The only word she'd spoken to him. She could feel his arousal pressing against her. He'd taken off his shirt, kept on just his jeans. His skin was hot and his muscles were strong. He was powerful and—

Dangerous.

She had kissed him, wanting the passion that had been between them to flare once more. When she made love with Tucker, the rest of the world faded away.

She had needed that. She needed their oblivion. She needed their pleasure. There was too much pain. Her stitches were gone but the jagged marks remained on her skin. The memories were burned into her soul and she needed something to numb them.

I need him. Tucker is what I need most.

So why did she fear him?

He had stripped her. Kissed her body. She trembled beneath him. She parted her legs for him. She shoved his jeans down.

"Baby, we can go slow . . ."

She turned her head away. That voice . . . Their voices were even similar. Dawn shook her head, frantic. She didn't want slow. Slow let her think too much. She'd wanted fast oblivion. She'd wanted the pleasure they'd had before. She'd wanted the life they'd had before. She wanted it all *back*.

But . . . *it's gone. Jason took it away.*

Tucker had moved between her legs. She felt the long, hard ridge of his arousal pressing against her.

"You're not ready." His words were a growl. *"I don't want to hurt you."*

No, she wasn't getting ready. Her body wasn't turned on because her mind was in chaos. But she needed *this*. Her nails bit even deeper into him and she arched her hips against him. Her head turned. Their eyes met—

Jason smiled.

"No!" Dawn shoved against Tucker, fear clawing at her. When he didn't let her go right away, she had screamed. She couldn't stop screaming when he touched her.

And that had been how it ended.

A tear slipped down her cheek as she stared up at the ceiling, coming back to the present. She'd fought for seven years to get her life back. To take control once more. And now a killer was back. A man who was trying to tear her world apart.

She couldn't let that happen. She couldn't be a victim again. She *wouldn't* let fear control her.

Not ever again.

CHAPTER NINE

He wasn't asleep. Tucker was in bed, staring up at the ceiling and trying not to think about just how close Dawn was to him.

When his door creaked open, every muscle in his body tensed. His gaze jerked toward that door and he saw her standing there, the light spilling behind her.

"Tucker?" her husky voice whispered to him.

He didn't move. "Is something wrong?" His own voice came out far too rough.

"Yes." She shut the door behind her. Immediately, the room was plunged into darkness. "I missed you." He could hear the faint rustles of sound as she came toward the bed.

Baby, be careful. I warned you . . . "Stop." He sat up in bed. "My control isn't going to hold." He wouldn't lie to her. "I want you more than I've ever wanted anyone. I'm trying to do this right. Trying to keep my distance and keep you safe—"

She touched him. Her fingers trailed over his bare shoulder. "I am safe with you."

She hadn't always believed that.

His shades were down, the thick curtains in his room covering them and blocking the lights from the city. He could only see the vaguest outline of her body. And that meant she could only see the same when she looked at him.

Did that make it better for her? Or worse?

"Is there someone else?" she asked as her fingers lingered against his skin. "If someone is waiting for you back in DC, tell me and I'll—"

"There is no one else." For him, there *never* was anyone else. She was the only one who'd gotten beneath his skin. Sure, he'd had other lovers. He had needs, and some nights he had to get relief. But in the dark . . .

They are always her.

And that made him feel even worse when he saw the dawn.

She leaned in closer to him and put her mouth to his. A light, tentative brush of her lips against his. His hands grabbed the bedding and fisted. "Dawn . . ."

Her tongue licked his lower lip. His mouth parted and she thrust her tongue inside. *Baby, I missed you, too.* His control was splintering. He should send her away. He was working on the case, pulling protective detail and—

It's her. I can't ever turn away from her. Not even if his damn job was on the line. She was the one dream he'd had all his life.

The one thing he wanted most.

The one fucking thing his brother had tried to take from him. And, now, finally, she was back in his arms. Kissing him, pressing her sweet mouth to his. Just like in his dreams, she wanted him again.

He wasn't going to stop. He tasted her. Explored her mouth. Got drunk on her the way he always had even as he kept his hands fisted at his sides. He'd swung his legs to the side of bed and she . . . she straddled them. Her body came closer to his, brushing against his chest, and that was when he realized that Dawn was naked.

She'd come to his room—naked.

He'd had that fantasy too many times. He'd woken up, without her, more nights than he could count.

Her knees slid toward his hips as her hands curled around his shoulders. Her breasts—her nipples tight—pushed against his chest. He wanted those nipples in his mouth. He'd always loved licking and sucking them and she'd been so responsive. She'd moan, choking out his name, and she'd get so wet for him when he sucked her sweet nipples.

I need her wet. I need her ready.

He wouldn't repeat the past. No way. "I want to . . . touch you," he rasped out. He wanted her to say it was okay. Needed those words. Because of their past.

Because of their present.

"Put your hands on me," she whispered. "Everywhere."

Slowly, his hands lifted. They curved around

her hips, carefully, lightly. Her head bent and she pressed a kiss to his throat, licking and then giving him a soft bite.

His teeth clenched. He'd always loved that one spot. His cock was rock hard beneath his sweats, so eager to sink into her the thing was about to start twitching. But she had to *want* him. Had to be desperate for him.

Because he wasn't going to have the same ending this time. *They* wouldn't end that way.

Her hands slid down his chest, her touch like silk. She reached the top of his sweats and she started to push down the cotton fabric—

"No."

Dawn froze.

"Not yet, baby. I'm already too close." And she wasn't. He lifted her up, turning his body and placing her on the bed. Then he moved on top of her, still slowly, waiting to hear her tell him to stop—

But in that darkness, in the dark where she couldn't see him, Dawn didn't tell him to stop. He stroked her breasts, teasing the nipples with his fingertips, then bending forward and licking her. She gave a quick gasp, one that just made him hungry for more, and he sucked her deeper. His heartbeat thundered in his ears, his muscles ached because they were clenched so tightly, but he moved carefully with her . . .

Don't fuck this up again. Can't fuck this up again.

He kissed a path down her body. When he got to the juncture of her legs, he hesitated.

"I want you." Her voice was certain, a husky temptation.

His fingers slid between her thighs. She was soft and hot, her skin slick to the touch, but . . .

I need more. I need her wild for me. He wanted her to be the way she'd been back in the beginning.

His hands settled between her legs. "If you get scared, stop me." Easy words to say in the dark.

"I won't stop you." Her promise, even huskier now.

He put his mouth on her. Her hips jerked and he held her there, using a light but steady grip. He licked her, he kissed her, he thrust his tongue over her clit, moving fast, stroking lightly, then harder, wanting to push her to the edge—

And over it.

He felt her first orgasm against his mouth. Heard the pleasure in her moan, and it made him desperate for more. He rose up, grabbing a condom from the wallet on the nightstand, and then he was ditching his sweats and shoving that condom on as fast as he could.

He went back between her thighs. He guided his cock to the entrance of her body. She was wet and hot and just as he'd wanted her.

But he hesitated. "Dawn?"

Too dark to see her eyes. Too dark to see her face.

Too dark for her to see my face.

"Don't make me wait longer, Tucker."

He wouldn't. He thrust into her, sinking deep and nearly losing his mind because she felt so utterly perfect around him. His hands slammed down onto the mattress, on either side of her body, and he withdrew, only to thrust again, harder, deeper into her.

Her legs rose and locked around his hips. She arched toward him, demanding, meeting him eagerly. There was no hesitation now, no room for fear. There was only the driving heat for them both as they raced toward the climax.

The bed shook beneath him. He grabbed her hips and lifted her even higher. He was rough now, too far gone to hold back.

It's Dawn. My Dawn.

He slid his cock over her clit and she cried out his name. Her sex squeezed around him and he knew her second orgasm was coming. He wanted to feel that orgasm all along his cock. He drove into her, even as his hand slid between them and pressed to her clit. He knew what she liked. He knew every inch of her body. He knew *her*.

She gave a little scream, one that he stopped with his kiss. Her sex squeezed around him, contractions of release that sent his own orgasm pounding through him. He stiffened, holding her too tight, but unable to stop.

The pleasure blasted through him, so good that

he could barely suck in a breath. He shuddered and held his body off hers even as her sex continued to contract around his cock.

Slowly, the madness faded. His drumming heartbeat settled and the frantic thunder stopped filling his ears. His breath came in pants as he strained to see her in the dark. "Dawn?"

"I missed you." The same words she'd uttered when she'd first slipped into his room.

He kissed her once more, then pulled away from her. Tucker went into the bathroom to ditch the condom. He turned on the water, making sure it was warm as he prepared a cloth for her. He'd clean her off, take care of her, and then . . .

Then we figure out what the hell we are doing next.

He opened the bathroom door. The light from the bathroom spilled onto the bed.

Dawn was gone.

Dawn stared at herself in the bathroom mirror. The bathroom that was connected to *her* room. Because the minute Tucker had left the bed, she'd fled.

Did that make her a coward?

Probably.

But . . .

She stared at herself. Her cheeks were flushed and her eyes were bright. Her lips still swollen from his kiss. She'd done it. She'd made love with Tucker again.

Was it love? Was it sex? Does it even matter?

A knock sounded on the bathroom door. "Dawn?"

Her fingers curled around the edge of the granite countertop.

"Are you okay?"

"Yes." She was not handling this well.

Silence. Then . . . "Did I hurt you?"

"No." She realized she'd spoken too softly. "No." *Straighten your shoulders. Open the door. Talk to him.* She'd put on one of the fluffy white robes that hung behind the door. Lifting her chin, she stepped from the sink and opened that door.

He stared at her. She stared straight at him. No darkness to hide behind this time.

"You ran."

She'd actually walked—rather quickly—to the other restroom.

"Is sex in the dark all you wanted?"

She didn't know what all she wanted. She just knew what she could have. And maybe it was time for some hard truth between them. "It's not you."

He took a step back and she saw pain flash on his face. That handsome face that haunted her best dreams—and her worst nightmares.

She grabbed his hand. "I have sex in the dark with all of my lovers. Not just you."

His face hardened and a muscle jerked along his jaw. "Your other lovers?" The words were a furious growl. "That's *not* what you want to be talking about with me right now."

She held him tighter. "Yes, it is. It's what you need to know. I didn't keep the lights off because . . . because of you." Dawn stumbled over those words. *Because you have his face. Because you have his eyes.* "I've had other lovers in the years since we've been apart. I need the dark. It . . . it helps me to hide."

"Why the hell would you want to hide?"

She let him go and walked around him, pacing toward the window and staring out at the city. Her curtains were pulled back so that she could see all of the glittering lights. "At first, I was hiding my scars. They were ugly, even when they stopped being so red. So jagged." Her breath whispered out. "And then . . . then I was hiding because no matter who I was with . . ." God, this was so hard to say.

He didn't speak behind her and the silence was stretching too long. Dawn eased out a slow breath and turned toward him.

"No matter who I was with, I was still afraid." *Truth.* "It became easier to stay in the dark." Maybe if she'd fallen in love with one of her other lovers, it would have been different. She'd tried to live a normal life. Tried to have relationships, but she put up too many barriers. She knew that.

It was hard to let men close. It was hard to trust.

Tucker stared at her, his eyes so bright and blue. Emotion swirled in those depths. He'd turned on all the lights in her room. *No more hiding in here.* He wore a pair of sweatpants around his hips, and his muscled chest was bare. Strong, determined Tucker. Her gaze drifted over him, staring at him fully in the light.

He had scars, too. But then, he'd always had them. Even when they'd been together before, she'd noticed his scars. Some were small, barely an inch long. Others were bigger, deeper. A few thick ones were on his back, just below his shoulders.

She'd asked about them before. She'd *kissed* them all before.

He'd told her they didn't matter. Accidents. Marks he'd gotten in battle. Wounds to be forgotten.

If only her own scars were so easily forgotten.

"Were you afraid when you were in my bed tonight?"

She'd been afraid going to his room. Been afraid as she stood just outside his door, but then he'd begun to touch her, and the feel of his callused fingertips had been so familiar. "No."

He nodded once, as if satisfied, then he was stalking toward her. One slow step at a time. She didn't retreat. Where was there to go? The window was behind her. He was in front of her.

And—

He reached behind her. Lowered the shade. Pulled the curtains closed. "Take off the robe."

"What?"

"I'm not your other lovers." Again, that muscle jerked in his jaw. "I'm not going to be some faceless man in the dark. That's not who I am to you. Take off your robe. Let me see you in the light."

It was so hard. The way his eyes were gleaming. The way his face had gone hard. The way—

He caught her chin in his hand. Tucker tilted her head up when she hadn't even realized that she'd turned away. "Who am I?"

"Tucker."

"Fucking right. Remember that. I'm not Jason. I'm not anyone you've been with in the past. I'm Tucker, and you can trust me."

Easy words to say.

"Take off the robe."

Her fingers fumbled with the belt. Slowly, she shrugged off the robe. It fell to a pool at her feet.

He sucked in a quick breath and then he took one step back as his hand fell away from her chin. His gaze—almost burning it was so bright—swept over her. Going first to her shoulder and to the cluster of three roses that had been tattooed there. The scar on her shoulder had been the worst, so Jinx had spent extra time layering the petals there.

Jinx.

She had to blink away tears.

His gaze slipped down to her right side. Another rose, one that curled over her hip. Then he looked at her stomach. Two more roses, twisting together there over the long, thin slice that had been left from Jason's blade.

She had three more roses on her body. One on the top of her thigh. He was staring at that one now. One on her back. One small rose along her inner arm.

"You are the most beautiful woman I've ever seen." His gaze was slowly moving over her as he spoke and his voice was a deep rumble. "You were made to be in the light. Made to be seen, not hidden away in the dark."

Her breath came too fast. Her heartbeat seemed to shake her chest.

His head cocked as his gaze met hers once more. "I'm going to touch you."

He'd touched her plenty in the other bedroom. He'd—

He pressed a kiss to the three roses on her shoulder. "And I'm going to have you . . . in the light."

It was too bright. Too many lights. And he—

"Say my name."

"T-Tucker."

He kissed her, a deep, drugging kiss. One that wasn't as gentle as the ones that had come before. One that took and demanded. One that made her ache.

"Still wet for me?"

She was still turned on from the sex before. He rocked against her, and he kissed her again. Harder. The thick length of his arousal shoved against her.

Her breasts were tight, her nipples aching, and she shouldn't want him again this quickly, *should she?*

"Your eyes are closed."

They flew open. She stared at him.

"This time, I need you to see me. Every second of *me.*"

He pulled back from her. Ditched his sweats but pulled a condom from the pocket. Staring straight at her, he rolled on that condom.

His cock was huge, thick and long, and she could still feel him inside of her.

She *would* be feeling him inside of her.

"Right here, Dawn. Right now." He came back to her. Lifted her up. Held her between his body and the window. "Keep your eyes on mine. Every minute. See *me*. Got it?"

She was seeing him right then. The flecks of gold hidden in the depths of his eyes. The passion on his face. The raw need.

He thrust into her.

"See me."

Their gazes held.

He withdrew, the length of his cock sliding along her sensitive skin.

"Because you're always what I've seen," he growled. "Only you."

She wouldn't look away from his eyes.

He thrust in, out, and he pinned her there with his body.

Her legs locked around his hips. Her hands clamped around his shoulders. This wasn't soft and tender. It was raw. Primitive.

Her breath came faster, her heart thundered and he drove into her again and again, pushing her ever closer to her release.

And when it came, the climax seemed to rip her apart.

"See me." He jerked inside of her and she saw the pleasure wash across his face. *"Me."*

Dawn had fallen asleep. Tucker's arm was wrapped around her body. He was in her bed, and he'd made sure that when she slept, she went to sleep with her body pressed to his.

Over the years, he'd seen many expressions in Dawn's eyes. Once, she'd even looked at him with love in her gaze.

Love.

Trust.

Fear.

Hate.

That night, he'd seen desire again. She'd stared at him and wanted the man that she'd seen.

Maybe it hadn't been fair to give in to the desire

they felt. He knew her emotions had been raw. The discovery of her friend Jinx had been brutal and she'd been desperate—probably looking for a way to escape the pain. A gentleman would have just given her comfort and walked away.

His father had made sure he hadn't raised a gentleman. He'd raised monsters instead.

His fingers slid over her arm. The softest silk. Did she know that he'd checked on her over the years? When the need got too great and he'd just had to make sure that she was all right? He'd been so relieved when she went to see the shrink. When she started training to be a PI, he'd been proud.

When she'd started to date again, he'd been a jealous bastard. When she'd gotten engaged briefly to that boring jerk of an accountant, he'd drunk his way to the bottom of a bottle—or three.

No other woman had ever gotten to him the way that she did. Dawn was beneath his skin. Soul deep. And that had been the problem. His brother had realized just how hard he'd fallen for her, and he'd attacked Dawn because of that attachment. She'd been targeted, she'd been hurt . . .

Because of me.

That guilt still twisted deep within him.

He pressed a kiss to her cheek, but Dawn didn't stir. After her day, the woman needed her sleep, and he needed to work because sleep sure as hell wasn't going to come easily for him. He slipped from the bed and padded into his room. A few moments later, he was booting up his laptop and pulling up the profile sketch that he'd created on their perp.

Organized killer. Meticulous. Closely followed the Iceman's exploits, possibly even received access to the case files that should not have been granted to a civilian. Because the cuts were too precise.

He kept typing his notes as his mind spun. He always worked best at night. Mostly because he had so much trouble sleeping. He'd been raised to sleep with one eye open because you never knew when an attack would come.

That same belief had followed him when he'd been a SEAL. *Don't sleep too deep. You might not see the threat until it's too late.*

Pity that the worst threats had been so close to home.

His fingers tapped over the keyboard as he considered all that he'd learned. He liked to get his thoughts down, to summarize his notes from the investigation and see where that led him.

Possibly seduced Jinx Donahue. Could be using charm in order to get close to his victims. If he seduced Jinx, then he may have used the same tactic on Heather Hartley. An agent needs to question those who knew her in Baton Rouge.

Baton Rouge. He hadn't been back there in years. There had been some talk from the folks there about putting up a headstone for his brother. What had been the fucking point of that? There was no body to dump in a grave. And no one to mourn around a headstone.

Jinx revealed details about Dawn to the perp. Number of tattoos. Potentially other intimate details. Killer is fixated on Dawn. Finishing Iceman's last kill?

His fingers stilled as he reread what he'd typed. Then his fingers began to tap once more.

Perp is linked to Iceman. Since the first victim we found here ties back to Baton Rouge, it's possible the man we're after knew Jason Frost.

And that made him wonder . . . wonder something that he had never thought before.

What if Jason Frost hadn't been working alone?

The killings had stopped when Jason went into the Mississippi River. But . . . that didn't mean there hadn't been an accomplice. And this perp that they were after now—perhaps he understood so much about Jason's crimes not because he'd read case files . . . but because he'd been there before, watching from the shadows. Helping?

A sudden, loud peal of music cut through the quiet suite. His gaze shot up. The sound was coming from Dawn's room. He surged to his feet and hurried inside just as Dawn grabbed for her phone. She'd turned on the bedside lamp and illumination spilled onto the bed.

"Jones?" One of her hands held the sheet to her

chest. "Wait . . . you found him? Where is he?" Her eyes had flared wide. "You are amazing. Yes, thank you. *Thank you.*" She hung up the phone. "Jones said one of his regulars just came by . . ."

He glanced at the clock on the nightstand. "It's one a.m."

"Yes, and in restaurant land, that's closing time. Jones always stays after the kitchen closes down to tally the day's accounts." She grabbed for her clothes, dressing quickly. "He gave out a meal a few minutes ago and asked the guy if he'd seen Red. Turns out our missing witness is bunking down at a motel tonight, probably making good use of that hundred I gave him."

Tucker watched her in silence. "Where's the motel?"

"Just under the overpass. Hard to miss because it's the one with the big red roof."

He nodded. "I'll be able to find it."

Dawn froze. "Um, excuse me?"

"I want you to stay here."

Her jaw dropped.

Yeah, this wasn't going over well. He knew that even before her cheeks reddened.

"*Tucker.* I thought we were working together on this, I thought—"

"I'll call Anthony and get him to meet me at the scene. I want you to stay here and stay safe for the night."

She paced toward him with an angry stride.

"We sleep together and now you're barking orders? I can handle myself."

"I don't doubt that."

"Then why—"

"Because this is my job. Keeping you safe. For tonight, you're staying here."

"Tucker, you can't—"

There was a knock at the door. "Just in time." Actually, the guy was *right* on time. He turned on his heel and marched for the door. Tucker glanced through the peephole and saw Bowen Murphy's stony visage staring back at him.

Bowen had texted him earlier and said when he'd be arriving. The fellow had a thing about being on time. Tucker opened the door.

Bowen cocked a brow. "Checking in before I crash. Just wanted you to know I was here—"

"There's been a change of plans. I need you to stay in this suite."

Bowen blinked. "Come again?"

"If you don't, she'll just try to leave."

Bowen's gaze took in Tucker's form, sliding over his still bare chest and noting his jogging pants. "She . . . Let me guess who that *she* is . . ."

Tucker backed away from the door.

"*She* is the woman who is currently feeling very pissed," Dawn muttered. She'd crossed her arms over her chest as she stood in the doorway to her room, and the glare on her face could have melted ice.

Bowen glanced between them. Then he nodded once and said to Tucker, "Bring me up to speed?"

"We just got a hit on a potential witness. I want to track the man down, but I need eyes on Dawn. Right now, she's the perp's next suspected target. She has to stay safe."

"This is bullshit," Dawn threw out. "You told me we were partners—"

Okay, time for the gloves to come off. He glanced at her. "I lied."

She flinched.

Shit. "When it comes to your safety, I'll do anything. You need to remember that. You just got a tip to where the guy is, you want to go running out to find him, but guess what? Our perp could be tracking him, too. The last thing I want is for you to show up and get in the killer's sights. He doesn't know where you are right now. I'm keeping it that way."

Her eyes showed her fury. "I've never lied to you, Tucker."

He'd told her too many lies over the years. That had been part of their problem. But . . . Now he stalked toward her. "Yes, baby, you have."

Her lips parted.

He made sure his voice carried only to her ears. "You told me that you didn't see a killer when you looked at me. And we both know that's not true."

She didn't speak.

What had he wanted? Her denial? That lie had always been between them.

"This is Agent Bowen Murphy." Now his voice was louder.

"Nice to meet you, ma'am," Bowen called.

She gave a little growl.

"He'll make sure no one gets in or *out* of this room until I get back." Tucker turned away from her, but Dawn's hand flew out and caught his arm.

"I'm not going to be the FBI's prisoner, Tucker."

For that night, she was. She didn't get it—he just wanted her safe.

She tightened her hold on him. "No more lies."

He couldn't make that promise. He pulled away and went to his room. He changed clothes, holstered his weapon and then he was heading for the door.

Bowen had made himself comfortable on the couch. Dawn still stood in her doorway. "She doesn't leave," Tucker said flatly as he pointed at Dawn.

Bowen waved him away. "Got it. Find the witness, and I'll take care of her."

He didn't look back, mostly because Tucker didn't want to face Dawn's fury. When he got into the elevator, he pulled out his phone and called Anthony. The detective answered on the second ring. "We've got a tip on Red's location," he said as the elevator doors slid closed. "Can you meet me?"

He'd left her. Benched her. Lied to her.

All after making love to me again.

What in the hell? Was he just trying to make her feel like shit or what? Making love with him had been a *big* deal for her. Life-changing big. *Because I didn't let any fear stop me. I fought for what I wanted.*

And then . . . he'd walked away.

Was it supposed to hurt that much? Because it felt as if her heart was being cut out of her chest. And she couldn't stop staring at that damn shut door. She kept thinking maybe it would magically reopen. Tucker would be there. He'd apologize, he'd tell her—

"His heart is in the right place."

It was the other agent. The blond guy. Bowen. The guy who was leaning back on the sofa looking as if he didn't have a care in the world.

She didn't think she liked Bowen. Actually, she didn't think that she liked Tucker much right then, either.

"I heard about your friend." Bowen's head turned and his dark gaze met hers. "I'm sorry."

The sympathy on his face was genuine, and she found herself softening toward him. *It's not Bowen's fault that Tucker is an ass.*

"You found one body today. Did you ever

consider that Tucker wants to make sure you don't have to discover another?"

She wasn't trying to understand Tucker's point of view right then. It hurt enough just understanding her own. "I can help on this investigation."

His gaze swept over her. "You look different, from your picture."

Some of the heat left her cheeks. *Crime scene pictures.* She'd met plenty of cops who'd seen those images of her worst time. Those cops usually handled her with kid gloves and stared at her with sympathy in their eyes. *Tucker is handling me that way, too. As if I'll break too easily. I won't.* "Victims always look different." Her gaze sharpened on him. "Let me guess . . . did you study my case before you came down to New Orleans? Were you told to do a brush-up on the Iceman and you saw what he'd done to me?"

"Absolutely. Wouldn't be doing my job if I hadn't stopped to review all the case files." He nodded, then rubbed his cheek. "But I wasn't talking about any crime scene photos. I was talking about the picture that Tucker keeps of you in his office. You look different in that picture." What could have been sadness flashed on his face. "You were smiling and your eyes were bright. For some reason, I thought that picture was taken after the attack, but . . . it was before, wasn't it? I can see that now. Your eyes . . . they're different."

She didn't move. "I don't know what picture you're talking about."

"You're standing in a field, looked like damn daisies, and you're smiling from ear to ear." His lips twisted. "I wanted that picture to be after. I needed it to be." His gaze fell. "I see too much pain in this job. I needed to know there was more happiness out there. That there *could* be more."

He'd kept the picture. For some reason, the pain in her heart eased a bit. "What has Tucker told you about me?"

"Not much. I learned what I could, like you said, from reading the Iceman's case files." But his attention shifted to her once again. "And I saw the picture in his office one day. I learned a lot from that . . ."

"Like what?" What could you possibly learn just from a photograph?

"Like . . . the way you were looking at the man who'd taken the picture. I know that look. Haven't seen it very much, certainly not directed my way," he murmured with a wry smile, "but it's a look a woman gets if she's in love."

Wasn't Bowen the chatty one? "That was a long time ago." Her voice sounded hollow to her own ears.

"Was it?"

"Yes."

He studied her in silence. She hated silence. In

silence, it was as if you were always waiting for something to happen. Something bad.

"He lied to keep you safe. He failed before, and I don't think he intends to fail again."

There was something Bowen needed to understand. Something that Tucker needed to see, too. "I'm not a victim this time. I *won't* be." She intended to fight back, not hide.

"People don't ever wake up wanting to be victims." Sadness was there, rumbling in his words. "They don't ask for bad things to happen to them. They don't ask for pain. For sorrow. Things happen. Attacks *happen.* It doesn't matter how strong you are, anyone can be hurt."

I'm ready to fight now. I will never be the woman who begs while a knife goes into my body.

"There's nothing wrong with being a victim," he continued carefully. "But I've never met anyone stronger than a survivor." His stare held her. "When I look at you, I don't see a victim. I don't think Tucker does, either. We both see a survivor, and Tucker? Well, the reason he's being such a controlling ass with you is because that man would do *anything* to make sure that you stay that way."

CHAPTER TEN

It was nice in the motel room. The bed was soft. The water in the shower was hot, and he could watch as much TV as he wanted.

Red liked the little room. He liked the way the sheets smelled. He liked the way he smelled when he got out of the shower.

The room had been thirty-nine, ninety-nine, plus tax. So he had money left. Money to buy breakfast. Lunch. Maybe dinner, too. He could have saved all of the money for food, but . . .

He'd wanted the room.

He'd wanted to be somewhere else for that night.

He'd tried to sleep but . . . he couldn't. His gaze kept darting around the room and he kept the TV playing because he didn't want to miss any shows. He'd already missed so much. There was a phone on the nightstand and he thought about picking it up. He still remembered his daughter's number. He could call her. Just check in. Maybe . . .

Maybe even go home. If she'd let him come back.

His hands were shaking. They did that. His hands shook and sometimes his thoughts got all cloudy. He'd had blackouts before, been told that he'd have them again.

There were pills he was supposed to take,

but the pills turned him into a damn ghost. He couldn't feel anything. Nothing but a thick fog that surrounded him. He didn't like that fog.

But he . . . he did miss his daughter. He reached for the phone.

Just as someone knocked at his door.

His heart jerked in his chest at that knock. It was so late . . . Who was coming to see him? No one ever came to see him. Most people barely looked at him when he was walking down the street. He'd gotten used to that.

I'm always a ghost.

"TV's too loud," a voice called through the thin wood of the door. "Management. Open up, *now.*"

Shit, shit. He was in trouble. He didn't want to get kicked out. Red scrambled toward the door, unlocking it. "Can't kick me out, I paid good money—"

Something shoved into his chest. At first, it felt hot, sharp, then . . .

Ice-cold.

He opened his mouth to scream but he could only manage a choked gurgle. His legs were giving way beneath him and the guy in front of him . . . he was *twisting* the knife he'd shoved into Red's chest.

"You won't talk to anyone." The guy smiled at him.

I know that face. He put the girl in the box. He came into my home.

"You won't talk, not ever again . . ." And he shoved the knife toward Red's throat. Red fell back.

The pain had been so intense, so consuming, but . . . but it was already fading. A heavy fog was sweeping around him. Just like the fog that came with his pills.

Had he taken his pills?

Because . . . because he sure felt . . . just like a ghost.

"How long have you been working with Tucker?" Dawn asked Bowen. She wasn't just going to go back into her room like a good little girl, so she figured grilling the other agent was an option she should pursue.

His lips pulled down as he seemed to ponder her question. "I've been in the unit with him for a couple of months now, but our paths have crossed in Violent Crimes more than a few times."

"The unit?"

He nodded. "Right. Our new experimental team. Samantha Dark is in charge, and she handpicked all of us for her team."

Samantha Dark. The name clicked for Dawn because Samantha had been in the news quite a bit recently. Cameron Latham, her former lover, had turned out to be a serial killer and Samantha had stopped him—and another killer—in Fairhope, Alabama, just a few months ago.

"Why were you all picked?" Curiosity filled her as she perched on the side of the couch.

"Because we all have . . . well, shall we say 'intimate' ties to killers?"

She just stared at him.

"I could tell by your face that you know Samantha's story. Her link to Cameron didn't make her an inferior profiler. Instead, it gave her insight that others didn't have. Closeness to a killer isn't a weakness. Samantha thinks it is a strength."

She waited, but he didn't say more. Obviously, the guy needed a push. "I get Tucker's link to a killer. What's yours?"

He smiled at her. "Am I supposed to tell you all my secrets as soon as we meet?"

She'd like for him to, yes, that was the point of her questions. "Macey's on this team, too."

His smile dimmed.

"Macey survived an attack," Dawn said. "That's her link?"

"She tell you that?"

No. I saw the scars on her skin and the pain in her eyes. "She didn't have to tell me."

Bowen nodded. "Macey is something special. Strong and smart. I knew she'd be on the team as soon as I heard about Samantha's promotion." He rolled one shoulder against the couch. "Meanwhile, I had to fight and bribe my way on. But when you see an opportunity coming, you don't let it pass you by."

The guy wasn't going to share about his past. She could respect that. After all, Dawn liked to keep her own secrets, too. She rubbed her arms, suddenly feeling chilled.

"You'd probably be a good addition to the unit, too."

Her head jerked up, surprise flashing through her. "I'm not meant for the FBI."

"Sure about that?"

"I'm a PI for a reason. I don't exactly play well with others." She liked taking the cases that appealed to her. Listening to someone else's orders? Following only the jobs that were assigned to her? *No, thank you.*

"But you want to work with us now."

"This is different, and you know it." Tucker knew it, too. "This is my life. I'm not going to hide away while some jerk hunts me down—or hurts more innocent people." The grief over Jinx was heavy, making her shoulders hunch. "She was my friend," she said, voice thickening. "She was dying below me and I didn't know. It's not right. She didn't deserve that."

"No, she didn't." He shifted his position on the couch, studying her with a hooded gaze. "I'm sorry about her death."

She blinked away the tears that were clouding her vision. "She didn't have any family. Jinx grew up in the foster system, bouncing around. She moved to New Orleans a few years ago.

Wanting a fresh start, same as me. I think she had a cousin in the area, but . . . they didn't exactly talk much."

He stared at her, and Dawn found that she wanted to keep talking about her friend. She needed to talk about her. "We met when she inked me."

His gaze slid over her. Her tattoos were covered. Her scars always covered—all except the thin one on her neck. That one was barely visible because Jason hadn't made it too deep. Just a little slice. *Let's get things started.* She'd been so stunned by the pain.

Jinx had wanted to cover that scar, too, but because it was so long and thin, Dawn had hesitated. *I can take care of it, Dawn. Turn it into something beautiful.* Jinx's voice drifted through her mind, so strong, as if her friend were sitting right beside her, talking in her ear.

But she wasn't. Jinx was gone.

"What tears me up the most . . ." Her voice had become a whisper. "He killed her because of me. I know that. She was a means to an end for me. I'm the end. If Jinx had never met me, then she'd still be alive."

Now Bowen rose, standing fully. His hands were loose at his sides. "That's the kind of thinking that will drive you insane. Trust me, I know that for certain."

Her stomach was in knots. "You see why I

can't stay on the sidelines? I can't let someone else die because of me. I *won't.*"

Every few moments, Tucker could hear the rush of wind overhead—that rush signaled a car sweeping across the overpass. He'd gotten to that little motel in near record time. A handful of vehicles were in the small lot, and the red sign near the little office flashed that there was a VACANCY. He started walking toward that office. He'd question the clerk inside, find out which room Red was in and then he'd question the guy. Anthony should be there any moment. Hell, he'd actually thought the detective might beat him to the scene.

But . . . Tucker stilled. He was about fifteen feet away from the motel's office, but he'd just noticed one of the room doors was halfway open. He turned, eyes narrowing. The light was on inside that room, he could see it shining through the blinds. He thought he could hear the murmur of . . . voices. Or was that a TV?

His heart rate kicked up. Could be nothing. Could be some guy who'd run out to get ice and he'd forgotten to close the room door behind him.

Could be nothing . . .

But Tucker found himself pulling his gun. "Hello?" he called out as he advanced toward that room. "Is everything okay in there?" His nostrils twitched because . . . a thick, cloying scent was hitting him.

Everything is not okay.

He hurried forward. He pushed that door farther open and then—

Blood.

Blood poured from the gaping wound in the man's throat. Blood matted in his long beard. Blood soaked his shirt. Blood coated the cheap carpet beneath him.

And—

The man's hand twitched.

He's still alive.

Tucker surged forward and dropped to his knees beside the guy. He knew he was staring at Red. The guy looked just as Dawn had described. *Only in her description the poor bastard wasn't carved up and bleeding out!*

"I'm FBI," Tucker said as his hands pressed to the gaping wound at the man's throat. Immediately, his fingers were soaked with blood. "Stay calm. I'm here to help—"

Red's eyes fluttered open. Did he even see Tucker? The fellow's gaze was bleary, pain-filled. His lips moved as if he'd speak.

You can't speak, buddy. Some bastard cut your throat open.

"Hold on," Tucker said. "I'm going to get you help. You're going to be okay—"

Footsteps rushed behind him, and Tucker looked up. He'd put his gun down when he ran to Red's side, and if the perp was coming back to attack again . . .

But, no, Anthony stood in the doorway. His eyes were wide, his weapon drawn. “I heard your voice,” he said, stepping closer as his frantic gaze took in the scene. “Fuck!”

“Call an ambulance!” Tucker barked.

Anthony yanked out his phone.

Red’s body jerked. His eyelids twitched then began to sink closed.

“Red?” Tucker said.

No response.

“Red!”

She was staring out at the city lights when she heard the ring of a phone behind her. Not her phone, though, because she didn’t recognize that ringtone, and a moment later she heard Bowen say, “Hey, man. She’s good. Got my eyes on her right now.” A brief pause. “Now tell me you found our witness.”

Silence.

“I see.” Bowen’s voice had become stilted. “Right. Yes, I know you made the right call. Never doubted it. No, no, don’t worry. I’m not going anyplace and neither is she.”

Her shoulders stiffened.

“I’ll be here when you get back. We’ll *both* be here.”

More silence as he ended the call. She kept staring out at the city. From her position, she could see a barge on the river. Lights were on that barge, but the river was just darkness beneath it. *Jason got lost in the darkness.*

The Mississippi was so strong. The authorities had sent dive teams in the water, but they hadn't found Jason's body. They'd said that gators might have gotten to him . . . or maybe his body had been pulled out by the current. Pulled deeper into the Mississippi . . . that he could have been taken all the way to the Gulf.

That it would be impossible to ever find his body.

She heard the squeak of the couch and the faint rustle of Bowen's steps behind her. "Let me guess," Dawn finally said as she stopped staring at the barge but instead caught sight of his reflection in the window as he approached her. "You get to keep babysitting me while Tucker and Anthony are interviewing Red?"

"No." A quick, curt response. His reflection looked big and dark, tense. Dawn glanced over her shoulder.

The man looked the exact same way. He exhaled. "Red is dead."

Shock beat through her body.

"When Tucker found him, Red had been stabbed in the chest and in the throat."

She forced her knees to stiffen. For a moment there, it had almost felt as if they wanted to give way.

"When Tucker got to him, Red was still alive, but the guy only lasted for mere seconds."

Dawn shook her head. "That's . . . that's not how Jason kills."

Bowen blinked at her. *"Jason?"*

Oh, shit. I slipped up. I'm not supposed to say that I think Jason is still out there. People think I'm crazy when I say stuff like that. Even Tucker didn't believe me. "That's not how the Iceman kills." Her words were very careful now. "He's never attacked a man. And he doesn't leave his victims behind. He lets them die in the freezer."

Bowen stared at her. "Maybe he didn't have an option this time. If he realized Red could identify him, then he would have needed to get rid of the guy right away."

Another death. "Why is this happening? After all these years, why now?" Just when she'd gotten her life together. Just when she'd found a place—people—that she could truly connect with. It seemed as if everything was falling apart.

"Our unit won't give up." Bowen's tone was flat. "Know that. Agent Dark is right when she says that our personal ties to killers are strengths. We understand just how devastating their attacks can be . . . and we know that victims need justice."

She couldn't just stand there with him any longer. "Excuse me. I'm . . . I'm tired." She brushed past him, made sure her steps were certain. Steady.

She shut the bedroom door behind her with a soft click.

Jinx. Red. Heather Hartley. Her lips trembled. And she let herself cry there, alone in the dark.

"Another body for Julia." Anthony gave a sad shake of his head. "I did not want the night to end this way. We needed Red to ID the perp."

The body had been taken away. The blood had been washed from Tucker's hands. Police lights still swirled at the scene, but the other folks at the motel had finally gone back into their rooms.

No one had seen anything. No one had heard anything. In that kind of place, folks tended to mind their own business. If you heard a strange sound, you didn't investigate.

And that meant a man died.

"How'd the perp know Red was in that room?" Anthony suddenly asked him. "I talked to the desk clerk. He said you didn't even come inside when you arrived . . ."

Tucker rolled his shoulders, trying to get rid of the heavy tension that had gathered there. "The door to room number 104 was open. It worried me, so I went to check it out." His gaze slid to Anthony. "That's when I found our guy." But the perp had been long gone. Damn it.

"You know this could be unrelated." Anthony put his hands on his hips. "Our homeless community is pretty big. Dawn gave the guy one hundred dollars. Maybe Red told the wrong person about that cash. I didn't see it in his room.

Maybe it was just a robbery gone wrong and not the copycat we're after."

"Red was a witness. He told Dawn what he saw and hours later, he's dead." Tucker didn't move. "I'm not buying that as a coincidence."

"But it doesn't fit the killer's MO. I mean, I get that I'm just some detective to you, but I read those case files. The Iceman doesn't attack this way—"

"MOs can change. Especially when circumstances demand that change." He was certain on this. "Red saw the killer, and now he's dead."

Anthony sighed. "Did Red say anything to you? I mean—"

Tucker gave a bitter laugh. "Hard to talk when your voice box is gone." Such a sad fucking waste. "He didn't get the chance to say anything."

Anthony looked a little green, but after a few deep breaths, he said, "There was a lot of blood spatter in there. Maybe the perp left evidence behind we can use."

Their techs were combing over the scene right then. "Maybe." Had Bowen already told Dawn? She'd wanted to come with him to the motel, but he'd been afraid the killer would be there. Waiting. Looking for her.

But the killer beat me here.

"Who gave you the tip on this place?" Anthony asked him.

"Jones." And they'd be talking to him. Seeing if

the guy had mentioned Red's location to anyone else. *This shouldn't have happened.*

Crime scene tape fluttered in the faint breeze.

The killer was moving too fast, striking too quickly. Almost taunting them. The perp was confident and determined, and the attack on Red proved that he wasn't afraid to make a kill right under the nose of the authorities.

Red was still alive. We missed the killer by minutes. Damn minutes. They'd already checked, hoping there was some kind of video surveillance system in place at the motel, but there was nothing.

Just blood left behind in a killer's wake.

"Dawn is safe, right?" Anthony questioned Tucker, and there was something in the detective's voice . . . a deeper edge of worry that had Tucker turning his head toward the other man and studying him a bit harder.

"She's safe," he replied curtly.

Anthony held his stare and stepped closer. "Is she?"

What in the fuck?

"Is Dawn really safe with you?" Anthony's voice had gone quiet and cold. "I know this has to be a damn nightmare for her. She and Jinx were close. Those two damn women lit up when they were together. Fastest friends you ever saw."

"I didn't realize you knew Jinx." *Is Dawn really safe with you?* The guy's words echoed in his head and Tucker found himself clenching his hands into fists.

Anthony's lips turned down. "Who do you think hooked up Dawn and Malone? The guy wanted help with his daughter, but Captain Hatch wasn't giving me the go-ahead for the investigation—and I knew Dawn would find that girl. She doesn't give up." Admiration lit his gaze. "And she doesn't back down."

The man sure seemed to know a lot about her.

"I knew Jinx and Malone long before Dawn did. And hell . . ." His fingers raked over his face. "I was the one who went to tell Malone about Jinx's death. That's why it took me so long to arrive here. I wanted to give him the news in person. Thought he deserved to hear it from me." Faint lines of strain bracketed his mouth. "I hate telling people their loved ones are gone. Worst fucking part of the job." He shook his head. "No, check that. Having a killer get away, knowing he's still out there, possibly hunting his next victim right this minute . . . *That's the worst.*" His eyes sharpened on Tucker. "So I ask you again . . . is Dawn safe with you?"

"I'm a former fucking SEAL, and a trained FBI agent. I know how to keep a victim safe." He had to bite back the fury rising in him. "I would never let anything happen to her."

"Because it's so personal to you." Anthony's voice was still quiet.

So was Tucker's. Lethally so. "All the more reason to keep her safe."

Anthony's lips tightened. "You think it's not personal for me, too?"

And there it was. The undercurrent that Tucker had sensed when Anthony was near Dawn.

"You're her past," Anthony said. "And when I talk about danger to Dawn, I'm not just meaning the prick out there killing. You're bad for her, Agent Frost. I know it. You know it. And so does she."

Fucking hell.

"So maybe someone else should be in charge of keeping Dawn safe. The NOPD knows how to protect victims, too." His eyes glittered. "And being with me wouldn't wreck the world that Dawn has built for herself."

Tucker took a step closer to the detective. There were eyes on them. Cops. Reporters. Local FBI agents. "Dawn isn't for you." The warning carried only to the man before him.

But Anthony gave a grunt. "You really think she'd ever be truly happy with you? You made the woman run screaming before. When she looks at you, deep down, we both know . . . she'll always see him."

Tucker's greatest fear. Right there.

Anthony glanced around, as if making sure they weren't being overheard, and then he said, "So how about you just focus on profiling this bastard. Let me take care of Dawn. Before you screw up her world even more."

Tucker's back teeth clenched. His control cracked. He reached out toward Anthony.

"Agent Frost."

He stiffened. Tucker knew that feminine voice, one rich with command. His gaze jerked to the left. Samantha Dark stepped forward from the shadows.

"Agent Frost . . . I got to the scene as fast as I could." She hurried toward him, her steps brisk and her heels clicking across the pavement. "Once my flight touched down, I went to see Macey and Dr. Bradford. Sorry I didn't get here faster when the call came in." Samantha's gaze swept toward Anthony. "And you must be . . . Detective Deveraux." She offered her hand. "Glad you called us in on this case."

"Yeah, me, too." Only he didn't sound especially glad as he shook her hand. "Though I wasn't expecting the bodies to pile up so fast on me."

"No." Her voice was emotionless. "And they shouldn't have. The fact that you have three dead in this city now—dead that could all be linked to the same killer—means that we are dealing with a very unstable predator."

Anthony's gaze trekked back to Tucker. "That's what I'm afraid of."

Another cop called out to him.

"Excuse me." Anthony stepped away.

Tucker watched him go.

"Your hands are fisted," Samantha noted.

He forced his hands to relax.

"It appeared to me as if you were about to lunge at an officer of the law." Again, no emotion was in her voice. "Something you want to tell me?"

Deveraux wants Dawn. He's not getting her. Not when her scent was still on Tucker's skin . . . the sweet scent that had finally pushed past the cloying stench of blood and death. Not when Tucker could still hear her sighs and her moans in his ears. Not when he could feel the silk of her skin.

Not when I want her more than anything else.

"Personal connections can work to our advantage. Your link to Jason and your understanding of his crimes is beneficial to this case." She reached out and touched his arm. "But your link to Dawn Alexander could be a liability."

Slowly, his head turned. His gaze met hers.

"If you're so consumed by her that you don't see the threat coming, you won't be any use to her. So I'm asking you—and I need you to tell me the truth right now—is your control in place when you're around her? Can I count on you to do your job?"

To protect Dawn? To hunt the killer? *"Yes,"* Tucker said with certainty.

But . . . was his control in place around her?

Hell, no. Only Tucker didn't see that as a weakness, either. The fact that she was the one person who made him wild, who pushed him over the edge . . . that just meant that he would do anything for her. He wouldn't rest until she was safe.

There were no limits for him, not when it came to Dawn.

Never when it came to her.

Tucker opened the door to the hotel suite. He took a few steps inside, his shoes sinking into the thick carpeting. If Dawn was sleeping, he didn't want to wake her.

"You should really let me know before you decide to waltz right in." A lamp flashed on and he saw Bowen sitting up on the couch, a gun cradled in his hand. "You know, knock politely at the door. Something to signal that you're coming inside and not just sneaking around like a perp in the dark."

Tucker stilled.

Bowen studied him a moment. "Judging by your face, I'm guessing it was one hell of a scene."

It was. More shit that would haunt his nightmares. "If I'd arrived just ten minutes sooner . . ."

Bowen stood up and holstered his gun.

"Red was still breathing when I arrived,"

Tucker added. "But I knew he was dying, and I knew there wasn't anything I could do to save him." He'd hated that helplessness. His gaze slid toward Dawn's room. The door was shut. "Did you tell her?"

"Yeah." Bowen ran his hand over his face. "She got quiet and went in her room. I don't think she's the kind of woman who lets others see her pain."

No. "Dawn's very private."

His hand dropped. "She was pissed as all hell at you for leaving her behind."

He paced toward her room, caught himself and stopped. "I'm glad you kept watch on her here. One dead body a day should be enough for anyone."

"You were afraid the killer would be there, that he'd be watching. That he'd go after her."

Tucker turned his head toward Bowen. "I'm still afraid of that." It was just the two of them, and he heard no sound from Dawn's room, so he figured he could speak freely to the other agent. "It's all about her. The first kill—Heather Hartley—she wasn't even living in this city. The killer brought her here."

"Because Dawn was here."

He nodded. "Dawn told me that she'd been feeling as if someone watched her for the last few weeks. That someone was in her home." *That son of a bitch will pay.* "I think the guy was accessing her place from Jinx's, coming and going as he wanted. Since Jinx was continuing on with her life as normal during that time, we have to assume the perp is someone she knew. Someone she felt comfortable giving the security code to her building . . . and a key to her house."

"A lover," Bowen surmised.

That's what Tucker thought, and it was good to talk over his theories with a teammate. He stepped away from Dawn's door as he focused more on Bowen. "He was using Jinx in order to get close to Dawn. When he was ready for his games to really start, that's when he eliminated Jinx and left those roses for Dawn. He wanted her to know that he'd been studying her. That he'd learned her secrets. Jinx probably told him everything she knew about Dawn, not realizing what was happening until it was too late."

Bowen swore. "That's one cold, methodical bastard you're talking about."

He absolutely was. "And we both know just how dangerous a guy like that truly is." He glanced at Dawn's shut door once more. He wanted to go in there and see her, touch her. Just make sure that she was safe, but . . .

You have a job to do. Do it. Protect her. He looked away from the door. "There's a possibility I never considered before."

Bowen lifted a brow.

"When Dawn first told me about her stalker, she wondered if it was Jason."

He saw Bowen's shoulders stiffen.

"I shot him in the chest. I know I did. Body or no, he's *dead.*" He was adamant on that. "But . . . fuck me, what if he wasn't working alone?"

Bowen gave a low whistle. "You know serial killing teams are extremely rare."

"But they do exist. One is usually the dominant, and the other follows his orders. Jason would have been the dominant partner of the team. And maybe . . . maybe with his death, the perp we're looking for now spiraled. For all we know, he could've suffered a mental break and been institutionalized for the past few years."

"Or been arrested," Bowen mused. "If his partner vanished, he would have been at loose ends."

Tucker began to pace. "And if that's the case, it would explain why the attacks are suddenly happening *now.* He's worked up his nerve. It took him this long, but he's back in action again. He knows how to mark the victims like the Iceman because he worked with the Iceman. He studied under him. See, at first, I was thinking the perp was someone who'd gotten access to the case files. Maybe someone even in law enforcement, but . . . but I think we have to consider that Jason Frost wasn't working alone."

"It would have certainly made his crimes easier," Bowen mused. "Moving the victim, securing the freezers . . ."

"Right. And now . . . hell, even his fixation on Dawn makes sense. If our guy had partnered with Jason before, then he's finishing the work that the Iceman started."

Bowen stared at him, seeming to absorb his words. "Who was your brother friends with, back in the day? Anyone standing out for you? I can start doing background investigations—"

Tucker gave a rough bark of laughter. "That's the problem. *I'm* the one he was close to back in the day. He didn't have a lot friends. The guy was a loner. An alpha type. He had lovers—too many of them—but they were disposable to him. He never formed a close attachment with anyone but me."

Bowen rubbed the back of his neck. "In order for your theory to work, we need an actual partner. There had to be someone, you just didn't know about it. The same way you didn't know that your brother was a cold-blooded killer."

But I did know. Tucker stared at him. Just stared.

Bowen's eyes widened. "Tuck?"

That nickname made him stiffen. Jason had always called him by that name. He licked his lips and tasted the fucking bitterness of regret. "Sometimes you see the danger coming, you feel it closing in, but you want to pretend it's not there. You want to pretend it's not real. Because it *can't* be, right?"

Pity flashed on Bowen's face.

"I was just nine when I realized how different my brother was." A day of blood and death and hell. "I knew there was evil inside but I thought . . . I thought Jason could fight it." *The same way I did.* "I saw it coming . . ." Guilt would follow him around until the day he died. "But I didn't stop it."

And the door to Dawn's room squeaked open. She stood there, fully dressed in her T-shirt and jeans. Her eyes were big and wide, stark, and her face was far too pale. "What?"

She'd been listening to their conversation, the whole time. She even had a glass still clutched in her hand. That old trick, putting a glass to the door so you could eavesdrop easier . . .

She dropped the glass to the floor. It bounced but didn't shatter in the thick carpeting. Dawn lunged toward him and grabbed his arms, holding tight. "What in the hell do you mean, *you knew?* You saw it coming?" Her nails bit into his skin. "He was going to kill me! You knew and you did *nothing?*"

Her pain was ripping him apart.

"Tucker? Tucker, say *something.*" But then she shook her head. "No, not something. Say that I'm wrong. Say that you never knew. Say that you never thought your brother would hurt me. *Say it.*"

He was silent, fighting for words.

She let go of him—only to shove her hands against his chest a moment later. A hard, powerful shove. *"Damn it! Say that you didn't know! Say that you didn't know he wanted to hurt me so badly!"*

He caught her shoulders in his hands and held her—so carefully. He'd had her in his bed that night, he'd been with her, skin to skin, he'd tasted heaven, but now hell was coming toward him in a fierce rush. A train, barreling straight for him, and there was no way to get off the tracks. "I knew he had . . . darkness inside."

Her breath choked out. He could feel Bowen watching him. Waiting. The other agent would want to know just what had gone down before with Jason.

He'll want to know if he can trust me.

Dawn will hate me.

But if this new killer was tied to Jason, he had to reveal everything from his past. There wasn't an option. Discovering the bastard's identity was key. Protecting Dawn took priority over protecting his own past.

"When people pissed him off . . . Jason always struck back." *Always.* "Some kids beat me up when I was nine. Made fun of my clothes, made fun of my lunch . . . called me a piece of trash." He swallowed, that memory so fresh that it still burned. "Jason found out. He went back and beat the shit out of them." Big brother, protecting him, but . . . "He killed their dog. Their cat. And a week later, a fire gutted the barn of one of the boys who'd been yelling at me the loudest."

Her mouth parted in shock.

"No one ever tied the animals and the fire to Jason. Mostly because I . . . I never said a word." She tried to back away. He let her go. "You don't know the full truth about my family. Folks only saw us from the outside. Jason was strong and tough." His lips twisted. "And I became that way. You had to be, in our house. Weakness wasn't allowed. Weakness was punished."

I'll never be caged again.

She just stared up at him.

"What are you saying, Tuck?" Bowen asked him.

He saw Dawn flinch at the nickname.

"My father . . ." He took a step back from Dawn. He wanted to look away from her when he finally told her this part, but he couldn't. "My father was a sadistic bastard. He loved inflicting pain on others. First he did it with my mother—my only memories are of her crying, of her trying to shield me and Jason from his fists and his belt. She tried to protect me . . . until I was five, and then she died and she couldn't protect me anymore."

Dawn's gasp was painful to hear.

"She was trying to leave him when she had that car crash," he said, remembering and hating that memory. "She was taking me and Jason away." And if she'd gotten them away, maybe everything would've been different. "But she was scared and driving too fast and she hit that big oak tree in the dead of night. She was bleeding and crying and he . . . he found her out there. He found us all out there on that damn godforsaken road."

Bowen swore.

"My father stood by the car . . . on that fucking lonely stretch of road. I was in the back seat, begging for help. Jason was with me, but he didn't say a word. She was crying . . . And my father just stood by that car, watching and waiting, until she wasn't crying anymore."

Dawn shook her head. "No," came her strangled whisper. "Tucker?"

"Jesus Christ," Bowen said. He came toward Tucker and put a hand on his shoulder. "I am so sorry."

He stiffened. Didn't Bowen see? Their father had been a twisted monster, one who had forced the darkness he carried onto his children. Jason had become a killer and Tucker . . .

"I can think like them," he said, glancing at Bowen. "Samantha knows that. She knows everything about my family. I told her about them before I agreed to join the unit." It was easier to look at Bowen. "I know how the killers think because I was supposed to be one of them."

"You're not," Bowen told him grimly.

Dawn hadn't said anything at all. Not since that broken whisper of his name.

Bowen glanced at her, then back at Tucker. "You and I will talk more in the morning." He inclined his head toward Dawn. "There are things the two of you need to say first. Without my ass here, watching." He grabbed his bag and headed for the door, but before he left, he paused. He glanced back at Tucker. "You're *not* one of them." Then he was gone.

The door closed softly behind him. Tucker made himself look back at Dawn. Beautiful, smart Dawn. Strong Dawn.

Dawn . . . who stared at him as if he were a stranger.

CHAPTER ELEVEN

"You've been keeping secrets," she said, tilting her head to study him. Then . . . then she shocked him by reaching out and touching his chest. "I know what those marks are now. They didn't make sense to me before—all of those faint, white scars. I . . . I thought you got them in battle."

Every muscle in his body had locked down. "They were marks from his belt buckle. After our mother died, there was no one to shield us. If we pissed him off, he'd beat us. Then he'd lock us in the closet. In the dark. For fucking hours." *Days.* Hot summer days had been the worst. He could keep them in that closet then, for as long as he wanted. There would be no calls from the school because they didn't show up. No people checking on them.

He and Jason had stayed in the dark, sweat soaking them, their lips cracked and dry. He'd vomited in that closet, again and again, but his father hadn't cared. They'd stayed in the dark, in the heat, with that mess all around them.

Hell. But their father had been careful. Just in case. "He'd never wanted to be caught, so . . . he took us out to the cabin."

She went white.

Yes, baby. I am so sorry. The same cabin that Jason took you to so long ago. "Neighbors would think we were going on a family trip, but we knew he was just going to kick our asses. To lock us up. He liked hurting us. When things went wrong for him—and they went wrong a lot—he took it out on us." In that fucking cabin.

He'd hated the place.

"It was so hot there during the summer. Sweat would soak us in minutes. We'd stay huddled in the closet and . . ." *This is the worst part. But I have to tell her.* "And Jason would swear that one day, he'd be surrounded by ice. He'd stay cold forever and the heat wouldn't touch him."

Her hand rose to her mouth. She stared at him, horrified understanding in her eyes.

"To get us through those long hours, he used to tell me to imagine that we were far away. Snow and ice were all around us. The ice was cooling us down, making us safe."

A tear tracked down her cheek.

"That's why he froze them. He wanted them to stay cold forever." He'd figured that out long ago. Just as he'd figured out so much about his brother. Too late. "When you're abused like that . . . when you grow up the way we did, your mind can get bent, Dawn."

She backed up a step. It hurt, but he understood. *She'll never want me touching her again.* He should have kept his hands off her. She was probably remembering what they'd done together—hours before—and hating him.

"Why didn't you tell me?" Her voice was a rasp.

"Because it was my fault." Truth. Savage. Dark. Ugly. The ugly truth that had kept him away from her for so long. "I knew what he was capable of doing—I knew what we were both capable of. I should have watched him closer. I thought . . . I'd found a way to channel myself. Maybe he had, too."

A furrow was between her brows.

"It was why I joined the Navy. I was going crazy on the inside. I needed risk. I needed the adrenaline rush and I needed to do something to make a fucking difference." His breath eased out slowly. "I was different—and it was seen. I was good at the missions, almost too good. I didn't slow down, didn't let emotions get in my way. I could be a perfect weapon."

"Y-you're not a weapon. You're a person."

When he'd been with her, he'd felt differently. He'd felt peace, not that terrible yawning emptiness.

"You told Samantha Dark your truth. But not me." Her eyes narrowed. "And you're only telling me now . . . because I heard you talking to your partner. You thought I was asleep. You thought I wouldn't know."

Don't lie. "Yes."

She shot toward him once more. Her hands lifted as if she'd touch him, but she froze, stopping herself. *Is she afraid to touch me now?*

"Why?" The one word was ragged, pain-filled. "Why do they get to know your secrets, but I don't?"

Because they don't matter to me the way you do. "They can look at me as if I'm a monster and it doesn't matter to me. But when you stare at me that way . . ." The way she was looking at him right then. "You rip me up inside."

Her lower lip trembled.

There's more, baby. So much more she didn't know. More that even Samantha didn't know. Some secrets were too dark to share.

"I should have stayed closer to my brother. I should have watched him better. I should have stopped him before the first girl was ever hurt." But after they'd gotten out of school, Jason had *seemed* better. Their father had been dead, burning in his hell, and everything had truly *seemed* better. Tucker had thought *he* was the dangerous one. So he'd enlisted in the Navy. He'd tried to get his life on track. Tried to be a better man.

And he'd seen—too late—what he'd left behind.

"I don't know who Jason may have gotten close with while I was gone. But those killings *only* happened while I was deployed. If he had a partner . . . he didn't bring the guy around me. He kept the SOB hidden, but I will find him. I won't stop until I do."

Dark shadows lined her eyes.

"Jason Frost is dead, and the guy out there hunting? He's going to be caught and locked away in jail for the rest of his life." *Caged.*

You know I can't survive in a cage. Jason's voice, floating through his head.

She looked down at her hands. Dawn had twisted them in front of her. "Are there more secrets?"

Yes.

She waited a moment, and when he didn't reply, Dawn gave a little shrug. "I thought we'd come back to each other."

He had to strain in order to hear her words.

She cleared her throat and spoke again. This time, her voice was stronger. "I missed you, so much, over the years."

His heart nearly stopped.

"I thought about you. I wished that I'd been stronger before . . . that I'd held on tighter to you. But I was afraid back then." Her head tilted back and she stared into his eyes. "When we were together tonight, I wasn't holding anything back from you. I stopped being afraid, but I don't think you did."

"Dawn . . ." He wanted to pull her into his arms. To hold her tight and *never* let go.

"You were the one holding back tonight. You

kept secrets before, and I didn't even realize it. You're doing it again." Her lips twisted down. "Do you know why?"

His fists were clenched so tightly they ached. *Because I want to protect you. Because I hate it when you look at me with so much pain. Because I still—*

"You don't trust me."

Shock pushed through him. "That's not it. There's no way I don't—"

"You don't think I'm strong enough to handle whatever it is that you're holding back from me." Anger sparked in her eyes, gleaming. A light flush coated her cheeks. "Just like you didn't think I was strong enough to handle your past before. You were abused. You were *hurt.* And you didn't tell me. You lied to me when I asked you about your scars."

"Because I didn't want that part of my life touching you." She'd been so perfect and pure. The best thing he'd had in his life, and he hadn't wanted her tainted.

But Jason had been determined to taint everything.

She gave a laugh. No, a sob. Shit, he didn't know—the sound was a twisted combination of a laugh and a sob as she yanked her shirt to the side, revealing the roses on her shoulder. "Guess what, Tucker? That part of your life did more than touch me."

His back teeth clenched.

"It touched me. It marked me. It changed me forever. I could have handled your secrets before. I would have understood about your past—I *loved* you then."

Then. Not now. Of course she didn't love him now. Too much time had passed, too much pain and—

"And I thought you might love me."

He sucked in a sharp breath.

"But without trust, there isn't love. There can't be. You held your secrets tight. You're *still* holding them tight, and I can't make you share them with me. No matter how hard I try, I just can't make you do that." She turned away from him and reached for the door to her room.

He grabbed her. An instinct. *Can't let her go.* His fingers curled around her shoulder and he held her, too tight. "You don't want my past. *I* don't want it touching you." Why couldn't she see that truth? He hadn't told her before because she'd been so fucking perfect and good.

She'd always been too good for him. He'd known that. But he hadn't been able to stay away from her. Not then. Not now.

"I wanted you touching me." She looked back at him. "I wanted you."

"Dawn . . ."

"No secrets. That's what I need. And that's what you can't give to me." She swallowed. The little click was painful to hear. "Let me go now. I need . . . I need to be away from you now."

Those words pierced straight to his soul.

And he let her go. After all, there was nothing in the world he wouldn't do for Dawn. She slipped into her room. She shut the door behind her.

She left him.

Left him alone with the monster that waited inside of him.

Baby, I can't tell you everything. You'll never want to see me. Never want to touch me. There are some secrets I have to take to my grave.

Her phone was vibrating. Dawn cracked open one eyelid and glared at the nightstand. She'd managed to sleep—finally. And her dreams had been nightmares. Horrible, twisted scenes of Tucker being hurt. Of Tucker . . .

Hurting others.

God, she was so messed up. Her hand shot out and she grabbed the phone. A text had just come through. One from Malone.

> Must talk to you immediately about Jinx. Come to Voodoo Tats.

Jinx. She sat up, cradling the phone. Reality slammed into her. Her friend was in a morgue now. Julia would have worked on her—or she *would* be working on her, depending on how long it took the body to thaw.

Oh, God. She had to thaw out Jinx's body.

Her eyes squeezed shut and she almost wished for the nightmares again. Because at least in those twisted dreams, she—

Her phone vibrated again.

Waiting at the shop. Hurry.

Her fingers tapped across the screen. Be there in twenty.

She jumped from the bed. She was still dressed—dressed in the clothes she'd worn yesterday. Maybe the cops would let her get in her place later that day so she could change. She felt like hell and she probably looked that way, too.

Her phone vibrated. Dawn glanced at the screen.

Come alone. No cops, no agents.

Malone had never been exactly wild about the police. He had a criminal record, and he'd been viewed with suspicion more than a few times. If he wanted to talk with her in confidence, she could see where he wouldn't want an audience around.

And she needed to talk to him. He'd been a father figure to Jinx. The guy was probably a wreck. She should have called him herself last night.

Dawn went to the bathroom and freshened up as much as she could. When she came back out—

Tucker was standing at the foot of her bed. His hair was wet, as if he'd just come from the shower. He wore khaki pants and a white button-down shirt. He lifted up a bag that he held in his hands. "I had clothes delivered for you."

She hurried forward and took the bag. Inside—*yes!*—she found her clothes. "Thank you." She turned away, heading for the bathroom.

"Dawn."

Her shoulders tensed. "I need to change, okay? Give me a minute." She pretty much ran into the bathroom. As fast as she could, she switched her clothes. And maybe . . . maybe she didn't look too hard at herself in the mirror. After everything that had happened, she didn't want to see herself. Not yet.

Some things don't change.

When she went back into the bedroom, he was still there.

"The team isn't quite done at your place," he said. "So you'll need to stay here—"

"I'm going to meet Malone." She lifted her chin. "I need to pay my respects to him. He was pretty much the only father Jinx had." She checked her phone, this time avoiding Tucker's gaze. "He texted. I told him I'd be there soon, so I need to go." She tried to brush around him.

He caught her wrist. And at his touch, an electric current seemed to travel through her whole body.

That was what he'd done to her. One night, and she was attuned to him again. When they'd been together in the past, their bodies had become so sensitive to each other. He'd been able to just touch her, and she'd reacted.

Fear had stopped that, for a time.

But the desire was back now. The passion that he stirred so effortlessly inside of her. It was there again, and even the fear couldn't hold it back.

She knew her emotions were twisted when it came to Tucker. She was twisted. Messed up. *Wrong?* Dawn didn't know. She just understood that he got to her, on a primitive level. She couldn't stop her feelings. When it came to Tucker, there was no holding back.

"I'm coming with you."

Dawn shook her head. "He doesn't want cops or FBI agents around. He's not exactly a fan of law enforcement."

His gaze sharpened. "Too bad. You're still under protective custody, and I'm not letting you walk out of here alone."

Not letting you. "That pisses me off."

Now his brows rose.

"You're taking over my life. A life I worked hard to build. You're locking me away." She glanced around the hotel suite. "You can't keep me sealed away from the rest of the world. You're not the only one who doesn't like a cage."

He swore—and he let her go. "I just want you safe. This bastard is gunning for you. You think I'm going to turn my back and let him take you away from me?"

His wording there . . . it was odd. Possessive.

"I have a job," she said flatly. "My own business. People who depend on me. I can't just hide and wait for some killer to be captured. That could take days. Weeks." *Months.*

"I'm going to get him." His eyes shone with determination. "I worked up his profile. We're going to a briefing with the coroner today. Our team is ready to hit the ground running. This is what we do, Dawn. We catch bastards like him and we lock them away."

"And I help people," she said quietly. "I find people who are missing. I help wives get justice. I help those who feel like they are out of options. My clients are counting on me, and I won't let them down." She nodded. "Just like I won't let Malone down. I'm going to see him."

"Dawn . . ." Frustration showed on his face. "I'm not doing any of this to hurt you. You're a target. To let you out on your own would be the height of irresponsible behavior. The bastard is *killing.* I can't have you becoming his next target."

Winding up dead wasn't on her to-do list. *And it hadn't been on Jinx's, either.* "What happened to Red?"

His jaw hardened. "He was stabbed in the chest and in the throat. No one at the motel saw or heard anything, and the poor bastard died choking on his own blood."

God. She sucked in a hard breath.

"I don't buy coincidences. I don't think that the only witness we had just randomly got killed in some robbery or some shit like that. The killer we're after . . . he found Red. He eliminated him. I don't want him doing the same to you." His shoulders squared. "So I get that Malone is your friend. I get that he doesn't like cops, but what you need to get . . . I won't risk you. I can't. So if you want to go and see him—fine. But you're doing it with a shadow. You're doing it with me."

Damn it. She *got* what he was saying, she really did. She didn't want to take unnecessary risks. But she also wasn't the hiding type. She wanted to fight. She wanted to catch that bastard who'd hurt her friend and so many others. She wanted to do *something.* And not just sit on her ass waiting for the bad guy to find her. So she nodded once, decisively, and said, "Then this is the way it will work." Not an argument, not a plea, just flat speech. "Be at my side, but don't cage me. Don't pull rank and cut me out of the investigation—that's not working for me. This is my life, and I'll stay with you." Dawn hesitated. "I'll stay with your team, but not as someone who sits on the sidelines. I *will* be a part of this investigation. I won't be a prisoner."

He was quiet a moment, and she didn't realize she was holding her breath until he nodded. "I'll clear it with Agent Dark."

What? Yes, hell, yes! "Good." She glanced at her phone. "Now we need to hurry. Malone is waiting, and that man does *not* like to wait. He's going to be pissed enough when you show up with me." She'd have to deal with that anger and calm Malone back down. She brushed by Tucker.

"We're not going to talk about it, are we?"

Dawn stilled. "It?"

"Last night. The sex. The secrets."

"No, we're not talking about that right now." Dawn glanced over at him. "Unless you've decided to really trust me?"

"I *do* trust you."

"Then stop holding back." She faced the front again. "Because you're the one pushing me away this time."

Voodoo Tats was dark. The closed sign hung from the front door, a bit crookedly.

Tucker stared at the building, his gaze sweeping over the windows. "Doesn't look to me like Malone is here."

"He's here." Her fingers swiped over her phone.

Tucker knew she'd gotten another text on the way there. "He said the back door is unlocked. To come in that way." Dawn slanted him a quick glance. "You can wait outside while I talk to him. The guy is going to be torn up, and Malone isn't exactly the kind of man who likes for others to see him hurting."

Yeah, he could buy that, based on his previous chat with the guy. Malone had struck him as the hard-as-nails type. But the place looked deserted, and the idea of Dawn just sauntering inside alone . . .

Hell, no.

"I need a few minutes to talk with him alone before you come in."

Without answering, he moved to the side of the building. A narrow alleyway waited there. Dawn slipped ahead of him, moving easily. It was so quiet out there. The streets were empty, the town barely awake. She turned up ahead, moving to the back of Voodoo Tats. Dawn reached for the door and, sure enough, the handle turned beneath her hand. She opened the door and started to walk inside.

"I don't like this." Tucker's gaze swept the alley. "I don't like this scene one bit."

She'd looked back at him. Her lips parted as if she'd argue with him.

"Take out your phone."

"Tucker . . ." A warning edge had slid into her voice.

"The phone, Dawn, now." And, yeah, he was biting off orders, but every instinct he had was screaming at him. The setup was wrong. The place was empty. The guy was telling her to come in the back door? All alone? *Fucking ambush.* That was what this felt like. Some kind of trap.

Glaring, she pulled the phone out.

"Call him," Tucker ordered. "Talk to him. Make sure your buddy Malone is here." He didn't want a text. He wanted to hear the guy's voice.

She dialed the number, putting it on speaker so he could hear the phone ring. The back door to the tattoo shop was open and—

He heard the phone ringing inside. Malone's phone was there, but the guy wasn't answering. He saw the worry flash on Dawn's face as the phone continued to ring.

And then voice mail picked up.

Her finger swiped over the screen, ending the call without leaving any message.

"You brought your gun, didn't you?" Tucker asked her softly.

"Yes." Her expression had changed completely. She didn't appear angry with him any longer. Now she was worried, tense—the same way he felt.

Tucker nodded. "I'm going in first." Because Malone could be in there . . . and if he wasn't answering his phone, the guy could be hurt. That was option one. Another option—this could be a trap and, in that case, he wanted them both to be ready. "Stay behind me."

He pushed the door open fully. "Malone!" Tucker called out. "It's Agent Frost! I want to talk with you, *now.*"

But there was no response.

He stepped forward and . . . his foot slipped on a piece of paper. He glanced down and saw . . . roses. A sketch of roses.

"That's my tattoo design," Dawn whispered from behind him.

His gaze slid along the hallway. There wasn't just one piece of paper there. Dozens of pages were scattered on the floor—copies, all of the same image. The cluster of roses that Dawn had on her shoulder.

"Malone!" Now his voice was a rough shout. "Show yourself!"

Nothing. Silence.

He strode forward. Turned to the right . . .

"This was Jinx's work room," Dawn said, her voice barely carrying to him.

The room had been trashed. Everything inside had been smashed. Mirrors broken, her tattoo inks thrown across the room. Utterly destroyed.

And right in the middle of that chaos, he saw a phone.

Tucker marched forward and stared down at the screen, making sure not to touch the phone. He didn't want to contaminate the scene and destroy evidence.

Missed Call.

Malone's phone. He whirled around.

Her phone vibrated. Another text.

She pulled out her phone, stared at the screen and blanched.

"Dawn?"

"It's . . . her. This time, the text is coming from Jinx's number. And it's *her.*"

He grabbed her phone—and saw that the image she'd been sent was of Jinx. A very *alive* Jinx. The woman was tied up and she was in the freezer, staring up with horror stamped on her face.

"He sent it from her phone. He has Jinx's phone."

The killer had her phone, and he'd lured Dawn to the tattoo shop. He'd set a trap and Tucker had let them both walk right into it. "We're leaving, now." He grabbed her elbow. "Come on—"

"No! We have to search the whole place! Malone could be here—he could be hurt. The bastard who killed Jinx and Red—he could have gone after Malone, too." She jerked away from him. "We have to search for him! We have to—"

Her phone vibrated again. Another text that had come from Jinx's phone.

I see you.

The SOB was watching them. Tucker caught Dawn's arm and dragged her from the back room. He did a fast sweep of that building, looking for Malone, but no one else was there. Just them . . .

And the longer we stay, the more danger we are in.

"We're getting out of here, now." He headed for the back door.

Her fucking phone vibrated again. Tucker looked back, glancing down at the screen.

You were supposed to be alone.

His eyes narrowed. Too bad. She's fucking not alone. "When we go outside, you stay behind me. We'll go straight to the SUV." He'd get her away from the scene and then he'd call in backup to search the shop and he'd get a crime scene team out to dust for prints. The team needed to find Malone, and he wanted to scout the area.

He rushed outside, moving fast, sweeping the scene, and Dawn was right with him. She didn't hesitate at all as they rounded the back of the building and then headed for that little alley.

He was going in first and—

A gunshot blasted. He saw the glint of the gun just before it fired and he jumped to the side, grabbing Dawn and taking her down with him. He felt the heat of the bullet burn across his arm, and then he heard the thunder of frantic footsteps, racing away.

Oh, no, you son of a bitch. You're not getting away that fast.

"Stay here," he snarled at Dawn and then he leaped to his feet. He took off running down that alley. He could see the guy in front of him, a guy wearing a black hoodie and running hell fast. Tucker pumped his legs faster, ignored the blood wetting his shirt and rushed after the bastard who'd dared to take a shot at them.

"Stay here?" Dawn jumped to her feet and stared after Tucker with her mouth hanging open. She was pretty sure the guy had been *shot.* And he'd just run away, acting as if he weren't hurt at all, but . . .

She looked down. That was definitely blood on her shirt. Blood that wasn't hers. She checked her gun. Good. She was—

Her phone vibrated, jerking on the pavement. It had fallen from her hand when she and Tucker had jumped for cover. She bent to stare at the screen.

Got you.

But . . . Tucker was racing after the guy who'd fired at them. So the shooter couldn't be texting—

She heard the faintest rustle of a footstep behind her. Dawn started to whirl around, but then she was hit from behind. Hit hard and fast. He shoved her forward and her head slammed into the brick wall on the side of the building. Her finger jerked on the trigger of her gun and she fired a wild shot, one that seemed to echo in her ears.

Tucker lunged forward and tackled the bastard who'd been running so fast. They'd already crossed the street and rushed into another alley. *This shit ends here.* He hit the perp hard and they tumbled onto the ground. He rolled the guy over, glaring down at the bastard. "FBI, you son of a bitch—"

It was a kid. A too-pale teen with acne on his face and terror in his eyes.

This isn't the killer.

"Who the fuck are you?" Tucker demanded.

The guy was shaking—shuddering. "I . . . I dropped the gun, man!"

Yeah, he'd dropped it when they were running. Dropped it—thrown it at Tucker. Same fucking thing.

"S-said he'd pay me if I fired . . . Just a shot to scare you . . . Didn't . . . didn't mean to hit you—"

And another gunshot blasted.

Tucker froze.

The kid was staring up at him in absolute horror and a gunshot was echoing in his ears. The blast had come from behind them.

Dawn is back there.

"Guy g-gave me a couple hundred." Spittle flew from the kid's mouth. "Just to scare you. Just to—"

Tucker yanked out his cuffs. He locked one cuff around the kid's wrist and the other he snapped around the pole on the side of a Dumpster. "You stay the fuck here." He jumped to his feet and spun around. His heart thundered in his chest as he ran back toward Dawn.

She could taste blood in her mouth. She'd busted her lip when he'd rammed her head into the bricks. He slammed her hand down hard, nearly breaking her wrist, and the gun dropped from her fingers.

Fine, you bastard. You want to play rough? She drove her left elbow back at him, hitting him as hard as she could. He grunted and eased his hold on her, just for a moment. The moment she needed. She lurched free of him and rushed toward the mouth of the alley.

"I'm going to teach you to like pain."

She stumbled.

"We'll get Tuck, and then the real fun will begin."

She whirled around. Those words were from

her nightmares, from the past that she wanted to forget.

He was there, holding her gun, his face covered by a black ski mask. His voice was rasping at her as he pointed that gun at her chest.

"You think you know him?" He laughed. *"Guess again."*

"Dawn!" Tucker bellowed her name.

The bastard in the mask lifted her gun and she threw her body to the side.

Footsteps thudded away. She pushed herself off the pile of garbage that she'd landed on as she realized that the guy was running away. Leaving her there. He hadn't even tried to shoot at her.

"Dawn!" Tucker's voice was closer. Desperate. She shoved to her feet and turned toward him.

"He was here!" She grabbed Tucker's arms. "He was just . . . here." She pointed toward the alley but the guy was gone. Tucker took off running and so did she. Her gun was gone—the bastard had taken it. When they got to the back of Voodoo Tats, she still didn't see him. Her head jerked to the left, to the right.

Where is he?

How had he vanished so fast?

And . . . *if he wanted me dead, then why didn't he take that shot?*

"He dropped the phone." Tucker pointed to the ground but didn't touch the phone that was there.

Probably because he didn't want to smudge any prints. *But the guy in the ski mask . . . he'd been wearing gloves.* "This way!" He headed down the small alleyway next to that phone. She followed him, but she didn't see any sign of the bastard who'd attacked her.

With every step she took, her heart grew heavier. *He was right there, and now he's gone.*

He'd wanted to take Dawn with him. To put her in the back of the vehicle he had waiting. To slip away with her into the city.

To spend hours working on her. Making her like the pain.

But she hadn't come alone. She hadn't followed the simple freaking instructions that he'd given to her.

So he'd had to improvise.

He slipped between the buildings, moving like a ghost. He could hear Frost yelling for him. He could hear the desperate tread of their feet as they searched.

They weren't going to find him. They weren't going to stop him. He would get away . . .

And he'd live to hunt Dawn another day.

You're afraid of me, Dawn. I saw it. You're afraid of me . . .

And you're afraid of him.

Just the way it should be.

Killing Dawn wasn't the point. If it had been,

she would be bleeding out in the alley. She needed to suffer. She needed to fear.

He needed to finish the work that Jason Frost had started.

And when he was done, Dawn would be frozen and Tucker would be destroyed.

He'd left Jinx's phone behind deliberately. Placed it into position before he ran the opposite way. He wanted them to find all the pictures he'd left on that phone. Another part of his plan.

The plan had been so long in the making. He'd been so careful, and soon . . . soon he'd get the ending he'd wanted all along.

CHAPTER TWELVE

"I'm going in that interrogation." Tucker glared toward the one-way mirror. "That little prick in there saw the killer. He took money from him to take a shot at me, and he's going to tell me exactly who we are after."

Dawn glanced between him and Anthony. The tension in the room was so thick it nearly suffocated her. The man in the ski mask had vanished, but the kid in the other room—the one with bleached-blond hair and too-pale skin who couldn't seem to stop shaking—he'd been arrested.

The guy didn't seem to get just how much trouble he was in. When you shot at an FBI agent, you didn't get to walk away. But the blond kept asking when he'd be let go.

No time soon.

Malone was okay, thank God. The cops had found him at his home. He'd left his phone at his office after he'd gotten the news about Jinx, and he'd gone on a serious bender. The uniforms who'd gone to his house had said he'd smelled like a case of cheap beer.

"The FBI has rank on this one," Tucker continued. "I want my run at him first, then you and your guys can have him."

Bowen stood beside Dawn, watching the scene

unfold. He'd been silent, just as she had, though she doubted it was for the same reason.

The guy got to me. He'd scared her in that little alleyway. Because the things he'd said . . . Jason had said them, too. How had the guy known that? Those words had been burned in her memory. *Word for word.*

Anthony inclined his head. "It's your show, but I'm telling you now . . . that kid is as high as a freaking kite. His pupils are pinpricks, he can't stop shaking and I caught the dumbass *singing* a few minutes ago. I don't think he's going to be able to give us jackshit."

Dawn's gaze slid back to the glass. That was her fear, too. She could see all the same telltale signs that Anthony had just noticed. She knew he was right.

Anthony headed toward her. He paused at her side, and his hand came up toward her face.

She stiffened. "Anthony?"

He almost touched her lip, but seemed to catch himself. "I'm sorry you were hurt." And he shot a glare toward Tucker. "I was assured your safety was a priority."

Over his shoulder, she saw Tucker's jaw clench.

"I'm okay." Her voice was flat. She wasn't going to let any emotion slip out.

"It's obvious he's after her." Finally, Bowen spoke. "He was trying to lure her out to him. We have to be on guard, no more mistakes."

Tucker marched toward the door. "No more mistakes." His words were clipped but she knew his anger was directed at himself. He'd barely stopped long enough to get his arm checked out. The bullet had clipped him, but he hadn't seemed to care about the pain. An EMT had patched him up at the scene, and Tucker had been stoically silent the whole time. A few quick stitches, no anesthesia. And right back to work he went.

He opened the door and headed out. Anthony cast one last look at Dawn, and then he followed on Tucker's heels.

Dawn's breath eased out slowly as she moved for a better position in the observation room. She'd never seen that blond guy before in her life. His gaze kept darting around the room, not lingering for more than a few seconds on anything. And his fingers were tapping on the table. *Tap. Tap. Tap.*

"He is higher than a damn kite," Bowen growled.

Yes, he was.

"You sure you're all right?"

She bit her lip. She hadn't told Tucker about the man's words . . . mostly because the bastard had been talking about Tucker and it had just—

No. Fear had kept her silent. Stupid fear. "A few bruises, nothing more." Her spine straightened. She wouldn't give in to the terror again. She wouldn't.

She saw the door to the interrogation room open. Tucker stepped inside, with Anthony right at his heels. The blond took one look at them, and terror flashed on his face. He jumped to his feet, throwing out his hands.

"Stay the hell away from me, man!" Spittle flew from his mouth. *"Get away!"*

Tucker raised a brow. "Calm down."

But the blond wasn't calming down. At Tucker's voice, he gave a yell and he . . . he launched right at Tucker.

Tucker just stood there, letting the guy come at him. At the last moment, he twisted his body so that the blond missed him totally. Then Tucker spun around and grabbed the kid's arms, jerking him back. Tucker wrapped one hand around the blond's throat and held him, effortlessly. "That's the second time you've attacked a federal agent, buddy. You must really want to spend the rest of your life in a cell." He let him go, putting his hands on his hips as he studied the younger fellow.

Anthony was silent as he shut the door to the interrogation room and watched the other men.

"No!" the blond yelled. "This isn't happening." He yanked up his hands and pressed his fingers to his eyes. He nearly jabbed his fingertips into his eye sockets. "Just scaring you. Just scaring you!"

"Who wanted you to scare him?" Anthony

asked. His voice was calm and cool. Easy. "Tell me, and we can help you out."

The blond stilled.

"We know your name, *Rowan*," Anthony continued. "Rowan Jacobs. You came up in our database. Seems you've had a few brushes with the law. Some small-time thefts, a drug possession . . . but you were a kid back then. According to the files I have, you turned eighteen two months ago." He whistled. "That means trouble for you, Rowan. Big trouble."

Rowan shook his head. "No. No!"

Tucker stepped toward him. "You said someone paid you. *That's* the man I want, Rowan. Tell me what he looked like. Talk to me, and I'll help you."

Rowan retreated until his back was pressed to the one-way glass.

"That kid is terrified," Bowen murmured.

Dawn couldn't take her gaze off the scene before her.

"B-blue eyes," Rowan stuttered suddenly. "Big, over six feet. Strong." His words came in rapid fire succession. "Dark hair."

Tucker's stare hardened on him. "Going to need a whole hell of a lot more than that, kid. You just described—"

"Him," Bowen said as his voice sharpened. "The kid's half-ass description could be Tucker."

"—about a million people," Tucker snapped at

the same time. "So you're going to have to get real specific, real quick—"

Rowan whirled to face the mirror. "He sees you."

He was staring straight at Dawn.

"He sees you," he said again and Rowan slammed his head into the mirror. Once, twice, and the mirror cracked beneath the impact of his blows. Dawn let out a horrified gasp as she saw the blood trickling over the glass. Blood poured down Rowan's face, but he pulled back, seemingly about to slam his head forward once more.

"Stop!" Dawn yelled.

Tucker had leaped forward. He grabbed Rowan.

"Medic!" Anthony was yelling. He'd yanked open the door to the interrogation room. "We need a medic in here!"

Dawn and Bowen ran out of the observation room. They rushed inside the interrogation room, crowding close to Tucker.

The kid was unconscious, the rough trembles of his body stilled. He barely seemed to be breathing. Blood poured from the gashes in his forehead.

"What in the fuck was that?" Bowen bent next to the fallen man.

Tucker looked up at Dawn. She stood there, heart racing, as more uniformed officers filled the room.

He sees you.

• • •

Tucker eased out a low breath and opened the door at the police station. The door led to a small conference room—and to Dawn. She stood up when he entered the room, worry flashing on her face.

Get your shit together, man. Do it now.

"We knew he was high . . . The kid is messed up. Rowan is being kept under medical supervision now." Because the guy had split his head wide-open. "We're not going to get anything from him for a while."

He moved closer to her. He could see the cut on her lower lip. The bruise on her cheek. The scrapes on her hands. Those marks pissed him off. They'd happened on *his* watch. He should have—

"I didn't tell you everything."

He stopped in front of her.

Her long lashes lifted and her gaze locked with his.

"I didn't tell you all the things he . . . he said to me in the alley."

He had to touch her. Carefully, the back of his hand slid over her cheek. That bruise didn't belong there. She should *never* have been—

Dawn caught his hand. "I didn't tell you everything that Jason said back then, either, and I . . . I didn't tell you everything that the man in the ski mask said today."

Shock pulsed through him.

"I didn't tell anyone all of the things that Jason said. No, no, that's not true. I told my psychiatrist." She licked her lips. "Just him. No one else. I was too afraid to tell the cops. I didn't . . . I didn't want them to look at you with suspicion."

He could only shake his head.

"Do you remember how I hid from you in those woods?" She blinked quickly and inhaled. "You shot Jason and I hid. You kept calling to me, but I didn't come out right away."

And he'd been fucking terrified. Yes, he remembered. As if he could ever forget.

"Jason said you were coming to the cabin to kill me. That you'd been using me all along."

Every muscle in his body tensed. Tucker shook his head, denying what she was saying. Denying that he'd *ever* hurt her.

"He said he was keeping me alive so that you could get there and join the fun. That you'd f-fucked me—" she tripped over that word "—and now you were going to kill me."

He stared at her as pain cut into his heart. "That's why you ran from me when I first got there." Why she'd fallen into the water.

"Jason said he wasn't acting alone. He said the press should call the two of you Icemen, not Iceman." She wet her lips. "He said he was working with someone . . . and that someone was *you*."

"No." The word came out too hard, too rough. But he needed her to understand. "It wasn't me. He was lying to you. He wanted to *hurt* you." *And me.* "I was never involved, baby, I swear it."

Her breath came in quick pants. "The man in the ski mask . . . he said the same thing to me. The words . . . they were Jason's words. *'I'm going to teach you to like pain.'*"

Those were words burned into Tucker's mind. Not because they were Jason's. But because they'd been their father's words.

I'll make you sorry pieces of shit like the pain. You'll stop screaming soon enough.

He had to swallow the lump in his throat.

"The man in the ski mask . . . he said he was waiting for you, so the fun could start."

Tucker didn't blink. He didn't move at all. The rage inside of him was so strong he was afraid if he moved, his control would shatter.

This case is wrecking me. "No." One word. That was all he could manage.

"Then the kid described someone who could be you." She lifted her hands and pressed them to his chest. "You look like Jason. Jason's body wasn't found. The words were the same, and I swear . . . even the voice sounded the same to me. He's back. I think Jason is back." Her voice broke.

A sharp knock sounded on the door.

"Agent Frost?" He recognized Samantha's voice. "We need to talk."

"I wasn't the only one holding back secrets." He said the words softly to Dawn.

"I didn't want the cops looking at you with suspicion. You'd been through enough. We both had."

"I was never working with him." He might have been screwed up, he might have enjoyed a taste for too much darkness, but he'd *never* turned into a cold-blooded killer. He would never hurt an innocent.

"Frost!" Samantha's voice was sharper. "I need you and Dawn in the meeting room, now." Her heels tapped smartly away from the door.

Tucker stepped away from Dawn. Stepped away when he wanted to pull her close. To wrap his arms around her and not let go.

But they were at the police station. His boss waited. And the case . . . the case came first.

Only she is the case. She's the priority.

He turned away from her and opened the door. He held it open while Dawn walked ahead of him. Their group had taken over the big meeting space at the end of the hall, and when he went inside, he saw the tactical board that the unit had prepared.

The victims' pictures were on that board. Pictures of them when they were alive, happy, and then pictures of them when the killer had finished with them.

"The reporters have this story." Samantha stood near the board. Macey and Bowen were seated at the table. No one else was in the room. She inclined her head toward Dawn. "And they have your past. They know who you are. They've made the connection. The headlines running today are that the Iceman is back. He's killing again."

"He's *dead,*" Tucker gritted. How many times would he have to say it? He blew out a breath and paced toward the tactical board. "It's not Jason we have to worry about. This killer . . . I think he's far more dangerous than Jason ever was." And that was saying one hell of a lot. "Jason had a certain victim type."

"Attractive young women," Bowen added. "College coeds."

Tucker's gaze slid to Dawn. She hadn't taken a seat. She stood just inside the doorway, watching them.

"Yes." He didn't move his gaze off her. "And he killed them in a ritualistic manner. He used his knife to cut them, marking them. Never slicing deep enough to kill. Just enough that his brand would always be on their skin."

She wasn't looking away from him.

"He put his victims in the freezer. Not because that was another form of torture, but because he wanted to keep the victims with him. To stop time. No decomposition, no destruction.

He would literally freeze the women when they were his. He meant for them to stay that way, forever." He pointed to the board, to the first victim, Heather Hartley. "This killer isn't focused on owning his victims. He's sending a message instead. I believe he called in the tip about the body because he didn't want time to be wasted. He wanted the cops to find the victim as soon as possible. He wanted us down here." No, that wasn't exactly true. His gaze slid to Samantha. "He wanted *me* down here. He wanted me here and he knew I'd come as soon as I heard about the type of kill that had been discovered."

There had been no option for him.

"He approached his second victim, Jinx Donahue, because of her tie to Dawn. He wanted access to Dawn's home, and he wanted to learn as much information about her as he could." His gaze cut to Jinx's picture. "Then he eliminated her."

"I don't remember seeing any men with Jinx," Dawn said softly. "She never brought anyone home, not that I saw. She never introduced me to anyone—"

"That would have been deliberate," Macey cut in. "He would have made sure that you never crossed paths. Not until he was ready."

"It's a trap." Tucker hated saying the truth. "Everything he's done . . . it's been to close his web around you." He rubbed the back of his neck. “And me. I’m just as much a part of this as you are. The guy wants me involved. He wanted me here, and he has me.” Now he moved toward the photo of Red. “Jason Frost would never have killed this way. Red wasn’t his victim type. The perp we’re after—he used a swift, brutal method to kill. He was eliminating a witness, nothing more, nothing less.”

Bowen’s fingers flattened on the tabletop. “In that case, we need to make sure our cop friends are keeping extra eyes on Rowan Jacobs. I would hate for another witness to vanish.”

“It’s doubtful Rowan will tell us anything,” Samantha said as her stare drifted over the tactical board. “When the drugs are out of his system, odds are high the guy will remember nothing. And as far as the current information that kid gave us—” her gaze cut to Tucker “—the description fits you and it fits Jason Frost.”

“And too many other people wandering the streets of New Orleans,” Bowen groused. “Useless.”

So far, yes, it was.

“Bowen.” Samantha turned toward him. “I want you in Baton Rouge today. Meet with Heather’s family. Her friends there. Learn everything that you possibly can about her.”

He nodded.

“Macey . . .” Samantha’s attention shifted to her. “You’re still working with the coroner?”

Macey's gaze dipped toward Dawn. "It's . . . a slow process with Jinx."

He saw Dawn pale. Dammit.

"Keep us updated," Samantha ordered. "I'm also waiting to hear back on the analysis our unit is doing on the gloves Dawn recovered. Maybe the perp was sloppy. Maybe we'll get a hit from the DNA database—something that can tell us who this guy is."

Then her attention shifted to Dawn.

"I can help," Dawn said as she stepped forward. "I *need* to help."

"I know you do." Samantha's voice was gentle. "But he tried to attack you today. He's gunning for you. Every moment that you are out in the open, that's a moment that you're at risk."

Dawn's chin lifted. "And every moment that I hide . . . that could be a moment when he's looking to make someone else a pawn in this sick game he's playing. You said he wanted me." She looked at Tucker. "You *both* said that. So what do you expect him to do? I'm not a profiler, but I'll tell you what I expect . . . I expect for him to keep hurting others as he tries to get to me." She exhaled on a ragged breath. "And I can't carry more guilt. I *won't*."

Samantha glanced at Tucker. Her eyes had gone dark and he knew she was pondering the situation. "I'd like a private word with you, Tucker," she murmured.

He nodded grimly. The others filed out, but Dawn lingered. Her gaze flickered between Samantha and Tucker. "As I've already told Tucker, I'm not going to be shoved to the side. I have contacts in this town—I'm the one who got you Red's location, remember that? Not using me would be a huge mistake, and I think you're both smarter than that." She turned on her heel and marched out.

The door closed quietly behind her.

He felt the weight of Samantha's stare on him. Rolling back his shoulders, he glanced her way.

"She's right," Samantha murmured. "Her ties in this city could be an asset to us."

"Anthony Deveraux has ties. His partner, Torez, has ties. Every damn cop in this PD has ties we can use."

Her head inclined toward him. "True, but the killer is after her . . . and that means he'll be focusing on the people close to her. People that 'every damn cop' won't know."

His jaw locked. "I want her safe," he gritted.

"Because your emotions are involved. That's the problem. And I worry it's too much of a problem." Samantha folded her arms across her chest and peered straight at him. "Blake Gamble and I don't work cases together any longer."

He knew Blake. One fine FBI agent—and Samantha's lover.

"We don't work them together because we're

too connected. Our emotions can get in the way. Instead of placing priority on victims . . ." Her lips twisted. "When we're together, we worry too much about each other's safety. That makes us a liability in the field."

"You think I'm a liability?"

"That's what I'm asking. I'm asking you—are your emotions controlled when you're around Dawn Alexander?"

No. He'd already crossed a line and slept with her—and he'd do it again if he had the chance. "She matters."

Samantha's gaze turned assessing. "Matters to the extent that you won't be able to do your job?"

"She *is* the job." He blew out a frustrated breath. "And Dawn isn't going to stay on the sidelines. Even if we turn her over to the PD for protection, she's going to be determined to get involved in this investigation. It's better if she stays with us, works with us . . . That way, I can keep an eye on her."

"It's a slippery slope," Samantha warned him. "The longer you're with her, the deeper your connection to her may become. I knew this was a risk when you came down here. But I thought since you hadn't seen her in so long that the ties were gone."

He wasn't sure his ties to Dawn would ever be gone.

"You're a target, too. I agree one hundred

percent with your assessment there. This perp wanted you down here—he wants you in his crosshairs. He sees both you and Dawn as his targets."

The guy had been smarter than Tucker anticipated that day—he'd deliberately divided them, trying to take Dawn away.

"This killer has already proved he won't hesitate to kill a man. Dawn may not be the next target—you very well could be. If this guy was working with Jason Frost, then his anger could be more focused on you. Potentially, Dawn could just be a means to an end."

Fuck, he didn't like where this was going . . .

"You're a good profiler, Tucker, so I'm sure you've considered the fact that this man . . . may want to hurt Dawn simply as a way of getting to you."

He swallowed. "That was why Jason targeted her."

Sympathy flashed on her face. "I know."

My fault. If she hadn't been with me, she would have been safe.

"I know that's why Jason went after her, and none of us can afford to overlook the possibility that this killer is doing the same thing. His rage could be more targeted on you than her. After all, you're the man who pulled the trigger. You are the one who killed the Iceman." Her gaze was unflinching. "This guy could want to destroy you and Dawn could be the means to that end."

I won't let it happen again. She won't be hurt because of me.

"You and Dawn are the ones he's after. So you know what I need you to do, Tucker?"

He waited. If she told him to stay away from Dawn . . .

Her face tensed. "Find the bastard before he has a chance to hurt anyone else. Use Dawn and her connections. Use everything that you both know. And *find* him."

"You all right?"

Dawn glanced up at the slightly hesitant question and found Detective Torez shuffling toward her. His dark head was bent forward and she could see the concern etched on his face.

"Just a few scratches." She offered him a wane smile. "Would have been a whole lot better if we'd caught the bastard."

He grunted. "I'm . . . sorry about Jinx."

She had to swallow twice before she could reply. "Thank you. I'm sorry, too." Sorry. Angry. Hurt.

He sat beside her on the little bench just outside the meeting room. Bowen stood a few feet away, watching them. Someone always seemed to be watching her these days.

"Cutting you out would be a mistake on their part." Torez's voice was low. "I think so, Anthony thinks so, hell, the whole department thinks so.

You get shit done—we've seen it before. And if some guy is gunning for you, then I think you deserve the chance to hunt him."

Her lips twisted. "I think so, too."

Torez leaned closer to her. "We checked Jinx's phone. There were other pictures on there. Pictures of your place. Pictures of the roses on your pillow."

Her stomach clenched.

"There were pictures of you from the crime scene yesterday."

Her gaze flew up to his.

"He was there, in that mass of reporters that gathered outside your home. He was in the crowd and he was snapping pictures of you. You and Tucker Frost."

He left that phone deliberately. He wanted me to know that he'd been there, all along.

"We didn't recover any prints from the phone. And Jinx's house—hell, he must have wiped that place down. This guy knows how to cover his tracks."

"The gloves," she whispered. "He left the gloves at the warehouse. Maybe he wasn't as careful there."

His gaze dipped to the closed meeting room door. "Hope so. The FBI has those—they're supposed to have the report back on them soon." He focused on her once more. "The roses in your room led us nowhere. They are sold everywhere down here—kids on the street sell them. Vendors in the park. Uniforms talked to everyone they could find, but we aren't getting a hit on the guy. Probably paid cash and walked away."

Because he was smart. No paper trail.

"Anthony's worried about you." His voice went lower. "He doesn't exactly trust your FBI buddy, Frost."

She wet her lips. "Tucker knows killers."

"Yeah, that's the part that worries Anthony. Sometimes blood tells, you know? Frost's brother was a psychopath. Cold as fucking ice, just like everyone says."

The door to the meeting room opened. Tucker stood there, staring at her. His blue eyes were so bright.

And cold. No emotion showed in them.

Cold as fucking ice.

"Don't forget that you have plenty of friends at the PD," Torez murmured. "And we'll have your back, always." He stood up and walked away.

She rose, too. Slowly.

Tucker and Samantha came toward her. Samantha delicately cleared her throat and said, "Agent Frost is going to speak with your friends Jones and Malone today. Since you know those individuals so well, I want you to accompany him during the questioning."

Damn straight.

Samantha stepped closer to her. "I've been

where you are." Her voice was low. "I know what it's like to be in the crosshairs of a killer. And when that happened to me, I couldn't just stand back and let others do the hunting. You're not a typical civilian—I've read your files and I know the type of training you've had. The type of work that you've done."

Hope tightened in Dawn's chest.

"Agent Frost is going to stay with you. You will have a guard with you until we learn more, but you *will* be working with us. So be careful out there. You're hunting, but so is the killer."

"I didn't call anyone else." Jones twisted his apron as he stared at Dawn and Tucker. "Just you. Just like you said. One of my regulars came in because he was hungry and I asked him about Red. He gave me the tip that he was at the motel, and I called you. That's all." He blew out a rough breath. "Then I saw the news this morning about the body at that motel, and I knew it was Red. Damn it."

Dawn put her hand on his and squeezed.

"My girl has too many dead on her table now." His lips twisted. "I wanted to help find the killer. I didn't want . . . I didn't want this."

"No one did," Tucker said quietly.

"The man who gave you the tip," Dawn prompted. "Your regular. What was his name? Where can we find him?"

"Young kid," Jones muttered, letting go of his

apron. “Blond guy, looks barely legal. He’s been on and off drugs for so long. I keep telling him to get clean, but . . .”

She stiffened. “Rowan?” That had been the boy’s name.

Jones’s gaze lit up. “Yeah, yeah, that’s it. He came by, desperate for food . . . and when I questioned him, the guy knew where Red was staying. Said he’d seen him go in the place.”

She shared a long look with Tucker, then she squeezed Jones’s hand once more. “Thank you.”

Dawn didn’t speak again, not until she and Tucker were away from the restaurant and back inside his rented SUV.

“Rowan is the link,” she said, voice excited. “We’ve got to get him to tell us more.”

Tucker cranked the vehicle. “Yeah, but he has to make fucking sense when he talks to us.”

“He knows who the killer is.” She was certain of this.

He drove them through the city. “According to him . . . I could be the killer. I look just like the bastard he described.” He gave a bitter laugh. “That’s a problem I have. Looking like a killer.”

She glanced down at her hands and saw they’d twisted in her lap.

For a moment, no one spoke.

Tucker exhaled slowly. “Malone is at Voodoo Tats. The crime scene guys finished up there, and I want to have another look around.” He turned at the light. "After we talk to him, maybe we can see Rowan again. Provided the guy isn't still trying to smash his own brains out."

He sees you. "I think he knows the killer was watching me."

"Rowan could have been spouting pure bullshit."

"Or he could have been telling us the exact truth." Being high didn't mean he was wrong. "Is there . . . is there a way I could talk to him?"

He made another turn. "Considering how violent he got during the last little chat, do you think that's a good idea?"

"I think he's the one with the most information. The one that we need right now." She reached out and touched his hand as he gripped the steering wheel. "You would be with me."

He stopped at the corner. Stared at her hand. "I didn't do such a good job of looking out for you last time." They were just down the street from Voodoo Tats. "Maybe Bowen should be the one watching you. Maybe Samantha is right . . . I'm too close to you."

"I want you close."

His gaze jerked up to hers.

"I like you close." A hushed admission. "I don't know Bowen. I don't know Macey. I don't know any of the others. You proved to me before that I could count on you." He'd made the ultimate sacrifice for her. "I want you close," she said again.

His eyes glittered. "And the secrets?"

"We have to stop them. Both of us. It's time." Past time. If there was any hope of a future for them, they had to face their past—every bit of it. No more secrets. No lies. No ghosts.

His hand lifted and curled under her chin. "If that's the case, then maybe I should enjoy this while I can."

"Tucker?"

He leaned toward her and pressed a soft kiss to her lips. So very careful. "You may not want me near you much longer."

Not true. Hadn't he heard her? He was the only agent that she felt comfortable with.

His forehead rested against hers. "It scared the shit out of me when I heard that gunshot. I couldn't get back to you fast enough."

"I'm okay." Now she was the one to press a soft kiss to his stubbled cheek.

"I keep thinking . . . what if I'd gotten back to that alley and you'd been gone? What if he'd taken you?" His head lifted as he pulled away from her. "Or what if you'd been dead when I got back?"

She shook her head. "I wasn't."

"Samantha said she worried my control weakens when I'm around you."

Her lips parted.

"She's wrong, though. It doesn't weaken."

His face had gone so hard.

"It fucking shatters."

CHAPTER THIRTEEN

Anthony nodded to the uniformed officer as he left Rowan's hospital room. That dumbass kid had needed over twenty stitches in his head. And he'd been jerking like crazy, spasming as the overdose riddled his body.

He hated what drugs could do to a person. He'd watched his own mother battle addiction for far too long. He'd seen it eat away at her.

And kill her.

Drugs made you weak. Drugs destroyed your whole world.

"Tony!"

Anthony looked up and saw Torez hurrying toward him. His partner was the only one who got away with calling him Tony. "How's the kid?"

Anthony glanced back at the room. "Not exactly talking, but at least he isn't slamming his head into the nearest wall." That was progress, of a sort.

Torez shook his head. "You think we're gonna be able to get anything out of him about the killer?"

"Damn unlikely. On good days, eyewitnesses don't remember much, and on days when those witnesses are jacked up on some drug . . ." He let the sentence trail away. "No dice." Frustration boiled in his blood. “I hate that Dawn is at risk like this. What happened to Jinx . . . it *can’t* happen to her.”

They walked away from the room, keeping their voices low.

“The FBI team has taken over,” Torez said and the faint lines near his mouth deepened. “Doesn’t really seem right, having them running the show in our town, but Captain Hatch gave the order for us to follow their lead.”

Anthony was so damn tired. He couldn’t remember the last time he’d slept. “I called the FBI in because I knew they were better trained to work with the serial. As soon as I saw the girl in that freezer, I *knew* we weren’t dealing with a simple murder.” He paused. “I thought they’d find him and stop him before anyone else was hurt, but it didn’t go down that way. The profilers haven’t done shit.” His breath heaved out. “I don’t want to be wrong about them.”

Torez studied him but didn’t speak. But then, his partner didn’t have to speak. He could easily read the other guy’s doubt. Torez didn’t like playing backup.

Neither did Anthony.

Anthony rolled back his shoulders. “I got to crash, man. You’re staying here for a while and keeping an eye on our perp?”

Torez nodded. “Yeah, yeah, man. I got him. You get some rest.”

"Thanks, buddy." Anthony turned away. "This case is exploding, and half the time, I'm afraid to see what is going to happen next." He stopped. "Because more is coming, I know it."

Malone was inside the tattoo shop, a broom in his hand and a scowl on his face.

"Don't know who made the worse mess . . . the jerk who broke in or the police team who came to look for fucking clues." He gestured around the place. "You think insurance is going to cover this crap? Hell, no. My business is wrecked, my best tattoo artist is dead and I—" He broke off, swallowing. "Jinx is dead." His voice was softer and the lines on his face appeared deeper. "Fucking hell, she's dead."

Dawn headed toward him and wrapped him in a hug. Tucker watched her. This was the second time Dawn had reached out to comfort one of her friends. Her touch was hesitant, as if she wasn't quite sure of herself. Her small body was nearly swallowed by Malone's as his hands came up and held her tight.

"I saw the story on the news. He *froze* her, Dawn." Malone's head lifted. His eyes looked damp. "He tortured her. Stabbed her. Just like—"

But he stopped.

She didn't. "Just like me," Dawn finished for him.

Malone's face tightened.

Slowly, Dawn pulled away from him. “Was Jinx seeing anyone?” she asked, voice careful. “Did she ever talk about someone to you?”

He started sweeping again.

“Malone?”

“She seemed . . . happier.” He bit out the one word as he worked. “In the last few weeks. I even asked her about it and teased her . . . asked her if she got laid.” His eyes squeezed shut. “She laughed. Wouldn’t tell me anything about the guy, but I knew she was seeing someone. If I’d had any fucking clue this would happen . . .”

“You didn’t know,” Tucker said grimly. “This isn’t on you.”

Malone’s eyes opened. “She never mentioned any name to me and I never saw her with anyone. Jinx was private, you know? Kept her secrets.”

Everyone seemed to be keeping them.

He huffed out a breath. “She did have a cousin in town, though. Guy who came around the shop a few times. I told her, though, that she needed to keep him the hell away.” His stare swung toward Dawn. “I don’t deal with users here, and that kid stayed sky-high. Every time he came around here, Jinx would get nervous. She wanted him clean, but the boy . . . Shit, I could tell that getting clean was the last thing on his mind.”

Tucker took a step toward Malone. “Did you happen to get that cousin’s name?”

“Rowan? Something like that.” Malone’s

shoulders sagged. "I saw what drug use does—I saw it rip my daughter apart. I warned Jinx. She had to be careful with that kid. Because he would drag her down with him if she wasn't careful. I gave her . . . gave her some support group names. Told her about some clinics in the area."

"She didn't mention him to me," Dawn said. "We were friends. Why didn't she tell me?"

"Sometimes, you try to cover up the things that hurt you in this world. You don't want the ones close to you seeing how much you hurt."

Or judging you.

"I think she wouldn't have told me, either, if the kid hadn't come around here."

"This Rowan . . ." Dawn wet her lips. "Did he have blond hair, brown eyes?"

"Yeah, yeah, that's him." Malone squinted as he looked back at her. "Sounds like you *do* know him."

Yes, they knew him. Everything kept circling back to Rowan.

"Caught him breaking into the shop about a month ago," Malone admitted. "Called the PD to haul his ass away. Since I called them, hell, you *know* how pissed I had to be."

"I know," she murmured.

He huffed and tightened his hold on the broom. "Jinx begged me not to press charges but I got the detective to try to scare the shit out of the fellow. Figured maybe that would help some."

Tucker's head cocked. "The detective? Just which detective was that?"

"Torez. He comes in here sometimes. Jinx gave him a nice tat a while back." His hand tightened on the broom. "Work of fucking art. Jinx was so good at her work. So fucking good . . ." His eyes teared up again. "Such a damn waste."

They talked a bit longer, then Tucker headed back outside with Dawn. He couldn't help tensing when he stepped onto the sidewalk. He'd been in that same place hours before, so frantic to get to her.

"Why didn't Torez mention that he knew Rowan?" Dawn asked.

Good fucking question. "I think we need to find out." He also thought every single lead they had circled back to that little punk Rowan, and it was time that they had another chat with him. The drugs should have cleared from the little prick's system by now. At least somewhat, anyway. Time for the truth.

From Rowan and from Torez.

Tucker shoved open the doors to the hospital corridor. His steps were fast, determined. He didn't know what kind of BS Torez was trying to pull, but the guy should have revealed that he knew who the fuck Rowan Jacobs was at the station.

Dawn was racing at his side, her steps just as

fast as his. They rounded the corner, going toward the room that he'd been directed to moments before by a helpful nurse and—

Torez was pacing a few feet away, a phone to his ear. "No, no, damn it, I don't know what the hell happened. He is *dead.*"

Tucker stopped. His gaze cut to the room on the right, room 603. Two uniformed cops were there, several nurses, a female doctor and—

"What in the hell is going on here?" Tucker demanded. "I want to talk with Rowan Jacobs, now." He flashed his badge and FBI identification.

The doctor shook her head. "I'm afraid Rowan won't be talking with anyone." Her lips tightened. "I'm sorry, but he appears to have suffered an aneurysm. We won't know conclusively until an autopsy is performed but the signs are indicating that he—"

"I *found* him like that," Torez growled as he marched toward Tucker and the doctor. "I went in the room, taking up my shift to watch his ass, and the guy was dead. Eyes open—staring at damn nothing." He shook his head. "Shit. I just called Anthony to tell him the news."

Their main link to the killer was gone? Tucker's eyes narrowed on Torez. "We need to talk, *now.*" He didn't wait for the other man to reply. Tucker just grabbed his arm and jerked Torez away from the hospital staff.

“Hey, *hey!*” Torez snapped. “Hands *off!* I don’t care if you are FBI, you don’t treat me like this. *You don’t put your hands on me.*”

Tucker caged Torez between him and the wall. Dawn had followed them, and she stood there, her gaze uneasy.

“When were you going to tell us that you knew Rowan?” Tucker demanded.

“What?” But Torez’s gaze had widened and his nervous stare darted over Tucker’s shoulder.

Dawn cleared her throat. “We just talked with Malone. He said Rowan broke into his shop a little while back and that you were called to the scene. He wanted you to scare the kid.”

Torez’s mouth dropped open.

“When were you going to tell us?” Tucker pushed.

“Fuck! I forgot! Didn’t even realize it was the same kid.” He raked his hand over his face. “I didn’t even file a report. Jinx—she begged me not to do it. Said he needed another chance. His hair . . . it was a lot longer then, not so peroxide-white.” His eyes squeezed shut. “And he wasn’t so goddamn rail thin. Didn’t even look like the same kid and I just— *Shit. I didn’t make the connection.*” His eyes flew open.

Tucker gazed at the cop, not sure he bought that story. Things were starting to look one hell of a bit too convenient. “And the guy just . . . died . . . when you walked into his room?”

Torez stiffened. "I don't think I like your tone."

"And I don't like the fact that a police detective is withholding facts on the investigation of multiple homicides." A cop like Torez, he would've had access to the Iceman's case files. He would have been able to see all of the details on the killings.

Suspicion mounted, a dark, twisting suspicion that coiled in Tucker's gut.

"I didn't know that Jinx had inked you." Dawn's voice was measured.

Torez stiffened. "It wasn't a big deal. I liked her work. If you wanted a good tat, everyone knew to go visit Jinx."

Tucker wasn't buying the guy's bit. At Dawn's question, Torez's gaze had turned nervous and the cop was sweating. "Just how well did you know Jinx?"

"No, man, *no.*" Torez surged toward Tucker and jabbed him in the chest. "You don't grill me like this. I'm not a suspect. I'm on *your* side. I didn't do anything to Jinx! I would have never hurt her!"

"Were you involved with her?" Tucker asked.

And he saw the truth—the quick, guilty flush on the guy's cheeks.

"You're married," Dawn said. "You have a wife. Two kids. And—"

"It was a one-time deal, okay?" Torez had dropped his voice and his hand. "I was drunk.

She was fucking gorgeous. And I didn't want anyone to know. Neither did she. *One-time deal.*"

The guy had just admitted to an intimate connection to one of the victims. And he'd just left the room that had their only witness—their dead witness.

Tucker stared into the cop's desperate gaze, and he wondered if he was looking straight into the eyes of a killer.

"This is bullshit!" Torez paced the PD interrogation room like a caged lion. "I didn't kill Jinx! I would never have put a hand on that woman!"

Anthony was at his partner's side. The police captain was there, a rep from the department was there, and it seemed like half a dozen uniforms were trying to surge into that little room.

Tucker stood with Dawn on one side of him and Samantha to his right. A face-off, and one that had him tensing. "You withheld pertinent details about your relationship with the victim and the witness. You think that doesn't justify some questioning from us?"

"I'm not a killer!" Torez was sweating, again. Not a good sign, especially with the way the air conditioning was icing that room. "I didn't remember Rowan—I've told you that several times."

"Didn't remember him," Tucker mocked. "But

it sure is convenient that you happened to be in the room with him when he died."

Silence. Even the police captain, Harold Hatch—an older man with thinning brown hair—glanced warily toward Torez.

"He died of natural causes—you heard the doc there!" Spittle flew from Torez's mouth. "Probably an aneurysm! That happens when people OD. We all know that kid was tripping hard on something!"

"We'll all know *exactly* how he died," Samantha interjected smoothly, "once an autopsy is completed."

Torez swore. "I can't believe this shit. I'm a cop. I help people—and you're trying to what? Say I'm the new Iceman?" He surged toward Tucker but Anthony caught his arm, pulling him back.

"Easy, buddy," Anthony soothed—or tried to soothe. "You have to stay cool."

"You stay fucking cool! No one is calling you a killer!" But he huffed out a rough breath. "I didn't want my wife to know, okay? If Gina finds out, she would leave me and take the kids. So I didn't say anything when I saw that Jinx was the victim. I just kept my mouth shut. I screwed the wrong woman. It's not a crime!"

Tucker saw Dawn take a step forward. He caught her wrist in his. His fingers stroked her wrist. "We're talking about a victim." His gaze slid to Dawn. "A friend." And he turned his glare back on Torez. "So speak about the dead with a little more fucking courtesy."

Torez flushed. "I'm sorry. Jinx—she was a nice woman. And I just— Shit, *this isn't happening. I didn't hurt anyone!*"

"You knew Rowan Jacobs. You had an intimate relationship with Jinx Donahue." Samantha's voice was flat. "You're going to have to answer plenty of questions for me. And you're going to need to back up everything you say . . . with alibis."

Torez looked frantically at his rep, then his captain. "They're calling me a suspect!"

"That's because," Samantha told him smoothly, "at this moment, you are one."

Samantha walked into the hallway with Tucker. Dawn had already filed out of the room a few moments before. "His rep is trying to close ranks on us, but I'm getting an interview with Torez."

"I want to be there—"

She shook her head. "You and Torez are too volatile when you're together." Then she gave him a sly smile. "Trust me, he won't see my threat coming. I know how to work guys like him."

He believed her.

"Take Dawn back to the suite. You two have been working all day. You could both use some down time."

"You're just trying to get me away from the station."

"I'm trying to get you both away." Her face was serious. "Reporters are about to beat the door down here. You and Dawn go out the back. You keep her secure, and when I learn more, I'll call you."

He glanced toward the end of the hallway. Dawn sat on the bench, her shoulders hunched. As he watched, Anthony approached her.

Anthony's steps were hesitant. He touched her shoulder lightly and murmured something to her. Dawn nodded.

"Partners usually know our secrets," Samantha said. She'd seen the exchange, too. "Makes me wonder . . . did Anthony know about the affair with Jinx?"

"You think he could be covering for Torez?"

Anthony was staring down at Dawn, his face tight.

"I think I'm going to find out." She turned away from Tucker and he headed for Dawn. As he drew closer, Anthony glanced up at him. Anger flashed in the other man's eyes.

"Torez is a good cop. He's been my partner ever since he transferred in last year, and he's *always* had my back."

Tucker took Dawn's hand and pulled her up beside him.

Anthony's gaze darted between the two of them.

"Did you know about the affair?" Dawn asked quietly.

Anthony's jaw hardened. "He's had more than one affair, okay? He has a weakness for pretty women, but that doesn't mean the guy is a killer. I don't like the way everyone is looking at him, grilling him."

Too fucking bad.

"I *know* him," Anthony added darkly. "Don't you think I'd know if my own partner was a killer? I'm not some blind asshole. I would *know.*"

"You don't always know." Tucker's voice was quiet. "Come on, Dawn. Let's go."

Her hand slipped into his.

Anthony blinked. "Dawn? It's . . . it's not him. Torez wouldn't do this to you. Trust me, okay? *It's not him.* I get that the situation looks bad, but the truth is going to come out. You'll see who the real monster is, and it won't be my partner."

Not your partner. I didn't want it to be my brother, either. Tucker and Dawn headed out the back, but Anthony followed them. Tucker's SUV was waiting out there. He'd parked the vehicle in the back because he'd seen the reporters swarming out front when they first arrived. He shut Dawn's door and started to walk around the vehicle.

Anthony stepped into Tucker's path. "I'm the one who called you guys down here. I'm the one who has been after this perp from day one."

Tucker stared at him.

"When I saw that girl in the freezer, all I could think about was Dawn. I made that fucking connection right away, and I wanted to make sure she wasn't hurt."

"She's in FBI custody."

"Yeah, well, your fucking *custody* wasn't so great before, was it? When the bastard nearly got her at Voodoo Tats." Anthony glared at him. "If anything happens to her on your watch . . ." His words trailed away, but the threat was clear in his eyes.

Tucker wasn't in the mood for any threats. He just wanted to get back to the suite with Dawn. To pull her away from the rest of the world and hold her tight. "Get out of my way."

"You're the one in my way," Anthony snarled, voice low and cutting. "But not for long."

Screw the idiot. Tucker shoved past him and jumped into the SUV. A few moments later, he and Dawn were driving fast through the city.

"Want to tell me what that was about?" Her question drifted to him.

He had a better question. "Want to tell me how long the guy has been in love with you?"

She sucked in a quick breath.

"Because it's pretty plain to see." He turned at the next light, aware that his hands gripped the steering wheel too tightly. "You two have a relationship that you want to tell me about?

Maybe something that you should have mentioned sooner?" *Because right now, I want to rip that jerk apart.*

"He's not in love with me."

That's not what I saw in his eyes.

"We went out on a few dates, nothing more."

He had to ask, even though he *hated* the question. "Did you have sex with him?"

Silence. The stark, twisting kind that told him she was pissed.

Shit. The FBI had already vetted her former fiancé—the guy hadn't even been in the country for the last four months so he was definitely not a suspect in the crimes. Now he had to wonder if they needed to take a closer look at any other lovers she'd had. *But I thought she hadn't gotten close to anyone since the fiancé.* Because, yeah, the FBI had checked that and—

"You haven't been in my life for seven years, Tucker. What I do—and who I spend my time with—that's not exactly your business."

He hit the brakes at the next light and his gaze snapped to her. Shadows slid over her face so he couldn't see her expression. "Bullshit. It's me and it's you. And everything about you has *always* been my business." He heaved out a hard breath. "We made love, Dawn, and you didn't mention anyone else. I thought you were coming back to me."

"The light's green."

"Fuck the light." But he hit the gas. "You're right. I shouldn't even ask about your life without me. Because *I hate to know who you've been with.* It makes me jealous. It makes me fucking crazy. It shouldn't be this way, but I still think of you as mine." That was the problem. He would always think of her that way.

"I didn't ask about your lovers."

"Ask. They weren't you. No one else will ever be you."

CHAPTER FOURTEEN

"I haven't slept with Anthony." They were back in the hotel suite, safely enclosed together, and Dawn turned to face Tucker. "We went out a few times," she continued, making sure to keep her voice low and steady. "But that was it. I'm very, very careful with my lovers, and I knew that Anthony and I would be working together. I don't like to mix my professional life and my business life."

His gaze seemed to burn as he stared at her.

"Anthony wanted more. I didn't. Simple."

He gave a grim nod.

"I want to fall in love."

She saw his shoulders give a little jerk. Determined, Dawn continued, "I want to trust someone completely. I want to share my life. I want to have a normal relationship, but normal hasn't exactly been in the cards for me."

His Adam's apple bobbed as he swallowed. "Believe it or not, I wanted all of that for you. I know I'm a fucking jealous bastard where you're concerned, but I wanted you to be happy. I kept thinking I'd hear of you marrying. Having a family. I knew it would rip my guts open, but I *wanted that* for you."

He didn't understand . . . Her problem was that

everything *she* wanted was twisted up in him. "I want to know your darkest secret."

His gaze became hooded.

"You and I are the only ones here. Whatever you tell me won't leave this room, but I want to know."

His hand reached out to her and his fingers skimmed over her cheek.

"I can touch you," he rasped, "without you flinching away. Do you know how long I wanted that *one* thing?"

Her hand rose and her fingers caught his. "You don't trust me." She felt him stiffen. "You think I'll turn away from you again. I get it. But I'm not the same girl I was then. I fought and clawed my way to the life I have now. I'm stronger."

"You've always been strong." His body came closer to her. His chest brushed against hers.

"Then tell me. No more secrets . . . not from you, not from me. I need this, Tucker. I need to know that you're the one person who shares everything with me." Because she wanted to share everything with him.

"I . . . don't want to lose you again."

His words had her heart squeezing in her chest.

"Not that I have you." His smile was bittersweet. "One night. That was what we had. We had—"

"We can have anything." She rose onto her toes, knowing that she had to be the one to take the first step. She had to show him that she could trust completely.

If she could do it, then so could he.

"Anything." Dawn's lips brushed over his.

And they were lost. Both of them. She felt the shudder that worked its way down his body. His lips parted beneath hers and his tongue thrust into her mouth. That wild desire—the fierce passion that would always connect them—surged to the surface. She tasted his need, the desperation, the lust.

And she wanted more.

Her hands shoved between them as she yanked at the buttons of his shirt. He'd removed his holster when they'd first entered the suite, so that wasn't in her way. She thought she heard a button pop. But Dawn didn't slow down.

She'd been going slowly for years. Playing things safe. She didn't have to play with Tucker. She didn't want to play at all.

She just wanted him.

Her hands touched his chest. That hot skin. She could feel his muscles and the power beneath her touch. Her fingers slid over his stomach, those incredible abs, and then she was fumbling with the button on his pants.

He pulled his mouth from hers. *"Dawn."*

Such hunger in that word. Raw need. She loved it.

"Baby, I want to be careful with you . . ."

No. She gave a shake of her head. "Enough of that." She slid away from him and hurried toward the light switch on the wall. She hit it, plunging them into darkness, and then she was yanking at her shirt because—

"No." He caught her in the dark. Pulled her close. "I told you before, there's no more hiding." And he backed her up against the wall. He pinned her between that wall and his body. His head lowered and she felt the stir of his breath against her neck. "There will never be any more hiding for either of us." His mouth pressed to her skin. He licked her. He sucked her. He had her moaning.

And he turned the lights back on.

She blinked against that sudden brightness and fear trickled through her. "Tucker . . ."

His head lifted. He stared into her eyes. "No hiding."

Her breath panted out.

"Do you want me?"

His eyes were a brilliant blue, his face etched into tight, hard lines. His body pushed against hers, and there was no missing the hard length of his arousal.

She stared into his blues eyes, she gazed at his handsome face, and she saw Tucker.

Tucker. Tucker's desire. Tucker's strength.

"Yes."

"Fucking, yes." He kissed her again. A kiss

that was a little wilder. A little rougher. Even hotter. His hand pushed between their bodies. He yanked open the snap of her jeans and jerked down the zipper. She barely heard the faint hiss of sound. Then his fingers were shoving the jeans down her legs and she kicked out of them and her shoes.

His hand slid under her underwear, coming up to stroke her, to thrust into her, and she shot onto her toes as her body tensed.

"Dawn?"

Her eyes stayed open and on his. *"More."*

He smiled at her. His dimple flashed.

She still only saw Tucker. The desire she felt for him was reflected in his eyes.

"I'll give you everything." His hand pulled back, and he thrust two fingers into her again. His thumb raked over her clit, drawing a ragged moan from her.

Desire shouldn't build so fast. Need shouldn't explode with a touch. But it did.

And she found she wasn't afraid. She was grateful. The passion she felt for him could make her forget everything else in the world. The killer. The death. The pain. For a few precious moments, all of that faded away.

Her panties ripped as he yanked them down. She didn't care. Her nails were raking over his chest. Her breasts were tight, her nipples aching, and she wanted his mouth on her.

She wanted—

Yes. He'd taken one nipple into his mouth. He was licking and sucking and her hips were riding his hand. She could feel her orgasm building. Her body was tensing and she struggled to catch her breath. Her heartbeat thundered in her ears.

His thumb pressed over her clit again, dragging a moan from her, but then he pulled back his hand.

"Right here," he growled. "Right *here*."

They were to the side of the window. No one would be able to see them.

He let her go just long enough to put on a condom, then he was back. He lifted her up, holding her so easily, then he drove into her. He filled her completely. Time seemed to freeze. She was staring into his eyes and Dawn couldn't look away. Her legs curled around his hips, he held her tightly with his fingers around her waist.

He withdrew, only to plunge deep again, sliding his cock right over her sensitive clit. Her breath came faster.

Withdraw.

Thrust.

The tension mounted inside of her.

He kissed her.

Withdraw.

Thrust.

Her nails clawed at him. She wanted faster. Harder.

He gave it to her. His hips drove against her as he plunged, as his control seemed to break away. He gave her everything that she needed and the pleasure hit her with a fury. It crashed over her and made her whole body tremble. Her mouth left his as she cried out his name.

He kept thrusting. The pleasure rolled through her, and then he was there. She felt his climax as it hit him. His muscles tightened. His grip turned almost bruising.

"Dawn." His gaze was bright with primitive pleasure. Lust. Release.

Possession.

Bowen parked in front of the apartment building in downtown Baton Rouge. Lights were on, gleaming from the second floor, and his intel told him that floor was home to the woman he needed to interview.

Catherine Peters, Heather Hartley's former college roommate. He'd been chasing leads for most of the evening and turning up jackshit. Hopefully, his night would be better. Because Catherine was the last name on his list, and if she didn't reveal any information for him . . .

Baton Rouge is a bust.

He walked toward the building and headed inside. He took the stairs quickly, frowning at the lack of security in the place. He always noticed things like that—side effect of the job. Most people walked around, thinking they were safe. Thinking that a flimsy lock on the door would keep monsters out.

They were wrong.

In moments, he was standing before Catherine's door. He lifted his hand and knocked. He could hear the pad of footsteps from inside, the creak of a floor . . . but the door didn't open.

He stared straight into the peephole. "My name is FBI Special Agent Bowen Murphy." He lifted his ID and badge, making sure both would be visible for the person on the other side of that peephole. "I need to speak with Catherine Peters."

The door opened, just a few inches, and a woman with short, reddish-blond hair peered at him. "FBI? Let me see that badge."

He gave her the ID. She studied it in silence a moment, then handed it back to him.

"Why does the FBI want to talk to me?"

He glanced around the hallway. No one else was out there. Bowen focused on Catherine once more. "I need to ask you a few questions about your former LSU roommate, Heather Hartley."

She blinked. Her eyes were a dark brown, and a faint spatter of freckles dotted her nose. "Heather? I haven't heard from Heather in ages, not since she left town to meet up with her boyfriend." She nibbled her lower lip. "Is . . . is everything all right with her? I mean, she and her boyfriend are okay, aren't they?"

Boyfriend. “Do you mind if I come inside?” he asked her. “Because we need to talk.”

They were showering together. The water beat down on Dawn as she stood beneath the spray. The lights were on in the bathroom. Tucker’s hands were sliding along her back. He was seeing all of her.

No hiding, not anymore.

She turned toward him and his fingers feathered over her left shoulder, lightly caressing the three rose tattoos that were there. Tattoos that would forever remind her of the friend she’d lost. As if she needed any reminder.

But it wasn’t her scars that she focused on right then. It was his. The small white scars that she’d seen before on his chest. His arms. His back.

She leaned forward and pressed soft kisses to his scars, those closest to her.

“Dawn.” His hold on her shoulder tightened. “You don’t have to—”

She kissed another small scar. It wasn’t about what she had to do. It was about what she wanted to do. And she wanted to do everything, with him.

The water kept pouring onto them. “How old were you?” she asked.

Because those marks looked so very old.

“Five . . . the first time. It was right after my mom was buried.”

Her heart ached for him.

"Fifteen . . . the last time."

Such a long, long time to suffer abuse. What did that long-term abuse do to a person?

Did it make Jason into a monster?

She looked up at Tucker's face.

What did it make you into, Tucker? What did it do to you?

His face seemed to harden as he stared at her, as if he could see the questions in her mind. Jaw locking, he reached out and turned off the flow of water with a hard jerk of his hand.

The water dripped down Dawn's body, sliding over her skin. Goose bumps rose on her arms as she stared at him.

"There won't be any going back." His voice was low and deep.

"Back is the last place I want to go." She turned from him and slipped from the shower. Dawn grabbed one of the towels and dried off quickly, but . . . she didn't cover herself when she was done. She let the towel drop to the floor. She was nervous, her knees nearly shaking, but she stood there before him. Not hiding. She wasn't going to hide.

She could do this.

He climbed from the shower, too, but his movements were slower. With his gaze on her, he toweled off. That hot, bright stare moved over every inch of her, and she felt it like a touch on her skin.

They'd had sex—hot, powerful sex. She shouldn't want him again.

She did.

More, she wanted to do so many things *to* him. Dawn wanted to knock down the last of the walls that held her back. She turned and went into her room, knowing he'd follow. When she entered that bedroom, her hand went instinctively to the light switch, but she caught herself.

Not now. Won't do it again.

She stood by the side of the bed.

He came up behind her. His hands curled around her waist and he pulled her back against his body. His mouth went to her neck, right on that sweet spot where her neck curved into her shoulder, where she was so sensitive that the touch of his lips had her nipples tightening.

One hand slid between her legs. Right between her folds. Then his fingers were pushing into her and her head tipped back against his shoulder. She knew she could come, just like that, with his fingers in her, with him behind her.

But she wanted something else. "Tucker . . ." She swallowed because her voice was so husky. "Get . . . get on the bed."

His fingers thrust into her once more, then his hand slid back, making a moan come from her lips.

He let her go. Her breath was coming too fast as she watched him slide onto the bed. His cock thrust toward her, full and swollen, bigger than her wrist. He lay down on that bed, put his hands behind his head, and his stare came back to her.

Not just hot now. Scorching.

"What do you need from me?" His voice was low, rough, and she knew he understood.

There were other lines she had to cross.

It's what I need from myself. Dawn eased onto the bed. She straddled his hips, staring down at him.

"Who do you see?" His hands were still behind his head. A deliberate move, she knew, one designed to make her feel safer. That was what Tucker always did. He tried to make her feel *safe.*

"I see you." She bent and pressed more kisses to those scars. So many of them. Scars that had changed a boy.

Changed a man.

She followed that trail down his chest. He'd tensed beneath her.

"Baby, be careful . . . When your mouth is on me, my control doesn't last."

She didn't need it to last. That was another of her tests—not for him, but for herself. To see what she did when he really let go.

Her hands curled around his cock and it jerked against her fingers. Her breath sighed out as she bent toward him, moving her body so that her mouth came close to the head of his arousal.

"Dawn." If possible, his voice was even darker. "Baby . . ."

She licked him. Licked him, kissed him, took that length into her mouth and thought only of him. She thought of the pleasure they gave each other. Of the way her body ignited for his. Of the way he made her feel, the way—

He'd moved in a flash. He was above her, pinning her beneath him to the mattress. His cock was at the entrance to her body, his eyes glittered. Savage desire. His touch wasn't careful. *He* wasn't careful.

"Need fucking *in* you."

"And I need you." His bare cock pushed at the entrance to her body. His control was disintegrating, and she still wasn't afraid. His face was savage in his need, and she still saw only him. "I'm on the pill. I'm clean. *I. Want. You.*"

His pupils stretched, filling his gaze. "Clean, too. Fuck—"

And he drove into her, a rough, deep thrust that lifted her off the bed. There was no holding back then, not for either of them. Her nails clawed down his back. She didn't even think about the stitches in his arm. His hands bit into her skin.

His cock drove in and out of her. She slammed up to meet him, fighting for the release.

No fear.

He kissed a hot path down her neck.

She started to scream when she came, but Dawn locked her lips together, fighting to hold back the sound. Fighting to make the pleasure last and last.

He erupted inside of her, and his release just made her climax stronger. Her head tipped back. He held her tight.

And she wasn't afraid.

She wouldn't be afraid. Not of him. *Not ever again.*

"Heather's dead?" Catherine shook her head. "I . . . Are you sure?"

"I'm afraid that I am." He always hated telling the news to friends and family. He was better at working the killers, not dealing with the victims. Their pain was too stark, too heavy to carry.

Catherine seemed to collapse into her chair. Silent tears trickled down her cheeks. "I am such a bitch."

Bowen frowned at her.

"I didn't even call her . . . didn't call to check on her. She left, and I just . . . I kept right on going with my life." She started to rock back and forth in her seat, a move that he didn't even think she was aware of making. He'd seen it before, an unconscious, comforting rock that victims made. "She was my roommate for a year, and I didn't even think about checking on her after she left. God." Her eyes squeezed shut. "I thought she was happy! I mean . . . she was always talking about her guy, how strong and smart he was and . . ." Her words just trailed away.

"I'd like the name of her boyfriend, Ms. Peters."

Her eyes opened. "Aren't you guys supposed to keep people safe?"

"We try, ma'am. We try very hard." *Sometimes, we just don't succeed.* It was the failures that haunted him.

"Then how did this happen?" Another tear leaked down her cheek. "Why didn't he keep *her* safe?"

"I'm not sure that I follow . . ."

"Her boyfriend! He was freaking FBI! She rushed down to New Orleans to meet him after he finished up a big case in Alabama."

Bowen stiffened.

"Why didn't he keep her safe?"

"Shit, baby, I hurt you." Tucker's voice was gruff as his index finger lightly touched her lip. "You're bleeding."

And the sight of that blood tore him up. Her busted lip. He should have been more careful. Damn it. He—

"I don't know that you did it." Her hand caught his wrist. "I think I bit my lip right before I came."

His heart slammed into his chest.

"I was trying to be quiet."

"You don't have to be quiet."

But she gave a sexy, husky laugh. "Trust me, I do. If your FBI buddies are close, I didn't want them hearing me."

He hated the sight of that blood on her lips. Tucker hurried into the bathroom and came back with a warm cloth. He dotted it against her mouth.

"You always took care of me."

He stared into her eyes.

"That was one of the things I liked so much about you. The way you'd surprise me at lunch. Or bring me my favorite energy drink when I was pulling an all-nighter at school." Her lips curved. "You brought me something every time we had a date. Books. Wine. Roses—"

But she broke off then, going silent. His gaze slid to her shoulder. To the three roses right there. Without another word, he got up and took the cloth back to the bathroom. When he returned to the bedroom, Tucker turned off the lights and slid into the bed with Dawn. She came toward him, curling her body against his, and he locked his arm around her, wanting to keep her right there.

He knew what she'd done tonight. She'd given him her trust—completely. He would do the same for her, even though he was the one who was afraid.

"The last time he hurt us . . . I was fifteen. Jason was seventeen, just about to turn eighteen." His voice sounded wooden, even to his own ears. "It was out at that godforsaken cabin. He thought he could keep pushing us around, keep controlling us, but we weren't kids any longer. We . . . I . . . fought back."

Her hand was pressed right over his heart. Seemed fitting. Did she get that she'd always held the fucking thing in her palm? That he'd gone a bit mad without her?

"I hit him. Punched him. Yanked that belt right out of his hand, and Jason was with me. Kicking and pounding at him. Soon our old man was on the floor." The rage he'd felt then had staggered him. He'd been shaking and a red haze had seemed to cover his vision. "He ran away from us, screaming that we'd pay. He jumped into his old truck and he shot off, careening down that old dirt road. I figured he'd go back to town. That he'd tell the cops what we'd done. He was always good at spinning stories. He'd tell them we attacked him and we'd go to jail."

He could feel her light breath against his skin.

"I wasn't afraid of jail. I was actually kind of relieved. At least I wouldn't be with him any longer. No one else ever understood the shit we put up with in his house. We always said our bruises came from football. Not his fists."

"I'm sorry. I was there. I saw you then, and I—"

He lifted her hand to his lips and pressed a kiss to her palm. "Nothing is on you. Remember that. Nothing is *ever* on you." Then he put her hand back where it belonged. Right over his heart.

"You probably heard the story about my dad dying . . . but what you heard, it wasn't the way things really went down." Dammit, this was hard. "What really happened . . . Hours passed while Jason and I were at that damn cabin, and the cops didn't show. Jason and I started to think he was teaching us a lesson, just leaving us out there in the fucking heat of summer. No food. No drinks. So we started walking. It was night so at least it wasn't so hot . . ." Such a lie. It was always hot in the summer, especially in the swamp. "We'd gone about two miles when we found him." And he had to stop because the memories were so strong. He could hear the crickets, all of the insects chirping around him. He could see the sky filled with a thousand stars. And he'd seen the truck, curled around that big old tree. "Fate."

"Tucker?"

"My first thought was that he'd gotten what he deserved. Twisted fucking fate. My mom drove away and died when he chased her. And now he . . . he was the one dead in the wreck. His truck had curled all the way around that tree. Never seen metal crunched that much. Jason ran to him, but I just stood for the longest time." *Staring at the crash. Fate.* And he'd thought, *This is what you get. This is what you deserve. Pain brings pain. Death brings death.*

Tucker looked up at the dark ceiling but he still saw that star-filled night. "Then Jason yelled that he wasn't dead." His brother's voice had cracked when he called out to Tucker. "My mom was trapped in her car, but our father was thrown from his truck. When I got to him, he was about fifteen feet away from the wreckage, like he'd been trying to crawl back toward us. He was covered in blood, choking on it, and he'd grabbed Jason's leg, holding tight to him."

"What . . . what did you do?"

"I watched him die." The words came out quietly. His darkest secret. "We didn't have a phone on us. Help wasn't nearby. There wasn't anything we could do . . ." His words trailed away. "That's what I told myself. But that was bullshit. We both watched him die. We didn't try to stop the blood. We didn't try to give him comfort in those last minutes. Bruises were still all over us from the last beating that bastard had tried to give us, and we just watched him." At the time, he hadn't felt any emotion. It had just seemed . . . fitting . . . the end that his father had. "We were still standing next to him when a sheriff came by the next day, a guy who'd come out patrolling. He thought we'd been in the wreck, too. That we were lucky to survive." Her touch was so warm on his skin. "Never told anyone differently." Until her.

He'd had to pass psych tests when he enlisted in the Navy, and then again when he'd been a SEAL. Life seemed like one big test . . . *Am I sane enough to handle what's coming?* It had been easy enough to give the right answers. After all, he'd gotten good at lying from an early age.

Pretending my father wasn't an abusive bastard. Pretending every single day wasn't a nightmare.

After Jason's death, when he'd gone to join the FBI, there had been more tests . . . He'd gotten past them, too. But if the docs had known the truth about his father's passing, about how he'd stood there and watched the man die, a grim smile on his lips, Tucker knew he wouldn't have passed a damn thing.

"Couldn't help but wonder," he rasped out, "did my father turn Jason into a monster . . . or did he just pass that shit on down to my brother? Is it in the blood?" Then his laughter came, bitter and mocking. "Is it in me? Is that what you wonder now? Is it—"

"No." Her voice was flat. And suddenly, she was even closer, pressing her body tightly to his. "I don't wonder that about you. I *see* you."

She didn't always. Not right after he'd killed Jason and she'd run into the woods . . . Not weeks later when she'd cried in his bed. Not—

Dawn kissed him. He could taste the salt of tears in her kiss. She'd been crying for him. Silent tears while he told her his dark secret.

"I see you," she said again. "And I know what you are."

• • •

"Catherine . . ." Bowen tried to keep his voice calm. The woman had been crying for the last ten minutes, not making any sense. He reached for her hands and pulled her up so that she stood right in front of him. "I need you to take a breath for me. Can you do that?"

Her breath shuddered out. She gave a nod. Her nose was red. Her eyes still streaming.

"You said that Heather's boyfriend worked for the FBI?"

"Y-yes . . . He'd just finished up a big case in Alabama . . . so he had some time off. He called. W-wanted her to meet him in New Orleans."

His heartbeat drummed in his chest. "I need a name, okay?"

She blinked.

"Give me his name. Just . . . tell me his name."

"Tuck." Her lips trembled. "She called him Tuck. Never heard his last name . . ."

Son of a bitch.

"Dawn!" He couldn't find her. His brother had fallen into the water and Dawn had run into the woods. She was hurt, terrified, and he couldn't fucking find her. "Dawn, I swear, I am not going to hurt you."

Insects chirped back at him. He could hear a gator croaking from the river, but there was no sign of Dawn. “Baby, please, come out.” He’d been searching for her, running desperately through those woods, but she seemed to have vanished.

Maybe she was unconscious. Maybe she couldn’t call back out to him. He didn’t know what all Jason had done to her.

Or maybe . . . maybe she was too afraid to call out.

She’s afraid of me.

“He’s gone. He’s never going to hurt you again.” Then Tucker heard a twig snap. He whipped around, looking to the left. “Dawn.” She was huddled against a big, arching oak tree, nearly hidden by its trunk and drooping limbs.

He rushed toward her.

Dawn threw up her hands. “No!” Her cry cut through the night. “Stay away from me!”

Tucker stilled. He needed her in his arms. “Jason is gone. He won’t ever hurt you again.”

Her hands dropped. He risked a step in her direction.

“Don’t be like him.” Her quiet plea. “Don’t hurt me.”

He took another step. Another. And he realized that she’d heard him calling for her all along, but she’d hidden. Not because she thought Jason was still out there.

But because she was afraid of me.

His jaw locked. He stood in front of her. Didn't touch her, not yet. Tucker offered her his hand as she huddled on her knees. "I swear on my life, I would never hurt you."

Slowly, her hand reached for his.

Tucker's eyes flew open. He stared up at the darkened ceiling as his heart raced in his chest. He could feel Dawn's body pressed against his, and he reached for the delicate hand that still lay over his chest.

He held her hand and hoped that she would always remember his promise.

CHAPTER FIFTEEN

Someone was pounding on the door.

Tucker frowned as he looked at his watch. Barely 7:00 a.m. He hurried toward the hotel suite door, wondering if there had been a break in the case. But he hadn't received any phone calls, and surely Bowen or Samantha would have notified him if they'd gotten a solid lead.

He checked the peephole.

Samantha. Bowen. Anthony.

And they all looked grim. What else was new? He flipped the lock and pulled open the door. "I'm guessing you have news that warranted an in-person talk?" An in-person group talk? *Not good.*

Samantha's gaze swept over him. "Where's Dawn?"

"In the shower. She should be coming out any moment." His stare shifted to Bowen. "You look dead on your feet, man. When is the last time you crashed?"

Bowen's jaw hardened. "We need to talk."

Obviously. That was why the little group was at his door. Tucker stepped back, waving them inside. He glanced toward Dawn's room, and just then, her door opened. She stood there, clad in a pair of jeans and a blue blouse, her hair still damp and her feet bare. “What’s going on?” Worry sharpened her voice as she hurried toward them. “Please, tell me no one else has been hurt.”

Samantha glanced at Bowen. If possible, his expression went even darker.

“Tell her,” Anthony snapped. “She needs to know what she’s dealing with.”

Dawn was at Tucker’s side. Her arm brushed against his.

Anthony noted that touch and his eyes turned to slits. “Be careful who you trust, Dawn.”

What in the hell was that supposed to mean?

Anthony took a step toward them, but Bowen threw out his arm, stopping him. “Cool down, Detective. Right now.”

But Anthony didn’t look cool. His cheeks had flushed. “You’re covering his ass because he’s one of yours.”

“We’re not covering anything,” Samantha threw right back. “I told you already, his DNA wasn’t a match.”

“Someone tell me what’s happening,” Tucker gritted. He didn’t like being in the dark.

Bowen glanced at Samantha. She nodded. With a sigh, he said, “I talked to Heather Hartley’s former college roommate last night. Turns out, Heather had a boyfriend, a guy she was supposed to meet up with down here.”

If possible, Anthony’s cheeks flushed an even darker red.

Voice low, Bowen continued, "According to Catherine Peters—that's the roommate—Heather's boyfriend was FBI."

Shock rolled through Tucker. "You're kidding me."

"Wish I fucking was," Bowen muttered. Then he cleared his throat. "According to Catherine, the guy had been working a case in Alabama—this was a few months back—and when the case wrapped up, he asked Heather to meet him in the Big Easy."

The sound of Tucker's heartbeat seemed far too loud as it drummed in his ears. He'd been working a case in Alabama just a few months ago. "We were in Fairhope," he said, inclining his head toward Samantha. He'd been working with her and several other agents. Coincidence, of course, but . . .

"Catherine never met the boyfriend." Bowen rubbed the back of his neck. The shadows under his eyes were dark. The guy had obviously pulled an all-nighter as he drove back from Baton Rouge. "But Heather told the roommate his name." Bowen's gaze darted to Dawn, then back to Tucker. "Heather called the guy Tuck."

He shook his head.

"I questioned her thoroughly." Bowen's stare was unflinching. "And she swears that Heather was dating an FBI agent named Tuck. The roommate never saw pictures of the boyfriend, never heard his full name. That was all she had to give me."

"It's not me," Tucker said flatly. "It's fucking obvious what you're thinking, but it's not—"

"We have a partial DNA match." Samantha's hands were at her sides. She leaned forward, rocking lightly on her feet. "It came from skin cells recovered in the gloves taken by Red. You know our team can be fast, and I gave them the order for a rush job. This screening was top priority. They moved heaven and earth to get the results this quickly for us."

Excitement heated his body. Good. Now they were getting somewhere. He'd hoped for more than partial results, but at least this was a start.

"To be clear," Samantha continued, "the DNA did *not* belong to Jason Frost."

"Because he's dead," Tucker snapped. He was sick of that refrain. He knew he'd killed his brother. *I wasn't letting him ever hurt Dawn again.*

Dawn's fingers found his.

"Dammit, you shouldn't trust him," Anthony snarled at her. "Dawn, don't you see what he's doing? You can't put your faith in him."

That guy was pushing him too far. Tucker's back teeth had clenched. His fingers threaded with Dawn's.

"The DNA was not Jason Frost's." Samantha eased out a low breath. "But as I said . . . it is a *partial* match. My techs believe that it's highly likely that a close relative of Jason's left that evidence behind. The DNA sample matched Jason's profile at most, but not all of the loci, and therefore the only conclusion that could be reached is that the killer we're after here is, in fact, genetically linked to Jason."

Linked. Related. A dull ringing filled his ears. "It's not me." He was the only relative left. His hold tightened on Dawn. He turned his head, needing to stare into her eyes as he said, *"It's not me."*

Her gaze was wide, stunned.

"No." Samantha spoke quickly. "Your DNA is also in the system, and . . . after Bowen called me from Baton Rouge, I had the techs triple-check the results for me."

Fucking triple-check? She doubted me, too?

"The DNA found on the gloves matches some of your loci, too, Tucker, but not all. Again . . . our data indicates that the killer is related to you."

He couldn't read the emotions in Dawn's eyes. He only knew his own disbelief and fury were about to tear him apart. Tucker swung his head back toward Samantha. "I have no relatives. My mother is dead, she was an only child, and my father is long gone, too. He had a brother, but the guy passed away when my father was ten. There is no other family. There was me. There was Jason. That was it."

There isn't another relative. There isn't another killer.

Yet . . .

There had to be.

"There is no mistake with these results," Samantha continued as her chin lifted. "The analysts are paid to be very, very thorough."

"I don't understand." Dawn's hand was still in Tucker's but her gaze had darted to Samantha. "You're saying Jason has . . . what? A cousin out there? Another family member who is picking up where he left off?"

"Tucker was in New Orleans." Anthony's rough voice. "Did he tell you that, Dawn?"

A furrow appeared between her brows.

Anthony stalked toward Tucker. Anger seemed to hum in the air around him. "I did some digging on you when Bowen called in with that story about Heather's boyfriend. I knew you and Samantha Dark were in Fairhope, Alabama, around that time. You guys made coverage in all the news outlets, didn't you? Stopping the Sorority Slasher." His lips twisted. "But you didn't go back to DC when the case was done, did you?"

Fuck. "No, I didn't." He squeezed Dawn's hand, but then he let her go. "I had some vacation days due and I took them."

Anthony was smirking. "Right. Vacation. And you want to tell Dawn just what town you decided to visit for that vacation?"

Samantha already knew. Bowen knew. He could see it in their eyes. Anthony had done his digging, all right, and he'd immediately told them what he'd found.

"You were more than ready to have *my* partner play the role of the killer." Anthony's gaze glittered. "But you were holding back truths about yourself the whole freaking time, weren't you?"

"It wasn't relevant." He locked down his control. He couldn't let his own rage out as he talked to Anthony. He had to play this right. *Stay focused.*

"Hell, yes, it was." Anthony pointed to Dawn. "Does she know that you were in New Orleans? That after you wrapped up your case in Alabama, you came here? Right at the same time Heather was supposedly visiting her FBI lover?"

Fuck me. "I never saw Heather. I didn't know the woman at all. The first time I saw her face . . . it was when I was looking at her crime scene photos."

"Why come back to New Orleans then? Why were you here?" Anthony pushed.

"Plenty of people come to New Orleans." It was the first time Dawn had spoken. Her voice was stilted. "Happens every day."

Anthony shook his head. "Bullshit. He came for you, Dawn." He paused a moment and his head cocked as he studied her. "You know how you said you felt watched?"

"She *was* being watched!" Tucker exploded. "The killer was in her home, he was—"

"*You* were watching her," Anthony accused grimly. "You came to New Orleans then because you wanted to see Dawn. Only that wasn't your first trip to spy on her, was it? I kept checking, kept digging through your travel history. Since she moved to the area, you've come at least once a year to keep tabs on her. To watch her." He swallowed. "You know what I'd call that shit? Stalking."

"Tucker?" Dawn's fingers touched his arm. "You were . . . here?"

Don't lie to her. But his gaze swept the group. Two agents on his own team and one NOPD detective who hated his guts. "Is this an interrogation?" His voice was mild because it had to be. If he played this scene wrong, he knew where he'd wind up. "I thought you just said my DNA wasn't a match to the killer's."

"Maybe you're covering for another family member," Anthony threw out. "Blood comes before anything else, right? Isn't that the way it always was for the Frost family?"

"Your DNA didn't match completely," Samantha affirmed. She exhaled on a sigh. "But we do need you to come down to the station and answer some questions for us."

This wasn't a briefing. It was them . . . coming for him. Coming to take him downtown. "And Dawn? What about her?"

"*I'll* take care of Dawn." Anthony was adamant. "And I won't be working my own agenda." Disgust was even thicker in his voice as he said, "You couldn't let go, could you? You could *never* let go."

This wasn't happening. "I'm not involved in these killings and I'm not protecting anyone."

"Torez got hauled in. You can bet your ass you'll get grilled, too," Anthony swore.

This time, he knew the cop was right. He was about to get grilled. And it wasn't going to be pretty.

"We should all head to the station." Samantha was the calm in the face of Anthony's storm. "You, too, Dawn. I'd like for you to accompany us."

"Tucker." Dawn's voice. Sharper now.

His shoulders stiffened.

"Were you here? Did you come to New Orleans?"

"Yes." He made himself look into her eyes. "I was here, and Anthony is right. I've been here before, too."

"Tucker . . ."

He locked his hands around her shoulders. "I was here, but not to stalk you. Not to scare you. Not to do anything to hurt you in *any* way, baby." The endearment slipped out and he knew the others heard it. Screw it. "I needed to check in and make sure you were all right. My brother tried to destroy you. I had to see you. I just had to know that you were okay."

"Why didn't you tell me? You never spoke to me in all of those years—"

"Because the last time we were together, you screamed when I touched you." A bitter truth he hated to say in front of the others. *"I just needed to see for myself that you were all right."*

"Sounds like an obsession to me," Anthony muttered. "Like I said, some guys can't let go, no matter what."

He didn't speak. Because maybe, maybe the guy was right. Maybe he was obsessed.

And when Dawn looked at him, did she see that truth?

He was afraid that she might.

The police station was a hum of activity. Phones were ringing. Voices were shouting out. Chaos reigned.

Dawn sat, hunched on a bench near the bullpen. Tucker had been taken to the back. He'd disappeared with Samantha and Anthony and the police captain. Bowen paced a few feet away, casting her curious glances every few moments.

"It's not Tucker." Her voice was harsh. So what? She felt harsh. And she was tired of sitting around, having everyone in the whole world seem to *watch* her. Dawn surged to her feet. "This isn't him. Someone is trying to set him up."

Bowen ran a hand through his hair. He didn't speak. Didn't offer up a quick, heartfelt affirmation that, no, his teammate *couldn't* be involved in the killings.

Silence could be its own condemnation.

"It's time for me to do what I actually do best." Her hands were shoved into the pockets of her jeans. "Investigate. So you stay here and you guys question Tucker all day if that's what you want to do, but I'm going to talk with Julia—Dr. Bradford. I want to know just what she's found in her autopsies." She turned on her heel and marched away from him.

"Dawn!"

She kept right on marching.

He caught her arm just as she was about to head out the gleaming glass doors at the front of the station. "You're under protective custody. You just can't—"

"I'm going to talk to the coroner. You want to tag your ass along, fine. But don't get in my way. Don't slow me down." Her emotions were rioting. *A partial DNA match.* There *couldn't* be another Frost out there. She knew the family—there weren't any other relatives in Baton Rouge. It had always just been the two brothers. No cousins. No one else.

When Tucker's father had died—*God, the truth he revealed will haunt me forever*—no one else had stepped forward to help the boys. Jason turned eighteen a few days after they'd buried their father, so he'd taken over custody of Tucker.

She shoved open the door and stepped out into the too-bright sunlight. She blinked quickly and wished she had a pair of sunglasses. The reporters weren't camped out in front of the station—a good thing because she didn't want to battle them. She'd heard Samantha and Anthony mentioning that a press conference was scheduled for later that day. Maybe the reporters were just biding their time until then.

"You're one hundred percent certain of the guy?"

Bowen had followed her. Big surprise.

"He's not the killer." She hurried down the street. She'd just caught sight of a news van. So at least *one* reporter was there. Dawn lowered her head and hunched her shoulders, not wanting to catch the attention of that crew.

Bowen kept pace with her. "But he . . . *is* a killer. We both know that. He killed Jason for you."

As soon as she crossed the street—and got away from that news van—Dawn spun to face Bowen. "Let's be clear. Tucker killed Jason to protect me. Not because he's some psychotic murderer, and, yes, I believe that with certainty. I trust him." She started marching again.

"You didn't trust him before. After Jason's attack on you, you kicked him out of your life.

Why? What happened to make you fear him so much then?"

"Really? Here? On the street? This is where you want to have this conversation?" At least they were far enough away from the station that prying eyes weren't on her, and, since it was early in the day, the area was fairly deserted. Her eyes narrowed on him. "Fine. But you already know this. I was a broken twenty-one-year-old girl. A serial killer had just spent hours torturing me and *telling* me that the man I loved was in on his crimes. He'd told me—"

"Wait." His face had gone grim. "Jason *said* Tucker was involved?"

Crap. Now she was making mistakes. "Jason Frost was a liar. A manipulator. He wanted to cause me maximum pain, and he did." *By breaking my heart.* "Tucker came. He saved me. He killed his brother to keep me safe so that—"

"Did you ever wonder if he killed his brother so that Jason couldn't tell you the truth about Tucker's involvement in the Iceman crimes?"

She felt sweat trickle down her back. It was early in the day, but the humidity was already like a blanket covering her. "Is this some kind of good cop, bad cop bit? Were you told to grill me and see if I had doubts about Tucker?"

He stared back at her. A car whizzed past them. "Do you?"

Her chin notched up. "Screw off, Agent

Murphy. If you won't back your own teammate, you're no good to me." She whirled away from him and hurried down the street.

"You understand, of course, why we needed to bring you in for questioning." It was Captain Harold Hatch who spoke. He rubbed his chin and assessed Tucker.

"Yeah, I get it." Didn't mean he liked it. Tucker waved his hand toward the others in the room. A watchful Samantha. A glowering Anthony. "You want to make sure I'm not some serial killer . . ."

"Or that you're not protecting one," Hatch murmured, his bushy brows lowering over his brown eyes.

"Again," Anthony added.

Tucker's fingers pressed lightly on the table. "I didn't protect Jason before. I don't know who this killer is, but I'm not doing anything to help him." *Partial match.* His head had been spinning ever since Samantha had dropped that bombshell. He didn't think the match was bullshit. He did wonder though . . .

Who is it?

Was it possible that Jason had a son out there? Or maybe . . . maybe their dad had even had another kid? They'd never seen their dad with another woman after their mom died, but, maybe . . .

"Have you been stalking Dawn Alexander?" Hatch asked.

He was leading the interview. Samantha had a personal relationship with Tucker, so she was hanging back, and Anthony . . . well, the captain had pulled rank on him.

"No," Tucker said quietly. "I haven't." Rage would get him nowhere. He had to answer the questions, play his cooperating role, and then he'd get back to Dawn.

"What about the trips you took to New Orleans? Were you just here because you enjoyed our jazz music?" Hatch's voice was doubting.

Samantha watched him with a hooded gaze. He should have told her about the trips. When she'd first come to him with the case, he should have mentioned that he'd been visiting New Orleans. But, shit, he'd thought it wouldn't matter.

He'd been wrong.

Tucker chose his words carefully. "My brother nearly destroyed Dawn's life. I checked up on her because I felt . . . protective where she was concerned." His response was calm. He knew how interrogations worked. And he knew how not to fuck one up. "I didn't think she wanted to see me, so I made sure not to intrude in her life."

"So . . . what?" Anthony butted in to ask. "You were some kind of guardian angel for her? Is that what you're saying?"

Tucker's head cocked as he studied the detective. "No. I'm saying I wanted to look out for a woman I'd cared about."

"Cared. Past tense."

Tucker didn't blink.

"Do you have a relationship with her now?" Hatch grilled him.

Watch yourself. They're trying to catch you in a lie. "Yes."

Hatch's eyes widened. What? Had the guy been expecting him to lie? Tucker knew better. He'd called Dawn "baby" in front of too many people earlier. He'd let his emotions slip out. Covering now would be senseless.

Hatch flattened his hands on the table as he leaned forward. "We found your prints inside Jinx Donahue's home."

"That's because I went inside with Dawn. We searched the place together."

"And *you* just happened to be present when the roses were found at Dawn's place."

"Right. I was there with her. She actually found them first, but I went in a few moments after her and saw them."

"You went in her bedroom," Anthony said.

Tucker raised his brows. "That's where the roses were left, yes."

"Dawn didn't tell me that someone had been watching her . . ." Anthony's cheeks were red. "She was friends with cops, but she didn't mention feeling watched, not until you came here and got back in her life. Why is that? Why only talk about what was happening *now?*"

"Because she didn't have proof. She didn't want to go to you without proof."

Anthony smirked. "Odd, isn't it? That there was no physical proof left behind, not until the moment you arrived in town."

"Not so odd, really. I came to town because of the killer. He was escalating, obviously. Perhaps my presence in Dawn's life even pushed him over an edge."

"Or perhaps you engineered everything that is happening here," Anthony said, voice cutting, "just so that Dawn would be afraid once more. So that she'd *need* you . . . and you could have a way back into her life. A way back to the relationship that you've never been able to let go."

"That's certainly one idea," Tucker murmured. "But it's the wrong idea." He kept his pose easy as he stared at the others. Showing aggression now would only work against him. It was a good thing he'd had so long to practice controlling his emotions. "You are the ones who contacted my team. I didn't come here on my own—"

"We contacted you because the scene looked *exactly* like the Iceman's kills. You could have staged that deliberately." Anthony had taken the lead from Hatch and, apparently, the captain wanted to see just where his detective would go with this line of questioning.

"And the DNA evidence?" Tucker asked, raising a brow. "Where did I find a partial match for—"

"Your father." Anthony smirked at him, eyes gleaming. "You're a smart son of a bitch. Had to be, right? Former SEAL. Highflier in the FBI. I'm betting you know plenty about evidence. Specifically, how to leave behind the evidence that you want others to find. I mean . . . I just didn't get it. Why would the killer leave his gloves for Red to take? Why do that, unless he *wanted* that evidence to eventually be discovered?"

Tucker didn't let his body stiffen.

"Maybe you kept DNA from your father. Hell, for all I know, maybe those *were* your father's gloves. You kept them, then you dumped them. Maybe they were your security in case we didn't call the FBI in right away. You were counting on the PD down here running tests on the gloves and then, when we did—bam—there would be a link to Jason Frost. You knew when we found the partial match we'd be calling your office. Calling you. Just like you'd planned all along."

"That's one interesting theory," Tucker murmured.

"Like it, do you?" Anthony gave him a cold smile. "Because I've got more."

Can't wait to hear this.

"You got to Red before I did. Before *anyone* else did. When I got to the motel, you were the one standing over that poor man as he took his last breath. At the time, I thought it was coincidence, but now . . . now I'm wondering

. . . did Red know too much about you? Did he see you with Heather's body? And you had to kill him?" A beat of silence. "It's such a fucking coincidence to me that Rowan Jacobs described the killer to us . . . a man who fit your description perfectly."

Tucker eased out a slow breath. One, then another. *Don't let him push too far.* "You have been working up a lot of theories." His voice wasn't mocking. It was flat. "But that's all they are. You want the truth?"

"That'd be nice," Hatch growled.

"I was in DC when I got the news about this case." He inclined his head toward Samantha. "My team leader briefed me, and I agreed to come down here because my job is to stop killers. I got on the plane and I got my ass down to New Orleans. I immediately started working the case, and, yes, that brought me into contact with Dawn." His gaze swept to Anthony's. "But you know that already."

Anthony grunted.

"I didn't plant evidence. I didn't kill Red. I tried to save him." Tucker's shoulders rolled back. "The real killer is out there. And by focusing on me, you're just wasting time."

It was cold in the coroner's office. Dawn shivered when she walked inside. "Julia?" Bowen was a few steps behind her, a shadow she couldn't seem to shake.

Dawn heard the murmur of voices, and when she rounded the corner, her gaze fell on Julia, clad in her white lab coat. Julia wasn't alone, though. Macey was at her side, and they were both hovering over a sheet-covered body.

"You shouldn't be here." Julia's eyes immediately filled with worry. "Dawn, I'm still working on the autopsy for Jinx. You don't *want* to be here."

Jinx was under that sheet?

Dawn stilled.

Julia pulled off her gloves, tossed them into the trash and then hurried toward Dawn. "You don't want to be here," she said again.

Dawn couldn't pull her gaze off the sheet.

Julia touched her arm. Dawn flinched.

"Let's go outside," Julia said quickly. "We can talk out there—"

"She suffered." The words were out before she could even think. "I saw—when I opened the freezer . . . he'd cut her." Marks that matched Dawn's. Or at least, that was what she'd thought at the time. "Were the marks . . . the same?"

Macey had come up behind Julia. Like the coroner, she was wearing a white lab coat and gloves. She took off her gloves and Dawn saw her gaze jump to Bowen.

"They were the same." Julia's face showed her sorrow. "I'm sorry."

"She worked so hard to cover up my scars." Her heart squeezed in her chest. "And he just marked her to match me." *Why?* "Did you hear . . . the FBI has a partial DNA match? They think the killer is someone related to Jason Frost."

Julia licked her lips. "I . . . heard that."

"Have you found any evidence to back that up?" Or, more important, any evidence to discredit that idea?

"I recovered skin cells," Julia murmured. "Just a few moments ago. From beneath Jinx's fingernails. Even though she was bound, she fought her attacker."

Jinx had always been a fighter. Once more, Dawn's gaze went helplessly to that white sheet.

Jinx is here. Heather is here. Red is here. And even that kid—Rowan—he's dead, too. So many dead.

"Macey, can we talk outside?" Bowen's deep voice asked.

Macey gave a quick nod, and they walked away. The lab doors swung shut behind them. Dawn's shoulders sagged a bit. Now, alone with Julia, she could lower her guard. "I hate this so much," Dawn whispered.

Julia nodded, swallowing.

"I need something to help me find this bastard. He's out there, hunting, and the cops took *Tucker* in for questioning." Her chin lifted. "He didn't do this. I know it."

"Sometimes, we don't know people as well as we think."

"I know him." She wouldn't let fear control her again. She'd just found her way back to Tucker. She wouldn't lose him again. "Those cells you found—they are going to prove his innocence."

Julia bit her lip, but didn't speak.

"The killer is someone that Jinx was seeing, romantically. Malone told me that she had a boyfriend—this was the guy. Tucker couldn't have been down here seeing Jinx. He was working cases with the FBI."

"Maybe he slipped away . . ."

"No." She was adamant. "It didn't happen." She was certain of this. "Jinx knew how I felt about Tucker." Because one drunken night she'd told her. Why was it that too much wine could always make secrets come out? "There are some lines that friends would never cross."

Julia glanced back toward the covered sheet. "You're so sure her lover and her killer are one and the same?"

No, she wasn't. Damn it. "Have you done Red's autopsy?"

Julia shook her head. "Not yet. It took so long to carefully thaw Jinx that—" She broke off. "Sorry. I shouldn't have said that."

"The killer attacked Red quickly. He didn't use the Iceman's MO. It was all about a fast kill with him. Since it was so fast, maybe he made a mistake. Left more evidence. I mean, if skin cells were found on Jinx, there has to be evidence on Red."

Julia paced toward her desk. “I’ll check him, Dawn. I’ll be as thorough as possible. You know how seriously I take my job.”

Yes, she did. Julia was the best there was. If evidence was on him, she’d find it.

“I do know . . .” Julia tapped a manila file that sat on the edge of her desk. “Based just on a visual look at the wounds, I think that Red’s killer was left-handed.”

Dawn’s eyes widened. “Jason was right-handed. Tucker is right-handed.”

“I have to do a more thorough exam. This was just a superficial survey while I was waiting on . . . on Jinx.” She stumbled a bit over those words. “But the wound in his neck is deepest on the right-hand side, and it becomes shallower as it slices to the left. That’s the typical strike pattern of a left-handed attacker. It was a frontal attack, judging by the blood spatter at the scene, and in a front attack from a *right*-handed perp, the deepest wound on the neck should have originated on the left-hand side.” She lifted her hands toward her own throat, indicating the pattern of the attack. “The killer would have been covered in blood . . .”

“Yes,” Tucker said carefully. “I found Red. I had his blood on me—I was trying to save the guy’s life! I wasn’t the one who attacked him. The killer beat me to his location. I wish that I had arrived sooner. I could have stopped the perp. I could have saved Red."

Silence. Still too much suspicion in the eyes of Hatch and Anthony. As for Samantha, he couldn't read her expression at all.

"Were you intimately involved with Jinx?" Anthony asked.

"No. I never even met the woman. I've been in DC, working cases." He gestured toward Samantha. "She can tell you I haven't had any time off recently to run down here."

"So it's been a long time since you came down here to spy on Dawn Alexander." Anthony looked oddly satisfied, as if the guy had just caught Tucker in a lie.

He'd caught nothing. "You can check my travel records—actually, I think you already have. The last time I was down here . . . it was right after we finished up the Sorority Slasher case. I made sure Dawn was doing well, and I left the city. End of story."

"But it's not the end," Anthony said. "You're here now . . . and the bodies are piling up."

"Suspicion is hitting Tucker hard," Bowen said as he paced outside the coroner's office. Macey didn't pace. She just stood still, her unusual eyes following him. "Someone is setting him up, I'm sure of it. For Heather to say an FBI agent named Tuck was her lover . . ." He gave a low whistle.

"This killer has been steps ahead of us all along. He wants Tucker to look guilty—"

"He's discrediting him." Macey pursed her lips as she seemed to consider all of the options. "There won't be enough evidence to prove Tucker's guilt. He's been in DC with us all for the last few months . . . he hasn't been down here checking on the body he had in a warehouse."

Bowen stopped pacing.

"We originally thought Dawn was the killer's end goal," she mused. "Maybe it's more about Tucker. Hurting him. Destroying what he values."

He loved that woman's mind. So deep and twisting. "Tucker values his job."

"And if suspicion is thrown on him . . . the first step will be his removal from the case and our team."

He nodded. "He's being questioned by the PD now. They were saying we were trying to cover for one of our own. Detective Deveraux demanded to be in the interrogation. After the way Tucker went after his partner, the guy was obviously wanting some payback."

"I don't think he's the only one." Her gaze cut to the closed lab doors. "Tucker doesn't have close ties to many folks. The only person that I think he truly cares about? She's in there."

He'd gotten that the first time he'd seen Dawn's picture.

"The killer knows that, too. Hurting Dawn is just another way of hurting Tucker."

She'd just said exactly what he thought. "The perp is going to try to kill her. Soon."

"Yes. And with all this focus on Tucker . . ." She shook her head. "Samantha won't have a choice. She'll have to remove him from duty. He won't be the one guarding Dawn any longer."

It would be them. "If anything happens to her . . ."

Tucker will lose it.

"We have to make sure nothing happens," Macey said. "We have to make certain that woman remains a survivor."

"Every witness in this case keeps winding up dead." Dawn couldn't rub the chill from her arms. "Red, Rowan . . ."

Julia had sat down behind her desk. "My father is blaming himself for Red *and* Rowan. He thinks he should have kept Rowan at his restaurant, and then called the cops."

"None of this is on Jones."

"You know how he is." Julia's lips tilted at the corners. "He wants to save the world."

"Reminds me of someone else I know."

The faint smile vanished from Julia's mouth. "You're not going to wind up on my table." She rose, and the wheels of her chair squeaked as she paced toward Dawn. "That's not going to happen."

A lump was in her throat. One that was very

hard to swallow. "Trust me, that's not on my to-do list."

No humor lightened Julia's eyes. "I look at Jinx, and I see you."

Because Jinx had been so close to her. *She knew me so well, but I didn't realize she was keeping secrets. We all keep them, don't we? And they don't do anything but eat us up on the inside.*

But maybe . . . maybe Jinx and her secrets could be the key to the crimes. "I need to go back to her place." *To my place. I've got the all clear now. The crime scene techs are done. I can head over and take a look around.* Maybe she'd see something that the cops had missed.

Once more, her gaze turned to the sheet-covered body. *I'll find him, Jinx. I'll stop him.* She hurried forward and gave Julia a quick hug. "Thanks for your help. The next time I'm here, I'll bring you a po'boy." She turned for the doors.

"I meant what I said, Dawn." Julia's voice trembled. "Don't wind up on my table."

Dawn looked back at her. "I won't. I promise." She shoved open the doors and found Macey and Bowen huddled together in the hallway. They both looked up at her, their expressions guarded.

"I'm going home." She kept her voice calm. "Tucker told me last night the police finished their investigation there."

Macey nodded. "They did, but . . . are you sure that's the place you want to be?"

It was exactly where she wanted to be.

Macey stepped closer. Dawn could see the worry in her eyes. “Are you sure you’re okay?” Macey pressed.

No, she wasn’t okay. “A killer is hunting me. Just how okay could I possibly be?” She was scared and she was pissed and she needed to do *something* before there was more violence and death.

Sympathy flashed on Macey’s face.

Dawn studied her and Bowen. “How do you feel about Tucker?”

And again, that guarded look came back to both of their faces.

“Do you think he could be involved?”

She was hoping for immediate denials. She got hesitations.

“I think . . .” Bowen spoke slowly. “I think Tucker Frost is a man with many layers. And secrets that he likes to keep.”

She knew all about his secrets, now.

“But do I think he’d torture women? Lock them in freezers and let them die?” He shook his head. “No. No, I have a real hard time believing the man I know would do that. But then . . . that’s why I’m not in the interrogation with him right now. I can’t be impartial.” He inclined his head toward Dawn. “And I don’t think you can be, either.”

“No, I can’t be.” That was part of the problem.

"Bowen's about to collapse," Macey said, pointing toward the other man. "He's been working this case all night. He's going to crash—"

Bowen frowned at her. "Dammit, Mace, stop worrying. I told you, I'm fine."

"*He's* going to crash," Macey continued doggedly, ignoring his words. "So I'll accompany you back to your place." Then she glanced at Bowen. "We're going to need you later. Rest now, all right?"

His face seemed to soften as he looked at her. "All right." But when he focused on Dawn, all that softening was gone. "Watch your ass."

"I intend to."

"Are we done?" Tucker asked as he glanced between Hatch and Anthony. He kept his voice mild, with an effort. He'd answered every question they had, again and again. He'd played the game the right way.

Hatch nodded grimly. "For now."

Tucker rose. "It's been real, gentleman." A real pain in his ass. *Someone is setting me up.* He followed Samantha out of the interrogation room. They'd only taken a few steps down that hallway when he spotted Detective Torez. Torez was leaning against the wall, arms crossed over his chest, and his face was locked in hard, tight lines.

When he saw Tucker, Torez straightened. "Not so fun, is it?"

"No, it's not." Tucker's gaze swept Torez. "But you learned that last night."

Torez lifted his chin. "I'm not the killer. I made a mistake, but I would have *never* hurt Jinx."

"And I didn't do it, either. That means the son of a bitch who did is still out there."

Some of the fury left Torez's eyes. "Jinx was a kind woman. Smart, with a heart that was too soft." Emotion thickened his voice. "She looked for the good in people. That was her fault. She always thought there was good inside. But sometimes, there isn't. Sometimes, people are just rotten straight to their core."

Samantha touched Tucker's shoulder. "We need to talk in my office."

Her office. Right. The NOPD had given her team work space. Tucker turned away from Torez and followed Samantha inside the little room to the right. As soon as the door shut behind them . . .

"Thanks for having my back," he said.

One dark brow rose. "Is that what you think happened in there? That I had your back?"

She hadn't been grilling him. She'd been silent, watchful, the entire time.

Now he studied her with a more careful gaze. "You think I'm guilty?"

She sat behind the desk. Her head tilted as she looked up at him. "Secrets are dangerous. The longer you keep them, the more power they have to hurt you. Or the ones you care about."

He stepped closer to her.

She never changed expression as she continued, "I had a very good friend who kept terrible secrets. He liked to hurt women. Liked to torture them and see how they reacted to the pain."

He knew she was talking about Dr. Cameron Latham. Her former lover. The man who'd been revealed to be the infamous Sorority Slasher.

"I didn't see him for what he was. For too long, I looked at Cameron, and I saw what I needed him to be. Because I missed the truth about him, I started to doubt myself. My beliefs about people, my judgments about their character. Trust . . ." Her lips twisted. "Trust is very hard for me even on good days."

"You don't trust me. You think I could be involved—"

"I think . . ." She sighed. "Because of my past—because of yours—we are under a special microscope here. The brass at the FBI is watching, and sometimes I wonder if they're waiting for us to fail."

He didn't know what to say.

"I have to remove you from this case now. You realize that. I know you do."

Fuck, yes, he'd known this was coming but that didn't mean—

"And I need you to stay away from Dawn Alexander."

"No." An immediate denial. When it came to Dawn, he knew *exactly* what to say.

Samantha held up her hand. "We're going to continue giving Dawn protection. Her safety isn't an issue."

"Samantha, this is bullshit. You originally wanted me on this case because of my personal involvement."

But she shook her head. "I wanted you on the case because I knew that you understood Jason Frost. Your tie to him would allow you to see if this killer was truly emulating the Iceman's crimes or not. It would allow us to potentially predict the killer's movements, but . . . this case isn't going the way I intended."

No, it wasn't going the way *anyone* had intended.

"A partial DNA match." She pressed her lips together. "I can't overlook that. The evidence we have points to the fact that one of your family members is the killer."

"I don't have any family—"

"Maybe you don't know about this person. Maybe your dad had an affair. Maybe it's a cousin you didn't know . . . But this killer is family, and I'll be damned if I keep you around and wind up causing you to have to kill another blood relation."

His eyes widened.

"You think I don't see the guilt you carry? I do. You had to make a choice. Your brother or the woman you loved."

The woman you loved. His shoulders stiffened. "I would make the same choice today."

"I know you would. That's why I want you away from here. You shouldn't have to make that choice."

There wasn't a choice for him. "This guy is pulling me in. He's deliberately trying to incriminate me. He gave Heather my name. Hell, he let her believe that he *was* me." His hands were fisted at his sides. "He's trying to make me look guilty, destroy all credibility I have. And you think I can just walk away from this? Get on a plane and head back to DC?"

"I think it's what you *should* do. Distancing yourself would undermine this perp's plan, and it's quite obvious to me that he's had a plan in place for some time."

"Because he's a cold, methodical killer." Tucker raked his hand over his face. "Only I didn't fully understand his motivation before. I thought it was about finishing what the Iceman had started. It's not . . . It's about . . . me. Me and Dawn."

"Your supposed connection to Heather Hartley will find its way to the media outlets. It's only a matter of time. Her roommate will talk . . . We're lucky Bowen got to her first. As soon as the press discovers her story, you're going to find yourself plagued by reporters. That much intensity will do nothing but hamper the investigation. I need you to back away from the case." Her face was solemn. "If I had my way, I'd send you back to DC on the next flight, but the NOPD has requested that you stay in town . . . because you're a person of interest for them."

Fuck. *Because they still see me as a suspect.* "Where is Dawn?" Was she still out in the bullpen? Was she waiting on him? He needed to talk to her and explain what was happening. *The perp is setting me up. And the cops seem to be falling for the ruse.*

Samantha took out her phone and read through a few texts. "She's with Macey. They're heading back to Dawn's place. I told you, we're going to make sure that Dawn is protected."

He wanted to be with her. He *needed* to be the one at her side.

"I want you to back away," Samantha said flatly. "And that's an *order*, Agent. So you need to tell Dawn that you're pulling back. From here on out, you're not part of the official investigation team."

No, he wasn't part of the unit hunting the killer. He was a fucking suspect.

CHAPTER SIXTEEN

"Okay, the place is clear," Dawn said, forcing a smile for Macey. "You've searched it thoroughly. I'm here, I'm good and I'm just going to crash for a few hours."

Macey frowned at her. "You're trying to get rid of me."

"Absolutely."

"Do you *want* to paint a target on yourself?"

"The way I figure it, I already have a target on me." *No painting necessary.* Her breath heaved out. "But no, the plan right now isn't to be bait. It's to have a few moments to myself so I can think. The building is secure. Hell, you and I both saw the patrol car parked outside. My safety is being monitored by the NOPD's finest. I'm good. And I just want to be alone in my own home." She didn't think that was too much to ask.

Macey opened her mouth to argue, but then there was a sharp knock at the door. Macey's eyes widened. "So much for the building being secure, huh? Seems as if someone just got past the security system downstairs. The system that *just* had the code changed." She turned for the door and checked through the peephole. Her hand had automatically gone to her holster. "Your detective . . ."

Her detective?

Macey opened the door. Anthony stood there, shoulders hunched, gaze worried. First, his stare focused on Macey, but then he glanced past her to find Dawn. "Patrol called and told me you were here." He seemed to hesitate. "I think we need to talk."

No wonder he got past the system downstairs. Anthony had been the one to change the code after the crime scene team finished up. He'd texted it to her that morning. He'd said that she shouldn't change the code, not until she got the go-ahead from the PD. The officers wanted to be able to access her building in case of an emergency.

Her gaze swept over him. Now she had a cop at her door *and* an FBI agent in her home. And she didn't particularly want either of them there. "Fine, let's talk." But she looked grimly at Macey. "I'm okay here. The patrol unit is downstairs. If I leave the building, I'll be sure to let you know."

"I'm supposed to stay with you . . ." Macey began.

Anthony frowned as he stepped forward. "That patrol is staying here. I'm the one who got them cleared with the captain. They'll be watching this house. If Dawn is here, she's safe." He blew out a breath. "Though I don't know why you came back to this place. After what happened to Jinx, I thought you'd be staying far away."

It was because of Jinx that she was back.

But, first . . . "Thanks for bringing me here, Macey. I appreciate your help." She would deal with one problem at a time. Very determinedly, she steered the agent toward the door. "I know Julia can use your help back at her lab. If she's going to find more evidence on those bodies, a backup pair of hands will be useful."

She could see the struggle on Macey's face.

"Go," Dawn said flatly. "I'm fine. I've got the NOPD keeping watch."

And, finally, *finally,* Macey left her. The door shut quietly behind her.

Dawn locked that door, then she turned to square off with Anthony. "Look, if you're here to attack Tucker—"

"The captain let him go. We don't have enough evidence to hold him. Just like we didn't have enough with Torez. Both men were questioned and released." He paced a few feet then swung back to face her. "How can you even bear to be here? Knowing the killer came in your home, your bedroom . . ."

"He can't get in any longer. That access point is closed." Courtesy of Bowen. He'd done that and told her about it. "And I'm here because I need fresh clothes. I need my things. I need my *home.*" Passion rang in her voice and Anthony looked back at her. "This is my place, and I won't be run away."

"You aren't scared?"

"I have room for more than just fear in my life."

He nodded. "I . . . need to ask you a few questions, Dawn. That's why I'm here. Not so much Tucker this time as it is . . . you."

"Me?" Her brows rose. "What do you possibly want to know about—"

"I was watching you when it was revealed that Tucker had been coming down to New Orleans at least once a year. You didn't look shocked."

Because she hadn't been. But now, she schooled her expression.

"You knew he was here those times, didn't you?" He frowned at her, his hands on his hips, his coat pulled back so that she could see the edge of his holster and the badge clipped to his hip. "You're one of the best PIs that I've ever encountered. If you're being watched, you know it, right?" He motioned to their surroundings. "That's how you knew the perp was here. You pick up on the small details. You saw Tucker when he was in the city, didn't you?"

Sometimes, it wasn't about seeing. It was about a primitive awareness. A knowledge that you were in someone's sights.

"You haven't answered my question."

"Yes." She licked her lips. "Yes, I knew he came down here."

"And you weren't alarmed by that?"

"Tucker doesn't alarm me."

He took two quick steps toward her, but then seemed to catch himself. "His brother tortured you. Someone is killing in the exact same method that Jason Frost used. You find out that Tucker has been stalking you—"

"He wasn't—"

"—and you're not alarmed?" His voice rose. "Why the hell not?"

"Because all Tucker has ever done is protect me."

"He's a killer," he rasped, staring at her in disbelief. "I got a friend to dig into his service records. Do you even know how many confirmed kills that man had when he was a SEAL?"

She didn't want to know. Or rather, she didn't want that news coming from Anthony. It was another tale for Tucker to share.

"He's a killer. His brother was a killer. And you magically think you're somehow safe with him?"

She crossed her arms over her chest. There wasn't anything magical about it. Tucker was a good man. She . . . trusted him.

"Jinx lived right below you. You make a living by learning the secrets that people keep . . ." His head cocked. "Am I truly supposed to believe you didn't notice that she was having an affair with someone? That you didn't try to learn the guy's identity?"

"I don't spy on friends," Dawn gritted out. "Jinx had her life and I had mine."

He nodded. "Right. Okay. Say I buy that . . . There are just . . . Things are bothering me, Dawn. Things aren't adding up."

Her phone rang, vibrating in her pocket.

"You found those gloves right away. Gloves that had basically been preserved so no evidence on them would be tainted."

"Red *gave* them to me—"

"Did he? Because he isn't around to back up that story."

She didn't like where this was going. Dawn pulled out her phone and glanced at the screen. *Tucker.* "I have to take this. Excuse me." She turned her back on Anthony. "Tucker? What's happening?"

"I'm off the case."

She'd expected that after the news about the DNA and Heather Hartley. Knew it had to be coming, but . . .

"And I'm supposed to stay the hell away from you."

Her heart squeezed in her chest. "I see."

"Reporters are closing in. Samantha says my presence will just draw more attention, that the brass at the FBI wants me to back the fuck off. It's an order, not a request."

She swallowed. "I . . . I understand."

"No, you don't. The last place I want to be is away from you, but at least Macey is there and—"

"Macey isn't here. I sent her away."

The floor creaked behind her. She looked over her shoulder and saw Anthony's frown.

"You *sent* her away?" Tucker's voice sounded strangled.

"Julia will need extra hands in her lab. She's slammed with all of the bodies, working day and night." Tension gathered at the base of Dawn's neck. "But look, Julia said she found skin cells beneath Jinx's fingernails. Those could give us the identity of the killer—and there could be more evidence. The victims are the key right now. So dealing with those bodies? That's priority." That was why Macey needed to be at the lab. Dawn forced her voice to lighten. "And I'm not alone. The NOPD has a patrol right outside my building. Anthony is here now—"

"What?"

"Dawn." Anthony's voice was sharp. "We aren't done."

"Apparently, he has questions for me. Maybe I'm the new suspect." She laughed and the sound was ragged to her own ears. "Wouldn't that be interesting? The only victim who survived the Iceman turns into a killer."

"You *aren't* a killer," Tucker snapped.

"I'll call you soon, okay?" *He has to stay away.* Why did that hurt so much?

"Dawn—"

She ended the call and faced Anthony once

again. "It seems Tucker is under orders to stay away from me."

"That's a good thing, Dawn."

Not to her.

She straightened her shoulders. "Did I have that last part right? You're here asking me questions because now I'm suddenly on the suspect list?"

He looked uncomfortable but said, "The questions have to be asked. You *did* have access to the inside of Jinx's condo. Maybe you slipped inside—"

"And killed my best friend? Why? Why in the hell would I do that?"

"Because you're an amazing PI. And you knew the identity of her lover. You knew that Jinx was sleeping with Tucker."

"This is bullshit." She moved toward the door. "I need you to leave, now."

But he didn't move. "What if I told you that during his interrogation today . . . Tucker Frost admitted that he was intimately involved with Jinx?"

Her heartbeat thundered in her chest. "Then I'd say you were lying."

He blinked.

"Don't play your games with me." Her heart raced even faster. "I've seen you do this—mislead suspects as you try to get them to slip up. It's not going to happen with me . . ."

"Because you're too careful to make mistakes?"

"Because I haven't done anything wrong, and neither has Tucker." She opened the door. "Goodbye."

He walked toward her, but stopped before exiting. "Do you think I *like* having to ask you these questions?"

"I have no idea."

"I *hate* it. But I have to do my job. My captain says interview you, says use our friendship to get close and find out the truth—"

She flinched.

"So I play my role. I come over here and I do my part, and I hate it." His breath expelled. "But I've got a morgue that's filling up with bodies. I have a killer to catch, and I will catch that perp, no matter what I have to do or who I have to hurt."

She inclined her head toward the door.

"How are you so certain he wasn't sleeping with Jinx? Why do you have this blind trust with him? That's not the way I thought it would be." Genuine confusion showed on his face. *"Why?"*

Because maybe I never stopped loving him. Maybe despite all the hell that came calling, I couldn't cut the link that bound us.

And I don't think he could, either.

"Sometimes—" her voice was soft "—you meet someone who seems to fit you so perfectly. As if a part of you has been missing and then—bam. It's there."

His brows rose. “He’s your fucking missing part?”

“No. I’m his.”

Confusion appeared again. She didn’t have time for his confusion. She guided Anthony out of her home, shut the door, locked it and then nearly collapsed against that door frame.

Her breath came too fast. Her heart was racing hard enough to rattle her chest. And her hands were damp with sweat.

Fear could do that to a woman. Fear could make your whole body shake and quake. But fear could *not* hold her back. She pushed away from the door and headed into her bedroom. She went straight for the closet. She yanked open the door, turned on the light and stared at the back wall, the wall that had been nailed shut by Bowen. Dawn studied that space for a moment, then she turned on her heel and marched into her small utility room. Her washer and dryer sat to the side, and her tool box . . . Ah, yes, there it was. Top shelf. She grabbed the tool box and shoved aside the assortment of screw drivers that she had.

Her fingers curled around her hammer.

Time to get to work.

Julia sat behind her desk. There were too many bodies. Too many dead. Too many victims. In the last few days, she’d seen too much violence.

Even when she wasn't at work, the victims haunted her. She could never seem to shut them out of her mind.

She needed to give them justice.

She rose to her feet. Julia started to reach for her gloves, but the door to her lab swung open. She tensed immediately. Was the guy at the check-in desk just letting a parade into her office?

"Baby, did I scare you?"

Her father gave her a big smile. The kind of smile that had always made her feel safe when she was a little girl.

"Sorry, Dad." To her, he was always just Dad. To the rest of the world, he was Jones. A force to be reckoned with. Her force. "This case . . . it has me a little jumpy." A little? Try a lot. Maybe it was because of Jinx. Because she looked at that woman and thought . . .

She's my age. We have the same friend. Live in the same town. Probably go to the same bars.

"The whole city will feel better when this Iceman is gone." He walked toward her desk and put a white paper bag on her calendar. One look, and she knew he'd brought her a po'boy. That was her dad—food was always a comfort. The way to heal any ill.

But she didn't have an appetite. Not that day. Not with Jinx's wounds still in her mind. "The Iceman is dead. I have to find clues to tell me who this guy is."

"Hmm . . . I read in the paper that it *was* the Iceman. That he was hunting again."

"You can't believe everything you read."

His head tilted as he studied her. "You always let the dead speak to you. You'll find your clues."

She wished she had his confidence.

"Is . . . Red here?"

She motioned to the back, to the cold storage. "Yes."

His hands twisted in front of him. Such big, strong hands. Hands that had always touched her with such gentleness. "And the other one . . . the boy?"

"He was brought in, but . . . I haven't been able to see him yet." *Too many bodies.* It was literally an all-hands-on-deck situation and she would be getting more backup in her lab.

"Wish I'd kept him with me. So many lost souls out there. We should be able to save them." Sadness flashed on his face. That was her dad—a heart as big as the world.

Julia went to him and gave him a tight hug. "Thanks for the po'boy."

"You eat it. Put more meat on your bones."

She couldn't promise to eat so she didn't say anything. She never lied to her father.

He pressed a kiss to her forehead. "When you get ready to go home, you call me. I'll be taking you."

"Dad, no, that's not—"

"A serial killer is in my city. You're the thing that matters most in the world to me. If you want me to sleep at all tonight, you'll call me."

And she knew he meant those words. "I'll call you."

Because Jinx's image was too strong. Jinx's pain was too real. Her father left a few moments later. She put on her lab coat. She put on her gloves. And then she turned on her music—soft, drifting music. Light jazz. The kind of music her father had raised her to love.

She went back to Jinx. Julia pulled back the sheet, studying the other woman's knife wounds. Measuring them, noting them. Then studying her body, looking for bruises that had developed. And there were plenty of bruises. She photographed them—the bruises and Jinx's tattoos. Her body had truly been a work of art.

Before he turned his knife on her.

Jinx was still clad in her bra and panties. Carefully, Julia took a pair of scissors from her instrument tray and cut the panties away. She'd had to wait until they thawed, too, because when Jinx had first come in, the cotton had nearly been melded to her flesh. But now the panties slid away as the scissors cut through the fabric.

Her eyes narrowed. Another tattoo had just been revealed. On the side of Jinx's hip, one that had been covered by the underwear. Julia pulled a light toward Jinx, shining it on her left hip. "Well, I'll be damned." Her gloved fingers hovered over the area—it was raised, scabbing . . . because the tattoo was fresh.

A heart. Jinx had gotten a heart tattooed on her hip. And there was a letter inside that heart. Not just one letter. Two. Initials? Yes, yes, they were initials. Initials in a flowing, cursive font. The heart was broken in two pieces, and thorn-tipped vines wrapped around the heart. The detail was incredible. Julia pulled out a magnifying glass just so she could study the tattoo more carefully. There was no mistaking those letters.

You got this tattoo recently. It's a heart and I'm betting those letters are your lover's initials.

And the first initial was a *T*.

Dawn pried the last nail free from the wall. She yanked down the heavy chunk of wood. Damn but that had taken too long. Bowen must have put twenty nails in the thing. She dropped the wood and picked up her flashlight, shining it down into the little corridor.

So dark. So still.

Her breath blew out and she knew there was no going back. She needed to search Jinx's place, but if she tried going through the door downstairs, one of the cops might see her—see her and stop her. Dawn made sure she had a gun, it was tucked into the back of her jeans, and with one hand still tightly gripping the flashlight, she climbed into the old chute. It was much bigger inside than she'd expected. The air tasted oddly stale inside, but there were no cobwebs. No dust.

Was that because the killer had used the secret entrance so much? Or because the cops had swept things down during their search?

Dawn moved slowly, inching along as she braced her body so that she wouldn't slide down too quickly. When she reached the bottom, she shone her light at the wall, trying to find the way out. She saw a section of paneling that looked different, and she knocked on it.

Hollow.

Her fingers fumbled and she hoped, really, desperately hoped, that Bowen hadn't been as thorough with the nailing down there and—

No nails.

The wood fell out when she shoved on it. Dawn moved easily through the space—and then she was standing in Jinx's closet. It was completely dark in the closet, but the area . . . it smelled like Jinx. Jinx had always used raspberry body lotion and that scent seemed to be everywhere. For a moment, tears stung Dawn's eyes, but she blinked them away. *Not now. Hurry. Do a search.*

She curled her left hand around the doorknob and eased open that closet door. The curtains were drawn in the bedroom, not letting in any light and not allowing anyone to peek inside. A good thing, considering she didn't want the cops watching her.

Or arresting her for trespassing.

She paused near Jinx's bed. The cops had searched thoroughly, but they didn't know Jinx like she did. Jinx had liked to hide things that mattered to her. She'd always been worried about a robbery. At her last place, someone had broken in and stolen her jewelry, so Jinx had been determined to keep the things that mattered most to her safe this time.

Dawn was betting her friend had a hidden spot for her valuables. She just had to find the spot. She headed toward the bed and the floor creaked beneath her feet.

Excitement fired Julia's blood. The tattoo on Jinx was fresh, and—obviously—it was one to recognize a lover. Those letters . . . those letters were a clue they needed.

She'd covered Jinx back up while she hurried to get her camera. She wanted to photograph the tattoo.

Macey had texted her just a bit ago, telling her that she'd be arriving any moment. She couldn't wait to show the agent what she'd found. She grabbed the camera and—

The lab door opened.

"Macey, hurry back here!" Julia called out. "There's a tattoo on Jinx, a fresh one by the look of things. It was on her left hip, hidden beneath her underwear, so I didn't see it at first. I removed the underwear during my exam and I found it—"

Something hit her. Hard, fast, a blow straight to the back of her head. Julia didn't have a chance to cry out. The camera flew from her fingers and her head slammed forward. Her cheek hit the side of the exam table, and she was thrust down, landing on the floor with a thud. For a moment, she didn't move at all, too stunned.

"I'm not Macey."

His voice sent terror clawing through her. Her hand fumbled out, trying to grab on to her instrument tray. It was just a few feet away.

He reached the tray before she did. He picked up her scalpel, and the light gleamed off its sharp edge.

She should scream. As loud as she could. Blood was pouring from her cheek and the back of her head hurt so much she thought she'd vomit right there.

Scream.

Julia opened her mouth.

"No one is going to hear you. You're fucking in the basement here. Scream as loud as you want."

She did. With every bit of power she had. And she kicked out at him as she tried to scramble across the floor.

But he laughed and that scalpel swung at her. The first cut was on her arm. Fast, deep, a slice.

The second was a stab—a sharp piercing into her shoulder.

Oh, my God. I know these wounds . . .

She'd measured them on Jinx. "No!" She kicked out at him again, aiming for his knee. He grunted and went down and she crawled away from him. Julia tried to stand up, but her head was spinning. Blood dripped down her chest. She staggered forward. He'd hit her too hard. She knew her own symptoms—blurred vision, sluggish movements, nausea . . . concussion. *He's given me a concussion.* If she didn't get away from there, she knew it would be so much worse—

"You aren't going anywhere." He yanked her back. Pressed the knife to her throat. "I've got plans for you."

He wrapped his arms around her and heaved her up against him. She fought him, twisting and punching, but he didn't even grunt. And she realized that her blows were too weak. She was too weak. Her mind was still functioning, but her body was sluggish. He'd planned that, incapacitated her from the first blow, and now—

He yanked open one of the storage lockers that she used for her bodies. Cold air rushed out, wrapping around her.

"Perfect," he whispered into her ear. "I'm going to make you like the pain . . ."

• • •

Dawn hadn't found anything under Jinx's bed. Not tucked away in her drawers, not hidden in the dark spaces of her closet. She'd gone into the guest bedroom that Jinx used for her tattoo art—she'd forever been sketching new tattoo designs. She'd sketch in her workroom at Voodoo Tats, and she'd sketch at home, too. Trying to perfect her art before she picked up her ink. The cops had left Jinx's sketchbook there. Dawn shuffled through the latest sketches in the book—a dragon, a snake, a heart. Beautiful work, and looking at those sketches made tears fill Dawn's eyes. She shut the book.

Nothing was out of the ordinary. *Nothing* was sticking out for her. Frustrated, Dawn headed back into Jinx's bedroom. As she neared the bed, the floor creaked beneath her feet again. She stilled and glanced down. Those wooden slats . . . Now her gaze started searching the floor, following the wood all around the room. And right there, near the wall to the right of the bed . . .

The slats there appeared brighter than the others. Newer? As if they'd been replaced recently?

Dawn hurried toward those slats. She knelt on the floor and pulled with her nails, trying to get a grip on a slat. It came up immediately, so very loose, nearly popping her in the face, and she stared down to see that a small dark space was under the slat.

A perfect hiding place. She reached inside and touched a metal box, one that felt cool beneath her fingertips. She pulled it up. *Fireproof safe.* She'd seen the kind in department stores. The key was still in the lock. *Thank you, Jinx!* She turned that key and the lid slowly lifted. Jewelry was inside. Rings. A heart-shaped necklace.

When she saw the necklace, Dawn stilled. Obviously, it was the kind of gift that a lover would give, but . . . there was something about it . . . The heart wasn't some simple design. It had vines snaking across the front of it. Thorns. A hard-edged, unique piece. One that would fit Jinx's style perfectly.

It was the same design that Dawn had seen sketched in Jinx's art room—in her tattoo sketchbook. *She was making a tattoo to match this necklace.*

The floor creaked behind her. *Oh, shit.* She knew that spot. She'd made the wood creak just like that when she walked across the room. Dawn sucked in a deep breath, then she lunged up to her feet. She threw the safe out of her hands and grabbed for her gun.

The man who'd been in the room rushed toward her.

Her gun pointed dead center at his chest. Her breath panted out—the quick pants seeming too loud in the silence of that room.

"You really want to shoot me?" Tucker asked her.

She'd locked her knees, but seeing that it was him—relief swept through her. She lowered the gun. "What are you doing here?"

He motioned behind him to the closet that she'd left open. "Following you."

Her gaze shot toward the window. "The cops out there—"

"You seriously think I can't manage to get past two rookies? And that's all they are. Freaking amateur hour out there. You *aren't* safe with them."

Her mouth had gone dry. She still gripped the gun in her hand. "I thought . . . You said you were supposed to stay away from me."

"I was."

"Then why are you here?"

He took another step toward her. "Because I need to be with you. I lost you before . . ." His lips twisted. "Saved you, lost you . . . all at the same time, and that shit gutted me. You were the one thing that I needed most in my life, and then suddenly, you were gone. *Everything* was gone." His hand lowered and curled around hers—around the hand that still gripped the gun. "I can't have that happen again. I won't. You are my priority."

"Your job—"

"You matter more."

She could see it in his eyes, the emotions he'd been holding back from her. She wanted to throw her arms around him. Wanted to hold him tight, but . . .

Not there. Not in Jinx's apartment. Not in a place that still carried her friend's scent. A place that was full of memories—good and terrifying. *Not there.* "I think I found something." She made herself step away from him. "Come with me . . ."

She led him back into the art room and grabbed for the sketches she'd seen before. "I found a heart necklace in Jinx's safe . . . and I'm sure I saw the same sketch for that necklace in here . . ."

Macey headed toward the coroner's lab. She'd stopped by the police station to talk with Samantha—she'd wanted to know more about the interrogation with Tucker. Samantha had been worried, saying the police captain seemed to just be focusing on Tucker, and if you focused too much on the wrong man . . .

You missed the killer right in front of you.

The lab doors swung open. Detective Torez rushed out, nearly hitting Macey.

"Oh, sorry!" He grabbed her arms, then quickly let her go. "Didn't mean to . . . um, collide with you."

She frowned at him. Samantha had told her that Torez had been questioned and released, but she hadn't expected to find him there. "Were you talking to Dr. Bradford?"

"No. Julia isn't in there." He rubbed the stubble

along his jaw. "Was hoping to find her. Anthony called and asked me to meet him down here so we could figure out what's happening with the case . . ."

She heard footsteps padding behind her, she glanced back—

Anthony was pacing toward her. He slowed when he saw her and Torez. "Did something happen? There a new lead?" Excitement lit his eyes.

But Torez shook his head as he walked away from the lab's entrance. "No, there's nothing. Julia must have stepped out and taken a break. Maybe even gone to her dad's place for a bite to eat." He shuffled toward his partner. "And I . . . Man, Jinx is in there. I just— I have to get some space, okay? I'll check back in with you later." He hurried down the hallway, not saying another word.

Macey watched him go and then she turned her head, glancing at Anthony.

He was staring straight at her. "I think we need to talk."

Her brows rose. "Then talk."

He glanced down the hallway. The check-in clerk was at his desk. The guy had been on break—he'd gotten back just when Macey arrived. Now the fellow was typing on his computer, not seeming to pay them much attention.

"How about," Anthony murmured, "we go

outside? It's always cold as ice down here. And to be honest, the place creeps me out. I'm not as comfortable with the dead as you are."

It wasn't about comfort. "Fine, let's step outside."

Some of the tension eased from his shoulders. Silent now, they walked outside. The day was growing late, but the heat was still as heavy as always in the city. It banished the chill from her skin.

"I need to talk to you about Dawn."

She kept her arms loose at her sides, waiting.

"I'm . . . worried."

"There's a serial killer loose in this town, a killer who seems to be targeting Dawn. I'm worried about her, too."

He looked away. "That's not what I mean."

She waited.

"I can't go to Tucker with this . . . Hell, he wouldn't believe me, anyway. He's so tied up in her, I didn't realize just how badly until I started seeing them together."

Her eyes narrowed. She'd been watching Tucker and Dawn together, too. There was a tension in the air between them. And the way Tucker looked at Dawn . . . *He never got over her. He tried, I think. But I don't think he ever let her go.*

"I stepped over the line."

She wasn't sure what that was supposed to mean.

"Friends don't dig into your past, right? Well, I dug into Dawn's."

Hardly the crime of the century. She'd dug into Dawn's past, too. "Dawn's past is out there for the world to see. Jason Frost took away her anonymity."

"You ever think he might have taken away more than that?"

"I'm not sure I follow you."

Deep lines bracketed either side of his mouth. "You know she was in counseling."

"Considering the nature of her attack, that's only natural." She'd been through her own counseling. During her darkest time, she needed that lifeline to keep her alive. "Most victims seek out counseling so that they can deal with the trauma of their attacks."

His gaze was hooded. "After her counseling, do you know that Dawn immediately started learning how to shoot? She enrolled in martial arts classes? She started studying to be a PI?"

"Sounds as if she gained strength—"

"It sounds as if she wanted to kick someone's ass."

Macey's brows lifted.

He cleared his throat. "I just . . . Shit, I think I need someone from outside to tell me that I'm being crazy. That the suspicions I'm having *can't* be the case."

She swept her gaze over him. His body

was tense. “What suspicions are you having, exactly?”

“I worry that . . . Dawn isn’t who she appears to be.” He thrust back his shoulders, as if preparing himself for some kind of battle. “I don’t think she stopped blaming Tucker.” His words came out in a fast rush. “I’ve known her for a while now and I’m telling you . . . that woman is layered up with secrets and emotions. She *doesn’t* let people get close. She keeps everyone—even the people she calls friends—at a careful distance. But I’m supposed to buy that after just a few days, she’s gone back to being intimately involved with the brother of the man who tried to kill her? The brother of the bastard who sadistically tortured her for hours?” He shook his head. “Calling bullshit. That’s not what victims do.”

“I think we can both agree Dawn isn’t a typical victim.” She kept her voice measured.

“She’s a woman who wants vengeance.” Sweat trickled down the side of his face. “She’s got a lot of rage inside of her . . . and she’s smart. So much smarter than people seem to realize. Do you know the woman went to LSU on a full scholarship? She was supposed to head to law school, already had her scholarships lined up for that, too, but the attack changed everything. It changed *her*.”

“Why don’t you just *tell* me what it is that you suspect—”

"It's too pat. Her finding those gloves. Them being so perfectly preserved that we could still get evidence off them. Jinx being right below her with that connecting dumbwaiter tunnel. We just have Dawn's word that she didn't know it was there. But . . . what if she did? What if she knew . . . What if Dawn has been involved in this mess from the very beginning?"

She shook her head. "No, that doesn't fit—"

"Doesn't fit what? The profile that you and *Tucker* made up? The guy is blinded by her. He looks at Dawn and sees the woman she was seven years ago. The victim. He doesn't see who she is now."

"But you see her?" she asked carefully.

His lips thinned. "I think I may be starting to. It was Captain Hatch who sent me to question her, just following procedure, but now that I've started lining up the dots . . ."

"What is it that you think you see?"

"A woman who is shaped by her past. A woman who has wanted to destroy the man she held responsible for her pain."

Her arms crossed over her chest. "You're saying she's after Tucker."

"I'm saying that she could be setting the man up for a very big fall. Revenge is a powerful motivator. It's not logical, it's not always sane, but it can consume you. I've seen it happen. I know what it's like when it destroys a life." He exhaled on a ragged sigh. "Think about it . . . maybe Tucker really was involved with Heather Hartley—"

"He denies that involvement."

"Because he might not want to look guilty as fuck! Look, if a woman I'd been screwing turned up dead, killed in the same manner my psycho brother used to off his victims, I might not be excited to have a full disclosure about our relationship, either. Maybe Tucker was involved with her, and then he ended things. But Dawn found out—she used Heather to draw him back to this city. She could be making every single move to incriminate Tucker."

"You truly believe she's the killer."

His face was serious. His tone hard and determined. Anthony swallowed. "I just think . . . sometimes we're blinded. We see only what we want to see. Dawn can make Tucker see exactly what she wants when she looks at him."

"A few hours ago, you were the one who seemed certain that Tucker was guilty. What's changed since then?" *Why the complete one-eighty?*

"She trusts him too much. She didn't have a moment of hesitation when we brought him in for questioning. I mean . . . why do that? Why . . . unless she knows something we don't. Unless she *knows* he can't be the killer."

Macey stared back at him.

He swore. "Look, I just needed to talk with

someone, okay? Torez isn't exactly impartial, and when I approached Dawn earlier—she kicked my ass out of her place. I left just moments after you did."

"Well, when you accuse someone of being a murderer that tends to piss them off."

He stepped closer to her. She didn't tense, but as a rule, Macey didn't like it when people came into her space. "What if she is a murderer?" Anthony asked. "Can you look me in the eyes and tell me it's not possible?"

"I believe we all have the potential for violence, but in Dawn's case . . . there is no way that she could have killed Red. She wouldn't have been able to get to the scene in time. She was watched by FBI Agent Bowen Murphy when Tucker went to investigate. She wasn't left alone at the suite. He was with her every moment."

He blinked.

"She has an airtight alibi for Red's murder."

He shook his head and suddenly seemed less certain. "I . . . I didn't realize she'd had a guard for that time. I thought . . . thought Tucker must have left her alone. I knew you were with Julia . . ."

"I was, but Bowen had arrived in town. He stayed with Dawn, and he wasn't a guard. She was under protective custody. There's a difference. So if the perp who killed Red *is* the same individual we're hunting here in the city, there is no way that person is Dawn Alexander."

Relief swept over his face. “Good—fucking great.” He backed away, running a hand through his already disheveled hair. “I needed to hear that.” Then he was reaching down toward his hip—not for his holster but for his phone. She saw that it was vibrating. He looked at the screen. “It’s the captain. I have to check in.”

He walked away before she could say anything else. Macey headed back inside the building, stopping to check with the clerk. “Is Dr. Bradford back yet?”

He frowned, peering up at her through his glasses. “She hasn’t checked out today.” He motioned toward his log. “She . . . should still be in the lab.”

She scanned over the names in the log, names that showed when individuals had checked in and out.

Dawn Alexander.

Jones Bradford.

Ronald Torez.

And her own name. Anthony’s name was just below hers. She initialed by the space next to her name once more and flashed her ID for verification. Then she was heading back toward the lab. She entered and the cold air inside wrapped around her. The place was so damn icy. She didn’t see how Julia could work there without being wrapped in layers.

Light jazz music drifted around her.

There was a po’boy on Julia’s desk. Maybe that

was where she'd been before, sneaking out and grabbing a quick bite and the clerk hadn't even noticed her absence because he'd been on a quick break, too. "Dr. Bradford?"

No answer.

"Julia? You in here?" She walked back to the exam area. Only . . .

There was blood on the floor. Some kind of accident?

But—

Her gaze turned toward the exam table. A body was still on the table. Julia wasn't there, but the body was. Since spending time with Julia, she'd realized how very by-the-book the other woman was. She certainly wasn't the type to leave a mess in her lab. To leave a victim partially covered—

Macey reached for the sheet. She lifted up the edge and a gasp tore from her.

Part of Jinx's hip was missing. A section of skin had just been *cut* away. But that wouldn't have caused the blood that she saw on the floor. Her head jerked up. *"Julia?"* Now worry pierced her because this scene . . . it was wrong. All wrong. When she looked closer at the floor, she saw that it appeared someone had tried to clean up the blood. Part of it was smeared across the tile.

"Julia? Julia, where the hell are you?" She rushed around, searching the lab, searching Julia's work area, but the woman wasn't there. The clerk said she hadn't left but Julia wasn't *inside* and—

And if she didn't leave, then she has to be hidden here somewhere.

"Oh, my God." She ran toward the wall of cold storage lockers, every instinct that she had screaming at her. She yanked open one locker—saw the body. Red. Jesus. She opened another, yanked out the gurney inside—Heather Hartley. Hell. She opened the third, pulling it out and—

Julia.

Her eyes closed, her body icy to the touch. "Julia!" Macey grabbed for the other woman, seeing the blood that coated her head.

Dear God, no!

Then Julia's eyes flew open.

Dawn climbed into her closet, grateful to leave that dark tunnel behind. "We need to call Julia and get her to search Jinx's body for that tattoo." Because she was sure now that Jinx had made that tattoo for herself. The necklace had been hers, so the tattoo would have been hers, too. "When something mattered to her, she made a tat." Her body had been covered in the art that was her life. "Her lover mattered, that's why she started that sketch of the tattoo. Maybe . . ." Tucker was right on her heels. "Maybe she even added more details when she inked herself." Hearts often had names in them, didn't they? Names or initials. That was kind of tradition.

"Macey and Julia have already been examining

her body." He shut the closet door. "Don't you think they would have noticed it if she'd had some guy's name on her by now?"

Not necessarily. Not if it had been hidden. She remembered that Jinx had been wearing her underwear when she'd been in that freezer. *He stripped you down to your underwear so you'd feel the cold surrounding you.* She walked across the room and opened her bedroom door. "I'm calling Julia. I'm—"

Her words stopped. She stopped. Because a man was waiting in her den.

"Hello, Dawn."

Detective Ronald Torez had his weapon drawn. He pointed it straight at her. Tucker was behind her, but Torez's gaze darted over her shoulder. "Hello, Agent Frost."

What in the hell?

"Why don't you both step forward and come out here to face me?" A muscle jerked in Torez's jaw. "Right the fuck *now.*"

Dawn inched forward. She'd put her gun down in her closet. Dammit. She just held her flashlight. Not much of a weapon against a gun. She had the flashlight and he had a gun.

"If you've got a weapon on you, Agent Frost," Torez continued coldly, "then you need to put it on the floor. I've got my gun trained dead center at Dawn's forehead, and if I see a weapon come at me, I will fire."

CHAPTER SEVENTEEN

The detective's gun was pointed at Dawn's head and Tucker could tell by the guy's lethal tone that he wasn't bluffing. Son of a bitch. Tucker had to put his weapon on the floor. There was no choice. Slowly, he put his gun on the carpet. Then he and Dawn both walked forward, moving closer to the cop, and Tucker kept his hands up.

That gun wasn't my only weapon. And when I see the right moment, I will be fighting back. As he advanced, he tried to position his body in front of Dawn's in order to better protect her.

"Don't," Torez bit out. "Freeze right there, both of you." His face was pale. "You went down to Jinx's place, didn't you? Snuck right back to the scene of the crime."

"How did you get into my home?" Dawn asked.

"I broke the lock. I knocked, pounded, but you didn't answer. I got worried so I broke in . . . and then I realized that you'd snuck downstairs." His eyes glittered at her. "Why? Why did you do it?"

That guy's finger was too close to the trigger.

"She didn't hurt anyone. Jinx was good. She was kind." The gun trembled in his grasp. "What the fuck did you do? Did you kill her together? Has this *always* been some weird twisted shit where the two of you were taking the victims *together?*"

Tucker blinked at him. "What are you talking about?"

"You went down there to destroy evidence!" Torez screamed. "Anthony warned me . . . said I should be careful around you both, but . . . Dawn . . ." His gaze swung back to her. "I never thought it could be you. You were her *friend.*"

"I don't know what you're talking about. I didn't hurt Jinx." Dawn's hands were up, too, but one of her hands still curled around a heavy flashlight. Torez hadn't told her to drop that light. His mistake.

Tucker could see that Torez was on the breaking point. The guy was spouting nonsense, and if his hand kept shaking around that gun . . . *He'll start firing.*

"You were in her place!" Spittle flew from Torez's mouth. "I went into your bedroom. I saw— Your closet was open—I realized you'd gone down there. How many times have you gone down there? Why the fuck are you doing this? *Is this some fucked-up game for you both?*"

"No one is playing a game." Tucker stepped in front of Dawn. That gun was shaking too much and if the guy fired, Tucker wanted to make sure that the bullet didn't hit her. "You need to calm down, Detective. You're confused. We just went down there to search—"

Torez gave a wild laugh. "Right. You went to search. At a closed crime scene. Bullshit.

You tried to set me up on this one, had my own brothers in blue doubting me . . . and you'd killed her!"

"No!" Dawn's voice called out. "We didn't! Look, just calm down. Call Anthony—"

"Already did. Called him as soon as I saw what the hell you had done. He'll be here soon and we'll take your asses in. You are going to *pay* for what you did." His eyes were wide and stark. *"You tortured her. You killed her. You—"*

"Drop the gun!" The cry had come from behind Torez. Fierce, sharp. Tucker recognized Anthony Deveraux's voice.

At Anthony's cry, Torez spun to face him. He didn't drop the gun. It was shaking in his hand, and he swung it around toward his partner.

Anthony fired. Once. Twice. Torez's body jerked as he stumbled back. Then he fell, slamming down onto the floor. His weapon dropped from his hand and skittered across the hardwood, stopping beneath the edge of Dawn's table.

Anthony's body was still crouched, his gun still up.

Time itself seemed to freeze.

Then Dawn was rushing around Tucker. She fell to her knees beside the fallen detective and immediately reached out for him. "Torez?"

Anthony sucked in a deep breath. He shook his head, as if he couldn't believe what he'd just done. "Is he dead?"

Tucker knew that he was. Dawn was trying to help the guy, but those shots had been clean and precise. The detective might have been dead even before he hit the floor.

"Dawn!" Anthony's voice thundered out. "Is he dead?"

Her hands were covered in Torez's blood. "Yes." Dazed, she looked up at Anthony. "Why wouldn't he listen? We didn't hurt Jinx. I didn't. Tucker didn't. We didn't do it! We were just searching her place. We found the sketch of her tattoo—"

And Tucker saw it happen. Anthony's face changed. The concerned mask vanished. He wasn't the worried cop any longer. Fury etched onto his face, hardening his jaw and narrowing his eyes. "Fucking bitch."

Dawn blinked.

Tucker had crouched down when Dawn went toward Torez. He was still crouched and his hand went to his right ankle, sliding under the edge of his pants. He touched the knife strapped there—

"I found the sketch at Voodoo Tats," Anthony muttered. "Thought it was the only one. Should have known she had another. She *always* was drawing shit." His gun lifted and aimed at Dawn. "Did that one have my fucking initials on it, too?"

Dawn blinked. "Anthony?"

He smiled at her. And when he smiled . . . a dimple flashed in his left cheek.

Fucking hell. "Dawn!" Tucker yelled as his fingers curled around the knife. "Get over here, get to me—"

Anthony swung the gun toward him. And he fired.

"You're going to be okay." Macey squeezed Julia's hand—her fingers were still ice-cold. They were racing out of the coroner's building. Julia was on a gurney and two EMTs were on either side of her. "You're safe. Everything is okay."

Such a lie. Julia's lips were blue. She was bleeding from at least four different wounds, but the cold . . . it had actually helped her. It had slowed down her blood loss.

I'm betting the asshole who did this to you didn't count on that.

The EMTs rushed Julia toward the waiting ambulance.

"*T-T* . . ." Julia's lips barely moved. "*T* . . . *D* . . ."

What?

"His . . . initials . . ."

Julia was in the back of the ambulance now. The EMTs pushed Macey back.

"Take care of her," she yelled, right before those doors closed.

T. D.

His . . . initials . . .

"Oh, my God." She grabbed for her phone. She called Tucker and the phone rang and rang and rang . . .

When Anthony fired at Tucker, Dawn lunged to her feet and raced toward the bastard. She swung the flashlight at Anthony as hard as she could, slamming it into the side of his head. He snarled and brought the gun up toward her—but not to shoot her.

Instead, he slammed the gun's handle against the side of her head. For a moment, she thought her cheek had broken. Stars danced before her eyes and she swayed.

Then he grabbed her. He yanked her forward and held her in front of his body. And the bastard—the man she'd mistakenly called her friend—jammed the barrel of the gun beneath her chin.

Her gaze—blurred and hazy because he'd hit so close to her left eye—sought Tucker. He was on the floor, slowly rising, and she could see the blood soaking the side of his shirt.

Her breath caught. Tucker was on his feet. Bleeding, but . . . he was coming toward her.

"Don't take so much as another step," Anthony snarled at him, "or I will kill her."

Tucker's head lifted. His blue eyes blazed as he stared at Anthony.

"Hello, brother," Anthony murmured.

Tucker flinched. "You're not my f-fucking brother . . ." His hand lifted to his shoulder and pressed to the wound there.

Anthony laughed. "Sure I am. Your half brother. Isn't that what the DNA match said? What? Did you think you and Jason were the only sons your bastard of a father had?"

Dawn's cheek burned and throbbed. Blood trickled down the side of her face.

"He knocked up my mom. Did it when he was still married to your bitch of a mother."

A snarl twisted Tucker's mouth. "Don't . . ."

But Anthony just laughed again. "Don't what? Don't talk about the dead? What are you gonna do? I'll tell you . . . *nothing*. Not while I've got your sweet piece of ass in my arms." And his hold on Dawn tightened. "I really thought you'd be over her by now. I mean, aren't you pissed at her? At least a little bit? She's the reason you had to kill Jason. You should hate her."

Tucker's gaze slid to Dawn's face. It almost hurt to look into his eyes. *So bright. My Tucker.* "I could never hate Dawn."

"No, right. I got that as soon as I saw you two together. Knew that I'd have to change my plans. See . . . before you two got together, I'd intended to pin all this shit on you. That's why I gave Heather your name. Why I got her to come down to New Orleans right after you closed that Sorority Slasher case in Fairhope. *You* were gonna be the fall guy. But then I saw you and Dawn together." His hot breath was on her neck. "And I knew you weren't the angry ex-lover that I needed you to be."

"Y-you wanted me to doubt him," Dawn managed, her voice husky. She wanted to pull Anthony's attention back to her. She knew Tucker was just looking for a chance to attack. If she could distract Anthony . . .

"Yeah, you were supposed to doubt him . . . but you fucking wouldn't!" The barrel jammed harder, shoving into her chin. "Why not, Dawn? Why the hell not? I even left those gloves, knowing they would give a partial DNA match. You were supposed to think he was covering for someone else. You were supposed to think he'd always tricked you. You were supposed to think he was the fucking bad guy!" He wrenched back her head, forcing her to look into his eyes. "Why the hell didn't you?"

She swallowed. "Because I trust him."

His lips twisted.

"Because . . . I love him." She needed to say those words. She needed for Tucker to hear them and to know they were true. She hadn't stopped loving him. She'd lost her way for a while—they both had—but what she felt for him had never died.

If anything, being with him again had made her love grow stronger.

We're different now. I thought we could have a chance this time. She'd been wrong.

Rage twisted Anthony's face. "I had everything planned . . . and you screwed it up. If I couldn't throw the blame on him, I was gonna put it on you. After all, you crumpled after your attack, didn't you? Let Jason break your mind?"

"No," Tucker growled, "she didn't."

"Bullshit. I broke into her shrink's office. I read all the files. She couldn't stand to look at you—she kept seeing dear old Jason in your place. Bet that made for some wild sex times."

"Let her go," Tucker roared.

"After you left her, she thought she was still seeing Jason. Did she ever tell you that? She was convinced he was following her . . . that was where I got the idea for a little stalking. A little sneaking into her house and rearranging things. But then Jinx fucking saw me, and I had to kill her." His jaw clenched. "She wasn't supposed to die. She was too good of a fuck for that."

Dawn's hands had fisted. She'd fought back the nausea that had risen after he'd slammed the gun into her head. Her body was steady and she wasn't going to let him use her any longer. As long as he had her against him, he knew Tucker wouldn't attack.

She knew it, too. And she knew why, though Tucker hadn't said the words. She'd always known.

He loves me.

When she'd told Anthony that she was Tucker's missing piece, she'd meant those words. She fit him. He fit her.

They'd survived hell before. They would again.

"That damn tat," Anthony snarled. "Didn't even realize she'd gotten it until I saw a sketch at Voodoo Tats. It had my initials in it . . . Can you believe that shit? So, of course, I had to bide my time. I had to wait until Julia was alone at the lab and I had to fucking *hope* that no one found the tat before I got there. Lucky fucking break, though, Julia was too busy with dead bodies to find it until the end . . . and then I took care of her. I stopped her from telling anyone else. And I cut that tattoo right off Jinx's hip. No one will ever know."

Her heart stuttered in her chest. "What did you do to Julia?"

"Exactly what the Iceman would have done . . . I gave her a very cold grave." He laughed.

Tucker took a step forward.

"Don't!" Anthony yelled. "Unless you want her to die right now. If I shoot her from this angle, the bullet will go straight up into her brain. If she's not dead when she hits the floor, she'll just be a fucking vegetable, that I promise you."

Tucker stilled. His hand wasn't at his shoulder any longer. It was at his side. For just a moment, she stared at him and remembered another time.

"Choose." Jason's voice. Filling her head. Hurting her heart. *"Choose right now and let her know it. Tell her the truth that we've always both known. Blood is thicker than anything else. Blood binds."*

No, blood didn't bind. Blood didn't link people more than anything else in the world. Love did that. "I love you," she said to Tucker and she smiled.

"How fucking sweet," Anthony mocked them both. "She loves you . . . She loves the man who is going to kill her."

Tucker shook his head.

"Oh, yes," Anthony promised. "That's how this is going down. The patrol outside? I sent them away when I arrived. So no one is going to come busting in here. No one has any clue what's happening. The tattoo is gone. If there's a sketch of it downstairs, I'll take care of that before I'm done . . . maybe I'll even torch the whole building . . ."

But the Iceman didn't like fire . . .

"You're going to kill her," Anthony said to Tucker. "Or at least, that's what it will look like. The Iceman's brother snapped and killed Jason's only surviving victim. Then, well, upstanding police detective that I am . . . I had no choice but to shoot you. To kill *you.*"

Dawn shook her head. The barrel scraped over her chin.

"I'll spin some story about Tucker getting my

gun and using it to kill poor Torez. But in the end, amazing cop that I am . . . I was able to stop the sadistic killer. You'll both die together."

"Why?" Dawn demanded. "Why are you doing this? Why—"

"It's in the blood," Tucker rasped. "I told you, Dawn. My father was a twisted son of a bitch. I wondered if he'd passed it down to me . . ."

He hadn't. Tucker was good. And Anthony?

He's been hiding the monster that he truly was all along.

"Our bastard of a father didn't want me!" Anthony yelled. "He wanted you and precious Jason, but he didn't want *me!* His mistake—his fucking mistake! The whole world will see—the two Frost boys were killers and I . . . I was the hero, all along."

No, he wasn't.

He was going to kill them both. He'd just admitted it—a dumb admission because Tucker had only been standing back because he didn't want Dawn to be hurt, she knew that.

But if Anthony was just going to kill them both, then she had nothing to lose. *I love you.* She mouthed those words at Tucker once more.

He gave a hard shake of his head but she was already moving. She drove her elbow back into Anthony's stomach as hard as she could. He grunted and his hold jerked on her. She slammed her right heel down on his foot and her left kicked back and rammed into his shin. He snarled but his grip finally loosened and she sprang to the side—

He fired. The bullet hit her in the back and she sprawled onto the floor as the pain of that hit burned through her.

She expected another bullet to slam into her. Expected to hear the rapid pounding of gunfire, but there was only silence. Silence and an odd . . . gurgle.

She turned her head to the side and looked to the right. Anthony was still on his feet but there was a knife in his throat. Tucker was in front of the guy—she hadn't even heard him move.

"I always choose her." Tucker snatched the gun from Anthony's slack fingers and he drove his fist into Anthony's face. Anthony fell back, hitting the floor. His fingers rose as he struggled to grab the hilt of that knife. He was choking, making that terrible gurgling sound.

He's dying.

Tucker grabbed the knife and yanked it out of Anthony's throat. Blood splattered. Anthony's body spasmed.

Tucker turned away from him. Tucker's frantic gaze found Dawn and she saw the terror there. He ran to her. She was still on her stomach, sprawled on the floor. Her back hurt, but she'd been lucky, the bullet had hit a few inches to the right of her spine. She could *feel* it in there. *Burning.*

But at least it hadn't slammed into her spine. She could move her body. She just *hurt.*

"Baby." Tucker dropped to his knees at her side and his hands reached out to her. "Just stay still. Let me check you out . . ." She could feel his hands trembling against her.

Her head was turned, pressed to the floor, and her gaze was on Anthony. He was still jerking. "He's . . . still alive . . ."

"He doesn't fucking matter. *You* matter. Baby, the bullet is still in you."

"I . . . I know."

"I'm calling an ambulance. You are losing too much blood."

Not as much blood as Anthony. "S-stop blood flow . . ."

"I am," he promised. She could feel the pressure on her back. "I've got you. You're going to be okay." Then he broke off and started barking orders into his phone, demanding that an ambulance get there right away. A moment later, he dropped the phone and he leaned closer to her. His lips feathered over her battered cheek. "Everything is going to be okay. Help is coming. I've got you."

He did, but she could still see Anthony. He was dying before her eyes. Was she just supposed to watch him . . .

The way Tucker's father had watched their mother die?

The way Tucker had watched his father die?

"You're . . . better . . ." She forced out the words. "Help him."

Tucker stiffened against her. "I'm helping *you.* You're bleeding too much. I'm not leaving you to help his sorry ass. I don't care if he is my brother . . . *you* are my everything. You're the only woman I've ever loved. The only person who has made me feel like I belong anywhere. I won't lose you, I *can't*—"

She caught his hand. "You won't." She made her lips curve for him. "I'm . . . not going anywhere. I'm . . . stronger . . . than I look."

He'd bent before her and now he blocked her view of Anthony. "I know you're strong." His face was grim. "But I can only help one of you and, by God, I will *always* choose you. I love you, Dawn. Now, forever. I need you in this world. I need you in my life. So don't ask me to turn away. You matter too much."

Just as he mattered to her. More than anything and that was why she couldn't let him watch again as someone else died. *Not another brother, even if he is a monster. Not another—*

Her broken front door banged open. She heard it slam against the wall. "FBI!" a female voice called out.

Macey? Macey's voice? And then footsteps were thundering toward her. Dawn tilted her head a bit and saw Macey. Macey sank to her knees beside Dawn. "I knew it was him!" Her voice broke a bit. "I knew it. *T. D.* Anthony—Tony Deveraux. He was at too many scenes . . . at the coroner's lab, deliberately keeping me outside because he wanted to give Julia time to die. He was at the motel with Red, he was there—"

Give Julia time to die . . . "Julia?" Dawn whispered, eyes tearing.

"She's all right," Macey said quickly. "She's at the hospital. I found her in time—"

Thank God.

"Look at her wound," Tucker cut through Macey's words. "Help her."

And Macey's fingers flew over her back. A sharp pain stabbed Dawn but she didn't cry out. Because Tucker had shifted to the side, she could see Anthony again. *"Help . . . him."*

This mattered. For Tucker . . . this mattered.

"Didn't hit anything vital," Macey said. "I'll keep pressure on her wound. She's going to be okay . . . But what about you, Tucker? Is that *your* blood?"

"I'm fine," Tucker growled. "Through and through shot."

"That's a lot of damn blood," Macey argued.

His jaw was clenched. "I'm fine . . ." Tucker stared down at Dawn. "Had much worse."

Tucker was going to make it. Dawn was determined to survive. And Anthony . . . *"Help . . . him,"* Dawn said again.

"Fuck! Don't move," Tucker ordered Macey with a glare. "She's the priority. You stay with her. You work on *her.*" His jaw locked. He turned to Anthony's jerking body. And then Tucker put his hands on Anthony's throat. He shoved his fingers down hard and Dawn knew he was applying pressure, trying to stop the blood flow.

Macey began yelling out orders about what Tucker needed to do.

Tucker's fingers turned red as Anthony jerked again and the blood kept pumping from his throat.

And in the distance, Dawn heard the scream of sirens.

She was being . . . wheeled . . . down a hallway. Dawn blinked against the lights. She was on her stomach, but there was no pain any longer.

"It's okay, baby," Tucker told her as he squeezed her hand. "You're going back for surgery. They're going to take that bullet out and you'll be good as new."

She could hear the screech of wheels and she glimpsed a few other people nearby—people in scrubs and wearing gloves. She tried to talk, but her tongue felt thick in her mouth. *Drugs. They've already given me drugs.* But before she passed out, she needed to say something. "You . . . you'll be here . . . when I wake up?" That was important. He was important.

She'd lost him once. She never wanted to lose him again.

His bright blue eyes locked on hers. His handsome face stared down at her. And he smiled, flashing his dimple.

Her Tucker.

"I'll never leave you again, I swear it."

She trusted him to keep his word. Satisfied, Dawn's lashes closed. When she woke up, she'd have another scar. Big deal.

When she woke up, she'd have Tucker. *That* was what mattered.

CHAPTER EIGHTEEN

Two weeks later.

"Are you sure you want to do this?" Samantha Dark asked Tucker as they stood in the narrow jail corridor. "You don't have to go in there with him. I'd more than understand if you didn't want to go through with this meeting."

Yes, she would understand, he knew that. Everyone on his team had been nothing but supportive over the last two grueling weeks. The nightmare was almost over now, all of the evidence collected, the threat eliminated.

"I need to go inside." For a final face-off with the brother he'd never known about. The bastard who'd tried to take Dawn from Tucker.

When will they learn? No one ever takes her from me.

"Besides—" Tucker cleared his throat "—Anthony called this little meeting. If he wants to confess, I'll let him finish burying himself."

She gave a nod. "Okay, then, but I'll be close."

Close, but not in the room with him because that had been part of the deal. Anthony Deveraux had said he'd talk freely with Tucker under the condition that no other FBI agents were present.

A little family chat.

Tucker squared his shoulders and entered the small room. The guards at the front of the jail had already taken his gun, so he went in unarmed. Anthony was seated at the small table in the middle of the room, his hands cuffed in front of him, and he was wearing a garish orange jumpsuit.

A jagged, bright red line—a scar—sliced across Anthony's throat.

A uniformed guard stood a few feet away from Anthony, but there was no attorney in that little room. No one else was present at all. But a video camera was perched in the upper right-hand corner of the room and their entire conversation would be monitored. He knew Samantha and the DA were both just down the hallway, settling in to watch the show.

Anthony raised his brows when he saw Tucker. "You sure took your sweet time getting here, *brother.*"

Tucker pulled out the chair across from Anthony. He stared at the other man, searching for similarities in their features. Maybe something he'd missed before. The hair was the same shade, he saw that now. Anthony's was cut a lot shorter than his, so Tucker couldn't tell if the texture would be the same. And maybe their jaws were similar. The dimple in their left cheeks—that was the same, too, but since it only appeared when Anthony smiled, he hadn't seen it much when he'd first met the guy.

Anthony gave him a slow smile and that dimple winked. "I knew you wouldn't be able to resist coming for a visit. Blood always tells, doesn't it?"

"No," Tucker growled back. "It doesn't. It doesn't tell a damn thing about a man."

Anthony's smile slowly disappeared. "You keep saying that to yourself." He leaned forward and his voice dropped to a whisper. "Keep saying it, especially late at night, when you're in bed with Dawn. You keep saying that blood doesn't tell. You keep telling yourself that you're not just like Jason. That you're not just like me."

Tucker didn't speak. An old interrogation technique. Just wait out your prey. He knew Anthony wanted to talk, so he was going to let the bastard talk himself blue.

Anger had the lines on Anthony's face deepening. "What was so fucking special about you? Why did dear old fucking Jamison Frost want you and Jason . . . but not me?"

Tucker laughed. "Is that really what this shit was all about? Your daddy issues? You were jealous because you weren't part of the screwed-up family unit?"

Anthony slammed his cuffed hands onto the tabletop.

The guard immediately stepped forward, but Tucker shook his head.

"You know *nothing* about me!" Anthony roared.

Actually, he did know plenty. Since Anthony's arrest, the FBI had torn the man's life apart. They'd found more than a few skeletons in his closet.

"Jamison Frost fucked my mother. When she got pregnant, he didn't believe that I was his. He thought she was just tricking him. She said . . . she said he told her to get rid of me. He did *nothing* for her. We were practically homeless my whole life. She was always on drugs, always so high she couldn't take care of herself—much less me. She screwed men for money so she could keep her habit going. I lived in *filth* and I had to try to pretend to the teachers at my school that everything was all right. That I was just fine while my father lived his life with you, and he never gave me a backward glance."

"And you think that's such a bad thing, right?" It was Tucker's turn for a smile.

"Better than a drug-addicted whore, better than sleeping on the ground, better than—"

"The beatings started when I was five. They didn't stop until my father was dead."

Anthony blinked. Then he sneered. "Poor little Tuck, he got spanked and he—"

"I was beaten by my father, I was locked in closets and left to starve. I was abused worse than any animal." He knew Samantha would hear his words but he didn't care. Right then, his words didn't matter. Anthony's did. "Believe me, if I could, I would have traded my life with yours."

"Bullshit."

"And if I'd known about you . . . when I turned eighteen . . . when I was working to get my life together . . . I would have come to find you, and I would have tried to help you."

Once more, Anthony leaned forward. "Like I wanted your help."

"No, no, I don't guess you did. It's strange, though. I mean, you've been a cop for almost seven years. Why? I thought you helped people, but that was just a lie. A mask."

"We both wear masks." Anthony cocked his head. "Seven years . . . easy to do the math. Seven years ago, I learned what Jason was."

"We *both* learned what he was that day." And Tucker had gone on to join the FBI, wanting to stop killers. On the surface, Anthony joining the PD appeared similar to his motivation, but . . .

We are nothing alike.

"I learned Jason was sloppy. He wasn't careful enough with his kills. He let you stop him. He thought you'd choose family over everything else, but you didn't. You chose *her*."

And once more, Tucker just waited for the guy to continue. Silence was key.

"I wanted to see what it was like." Anthony dipped his head forward. "To take a life. I wanted to see if I could get away with it. Being a cop . . . it was training for me. I learned about the crime scenes. I learned about investigations. I learned how to make evidence go away." He gave a whistle. "I also learned which prey to use. If you don't want to catch attention, don't go for the pretty college coed. Go for the people who live in the shadows. The ones no one will miss."

Tucker's gut clenched. "How many have you killed?"

Anthony widened his eyes. "I'm not saying that I've killed anyone during those seven years. But if I *had* killed, I would have chosen prey that lived on the edges of society. The useless addicts. The ones who wouldn't even have the sense to fight back."

"Addicts . . . like your mother?"

"My mother died of a drug overdose." Anthony shrugged. "That happens with addicts."

"Just like it happened with Rowan Jacobs."

Another shrug.

"Bullshit." Anger seethed in him, but Tucker didn't let that rage out. He wasn't the one who was going to break in this interview. "You killed Rowan, when you were supposed to be guarding him. You were afraid the guy would be able to tell everyone that *you* were the one who paid him to shoot at me, so you got a needle and you pumped that kid's veins full, didn't you? Julia found the needle mark. She checked his blood, she knows—"

"So glad she survived her attack," Anthony murmured. "Always rather liked her."

"You liked her so much that you hit her over the head and threw her in a body locker."

Anthony's cuffed hands lifted as he rubbed his chin. "Why did Jason choose the freezers? I've always wondered that. Doesn't make sense . . . I mean, Louisiana is fucking hot. Why go cold with the kills?"

"Because our father left us in that heat. For days and days. We'd sweat and we'd vomit and we'd be sure that we were going to die. Jason talked to me during that time. He'd talk to me for hours—until his voice was gone. He'd tell me that we didn't really feel all that heat. That it was mind over matter. That we were in ice. Protected. Forever safe . . . in the ice."

Anthony didn't blink. "Sounds like your brother loved you."

"He did, as much as he was able to love anyone."

"And you still killed him."

Tucker looked over Anthony's shoulder. A one-way mirror was there, and his reflection peered back at him. For a moment, he saw Jason.

Maybe I will always see him. "Yes, I still killed him." Time to take off the fucking gloves. Tucker leaned forward. His voice dropped. "Just like I would have killed you."

Anthony swallowed and his Adam's apple bobbed. "I heard . . . heard you saved me. You stopped me from bleeding out."

"Because Dawn didn't want me killing another brother. She thought I couldn't live with that on my soul." He smiled. In the mirror, his dimple flashed. Jason's dimple. "But I'll tell you a secret."

Anthony's eyes gleamed. "Please do . . ."

"I don't give a fuck about you. If I hadn't been so fixed on getting to Dawn, on saving *her,* I would have used my knife to cut your throat wide-open. I would have stared down at you and watched as you choked on your blood."

Anthony's eyes weren't gleaming any longer.

"You made a mistake. You went after Dawn. No one does that. She *is* my family. You really should have learned from Jason's mistake."

The guard was watching them. Tucker and Anthony were both still in their seats. It was hot in the room. Too hot.

Imagine we're in ice. Safe, so far away . . .

"You're going to spend the rest of your life in a cage." And, once more, Jason's voice drifted through Tucker's mind. *You don't want me in a cell? A cage? We've both been in a cage before. We swore neither of us would go back.*

It was Anthony's turn to go in the cage.

"We've got you on the murder of Detective Ronald Torez. We have you on the murder of Jinx Donahue and Rowan Jacobs. On the *attempted* murder of Dr. Julia Bradford. And thanks to your not-so-clever ass leaving your gloves and DNA at Heather Hartley's crime scene, we have you for her death, too."

"I wanted you to know I was out there. Another brother, hunting. Another brother, killing."

"Don't worry, I know. The whole world knows." He stood up. "Hope you enjoy them all knowing . . . while you're living in a cell. Though if I were you, I'd be watching my back. Once you get sentenced and head off to Angola Prison, you're in for real hell. The inmates there don't take too kindly to cops, especially the killing kind." Tucker turned away.

"What the fuck was so special about *you?*"

Tucker rolled his shoulders and turned back to stare at the man who was his half brother.

"You got close to Dawn. You had his face and she still loved you. But I go to her . . . and she wouldn't give me the time of day. I was a cop, I should've been a freaking hero in her eyes . . . and she shut me down."

And that had been when the Iceman game began. Another piece of the puzzle fell into place. "I'm not special. I am lucky. A very lucky bastard because she loved me back then . . . and she loves me now."

"Fucker."

Tucker smiled. "I thought she was afraid of my darkness, but she wasn't. The first time I saw her, I wanted to protect her. She seemed so delicate and perfect. An angel in my hell."

Anthony's face twisted in disgust.

"Then I realized she was so much more. Dawn made me want to be a better man. She brought me into her light. She filled the holes that I had inside." And the darkness had eased. "She fit me." He'd been unfinished and then Dawn had changed him.

Made him into a better man.

Hell, yes, he'd kill to protect her.

Once more, he turned away. Another deliberate tactic. He took a few steps toward the door.

"You're a killer, too! Deep inside! I know you are! I know you have to be! I read about what you did while you were a SEAL. Your confirmed kills. You liked it, didn't you? You liked that rush, you liked—"

"No, I didn't. I never enjoyed taking a life." He glanced back. "Because I'm not you and I'm not Jason and I'm not fucked in the head."

Anthony jumped to his feet. The guard tensed.

"We found your case files, by the way," Tucker said.

Anthony paled.

"Did you think you were clever, hiding them at Torez's cabin? I mean . . . he was selling the place to you. Probably thought it was the perfect spot, didn't you? A cabin in the swamp, one just like the one Jason had used." Disgust tightened his mouth. "Case files," he said again, shaking his head. "As if those poor people were criminals. You took their pictures, you listed their death dates . . . I counted five of them. Five kids, all just like Rowan. Drug addicts. People who—when their bodies were discovered—didn't even have autopsies performed on them because *you* were the investigating detective and you ruled them as ODs."

"I got away with killing them," Anthony boasted. "For years. Not like Jason. I was better. I killed them and no one noticed. I—"

He'd gotten a confession for those five victims. He'd done his job. "You're not better than Jason. That's what's sad. You could have been. But you're just as screwed up as he was. You're just as much of a monster." And there was nothing else to say. This time, when he turned away, it was because he truly was done.

Tucker headed for the door.

"So are you!" Anthony yelled after him. "You can pretend all you want . . . but I know the truth! You're just like me! You're a killer inside! You're a monster! The Frost curse! We're all fucking monsters! *So. Are. You!* You think you get to live happily-fucking-after with Dawn? What if you have a kid? Huh? What then? The baby would wind up like me—or Jason! *You're one of us. You can't ever escape that!*"

Tucker entered the hallway. He heard a door open a few feet away, and Samantha appeared. She came toward him, her heels clicking on the floor. "You all right?"

"Of course. Never better. I got the confession, didn't I?"

She nodded.

"Then I'm done for now. I'll be taking the vacation time I have coming." And he'd be spending that time with Dawn. *Away* from killers and crime scenes. He started to walk away, but Samantha moved into his path.

He stilled.

"You know he was wrong."

Do I? "Nature or nurture," he murmured. "The eternal debate. What makes a killer? Sometimes, though, it can be both. Nature and nurture, and when you've got both working against you, is there even a fighting chance?"

"There is. Absolutely there is. Look at you. You put killers away. You help people. Nature, nurture . . . maybe it's more about the soul inside. And your soul, Tucker? It's a good one. I could see it the first time I met you."

She sounded as if she meant that. "Thanks, Samantha."

Her expression didn't lighten. "If you ever need a friend to talk with, I hope you know I'm here. Everyone faces the darkness sometimes. It's just easier when you know you're not alone in those shadows."

Yeah, it was easier. He'd realized that truth when he'd met Dawn.

Tucker didn't rush out of that jail. He took his

time, collected his weapon and then he headed outside. He drove back through New Orleans and parked across the street from Dawn's PI office. He climbed from his SUV, the heat from the city immediately surrounding him, and he turned to look over at the big stone building.

A man was in front of that building, a man close to Tucker's height, with his build and with his dark hair.

The man was turned away from Tucker, but he seemed so familiar in that instant . . .

Jason?

Tucker stepped forward but a car horn honked, blasting loudly, and he realized he'd nearly gone straight into the street. At that horn, the man glanced up.

And it wasn't Jason. It was a stranger.

Because his brother was dead. The nightmare was over.

Dawn was sleeping in his arms. She was soft against him. Warm. Her hand was over his heart, just where it belonged.

His fingers slid over the silk of her arm. She was so perfect to him. When he thought of losing her, every muscle in his body tensed. Tucker didn't want to think of a life that didn't include Dawn.

"It's your fault this is happening to her." The voice came from the darkness near the foot of the bed.

"You knew it would happen," Jason said. Jason. That was Jason's voice. *"Only a matter of time, for us both. The urge was always there. The violence—it's a rush, isn't it?"*

No, it wasn't a fucking rush. And this wasn't happening.

"You won't believe what I've learned. I want to show it to you. Share it with you."

"Get . . . out . . ." Tucker growled. The sound of his own voice was off . . . odd.

"She's messing things up."

No, Dawn was making his life better.

"So it's time I killed her. Long past time . . ." And Jason lunged toward Dawn.

"No!" Tucker shouted and he surged up, ready to fight and attack, ready to destroy. He jumped out of the bed and took a few frantic steps forward.

But Jason didn't wait at the foot of the bed. No monster was there.

Dawn turned on the light and the shadows vanished.

Sweat covered Tucker's body and his breath surged in and out, burning his lungs.

"Are you okay?" Her husky voice, pulling him back from the edge.

Tucker glanced at her, ashamed. "Bad dream."

She patted the bed beside her. "I've got a lot of experience with those."

So did he, unfortunately.

"Maybe we can help each other to have better dreams."

He slid back into the bed. She curled around him. Her hand went back to its place over his heart. "I should turn off the light," Tucker muttered.

"No, let's leave it on. Because of you, I've started to like the light."

He pressed a kiss to her cheek. "I wish so many times . . . that you'd never been hurt. I'm so fucking sorry. I let you down." He'd failed her. And wasn't that what his nightmares were about? Not keeping her safe? Not stopping the threat.

She slid even closer to him. "You didn't let me down, Tucker. You never have. You never will."

Her faith in him . . . God, did she have any clue just how much she owned his very soul? "Will you . . . will you come with me back to DC?" But even as he asked the question, he hesitated. "No, wait, I can transfer down here if you want to stay in New Orleans. I can join the local FBI branch and—"

"I think a new city would be good for us both." Her breath stirred lightly against his neck. "And I'm sure there will be plenty of cases that a good PI can solve in DC."

She was going to come with him. Hell, yes. His heart thundered in his chest.

"I want us to have a chance, Tucker. Me and you . . . the future that we used to talk about. I want to try for that."

He did, too. So much. He turned and put his hand under her chin, tipping her head back. “I would give you anything.”

“I know.”

He kissed her, carefully, tenderly. “I love you, Dawn.”

His Dawn. He finally had her back in his arms, and he wasn’t going to lose her again—not to a killer in the shadows, not to a monster in his mind. He’d fight for their future. He’d fight for their life.

And he’d fight for the happy ending that she deserved. No more pain.

Just hope.

EPILOGUE

Six months later . . .

"Tucker . . . I need a word."

Tucker glanced up at Bowen, impatient. "My bride is about to walk down the aisle. This is not the time for a word."

But Bowen's face was serious. "There's something . . . Shit, no, you're right. This isn't the time. Never mind. I'll tell you when you get back from the honeymoon." Bowen turned away.

But Tucker snagged his arm. "What's happening?"

Bowen's mouth tightened. "They found him."

"Who?" He was lost.

"Jason Frost. His remains were found off the coast of Biloxi by some divers. There wasn't much left, not after all this time, but . . . he was positively identified this morning."

Jason Frost.

"I just . . . I got the call a few minutes ago and I thought you would want to know right away." But Bowen raked a hand over his face. "I should have waited. Shit. I have terrible timing. You know that. You—"

Tucker clapped his hand over Bowen's shoulder. "You're a good friend. And thank you."

He eased out a breath and it just seemed . . . it seemed as if his shoulders felt lighter.

They found Jason.

He heard the wedding music begin to play. Music for him. Music for Dawn.

He took his place near the minister. Bowen followed at his side.

They found Jason. After all of those years, now Dawn would finally have the proof that Jason would never come after her again. She was safe. Their past was truly dead.

Dawn appeared, wearing her dress of white, a big smile on her face, and her gaze locked solely on him.

And he forgot about Jason, just as he knew Dawn had . . . she didn't see the ghost of his brother any longer. Neither did he.

He just saw his future.

And it was fucking beautiful.

Books are produced in the United States using U.S.-based materials

Books are printed using a revolutionary new process called THINKtech™ that lowers energy usage by 70% and increases overall quality

Books are durable and flexible because of smythe-sewing

Paper is sourced using environmentally responsible foresting methods and the paper is acid-free

Center Point Large Print
600 Brooks Road / PO Box 1
Thorndike, ME 04986-0001 USA

(207) 568-3717

US & Canada:
1 800 929-9108
www.centerpointlargeprint.com